FIRST WALTZ

The music swelled above them like a rosy cloud, enveloping them in breathtaking waves of harmony. Never in her life had Angel felt so light. It was as if she were walking on air.

Still, she was unable to lift her gaze beyond the sapphire in Sebastian's pristine cravat. The waltz seemed so personal, bringing the two of them together in such an intimate fashion that mere inches separated their bodies.

She tried to move back slightly, but was caught off guard when his arms tightened about her. Her gaze flew to his and she found him staring down at her. Cheeks burning, Angel dropped her gaze to his neck, but found that the slight blue-black shading of his shaven skin was almost as sensually devastating as the fire in his eyes.

Her breath, coming in little gasps, made the lace at his throat flutter slightly. What would it be like to touch the shadows beneath his chin?

And what would it feel like if she brushed his neck with her lips . . . ?

ZEBRA'S REGENCY ROMANCES
DAZZLE AND DELIGHT

Rebecca Robbins
A Guardian for Angel

ZEBRA BOOKS
KENSINGTON PUBLISHING CORP.

ZEBRA BOOKS are published by

Kensington Publishing Corp.
850 Third Avenue
New York, NY 10022

Zebra and the Z logo Reg. U.S. Pat. & TM Off.

First Printing: January, 1996

Printed in the United States of America

Chapter One

England 1815

Sebastian Maximilian Hughes, sixth earl of Darcy, leaned idly against the trunk of an ancient, twisted oak as he waited for the start of the horse race. Although the match was only a country trot, he was nonetheless excited about it (though no one would have known as much by his cultivatedly dispassionate demeanor).

Lord Darcy had carefully watched the young stallion entered in that afternoon's race for the past five years. In that time he had become convinced that Hughes Pride was his ticket to obtaining the coveted Grand London Gold Cup—a feat both he and his father, deceased three years earlier, had longed to achieve all their lives.

Today's event would be Hughes Pride's first real race.

Glancing around at the stallion's competition, Sebastian knew it was a given that the black would win, even though the course was not a flat one such as Hughes Pride had been bred and trained for, but more of a mix between flat and steeple-chasing paths. As a result it contained several stone fences, tall green hedges, and wide streams. But none of these obstacles even registered in Sebastian's mind. To him, the only question was by how many lengths Hughes Pride would cross the line before the rest of the pack.

A familiar flutter of excitement, such as he always felt before a race, rose like champagne bubbles in his belly. Glancing at his two companions, turf fanciers like himself, he addressed the taller of the gentlemen. "Care to make a little wager on the outcome, Simon?"

Blue eyes crinkling amiably at the corners, Lord Evanstone shook his head. In his curly beaver hat he looked at least a foot taller than his six foot five inches.

"Not on your life, Seb," he replied with a laugh. "I watched as they brought Hughes Pride to the course today. Looked like Beelzebub himself. Stomping and kicking like he wanted to smash his competitors into the ground." Then he looked hopeful. "Unless, of course, you're willing to back someone else's horse."

Sebastian grinned but did not reply. Turning to his other friend, Lord Barstow, he raised his brows. "How about you, Horatio? Care to bet a bit of gold?"

The short, black-haired lord also declined. "No. I agree with Simon. I think it only fair that you let us back your stallion while you back another. After all, you will come out the winner either way. If you place your bet on another stallion you shall fleece us when Hughes Pride loses, and on the other hand, if Hughes Pride wins, you also come out ahead since your horse will move one track closer to taking the Grand London Gold Cup."

Chuckling, Sebastian glanced toward the separate paddocks containing the restless thoroughbreds. It was necessary to separate the stallions in order to avoid fights.

"Sorry, gentlemen. I never back anything but my own stock."

"Then you must not blame us for backing Hughes Pride as well," Evanstone declared, "for there isn't another worthy mount in the lot."

Nodding his understanding, Sebastian lifted his gaze from the milling horses and searched the small crowd of men gathered about the clearing. There were no ladies present, although one gentleman had brought along his brassy-headed pocket Venus. It was considered taboo for a lady of Quality to frequent such sporting events, although ladies were allowed to attend larger races such as the Gold Cup and Ascot.

Pulling a gold watch from his pocket, he glanced at it and frowned. "I wonder what we're waiting for. The race was supposed to have started five minutes ago. I want to leave on our journey for Lord Appleby's as soon as possible, in order to reach the estate before dark. It wouldn't do to arrive late for his daughter's birthday fete."

Barstow peered at him curiously. "Since when did you worry about reaching a chit's birthday celebration on time, Sebastian? They're always such deadly dull affairs. God knows if my mother hadn't promised Lady Appleby I'd attend so she'd have enough unmarried chaps to squire the debs, I'd sooner eat lye soap."

"The devil you say," Sebastian growled. "And what is it, precisely, that you dislike about Lady Sarah?"

"Oh, I've nothing against the gel," Barstow assured him. "She's a pretty little thing, charming as six pence, and her pockets are overflowing to boot. But her father, Lord Appleby, like all the rest of the Moreton clan, is one of the most tedious chaps I've ever had the misfortune to meet. Take his peculiar hobbies—collecting beetles, for example. The man can run on for an hour or more on the subject, and never seems to notice that no one is interested. Fellow could bore the scales off a fish. Besides, the party doesn't start until tomorrow. What's the hurry? I had hoped to get in a morning's fly fishing on the Aire before having to do the pretty."

Sebastian's voice took on a slightly menacing tone. "Lady Sarah specifically asked me to arrive the evening before the party. And, since I have decided to make her my countess, I'll thank you not to speak ill of my future father-in-law."

Eyes widening, Barstow chortled. "You old devil!" he cried, slapping Sebastian on the back. "You're going to marry the chit? I thought you were a confirmed bachelor like myself!"

"Every eldest son must marry in order to secure an heir. Mark my words, Horatio, even you will come around someday," Sebastian responded easily. "As for Lady Sarah, she struck me as likely a candidate as any."

"That's as may be," Barstow countered, still grinning. "But I hope you like beetles. You're bound to hear a great deal about them in the future. So, when is the leg-shackling to take place?"

"The date hasn't been set. Lady Sarah wishes to enjoy another Season before settling down to the life of a matron, and I am inclined to indulge her whim."

Lord Evanstone cleared his throat. His gaunt face was oddly pale. "I was not aware you and Lady Sarah were engaged, Seb. Why did you not tell us before?"

Sebastian shrugged. "It slipped my mind."

Barstow tilted his dark head so that his face left the shadow of his hat's brim. His eyes slivered against the bright afternoon sun. "Slipped your mind? Then you cannot be in love with her. Have you ulterior motives for the match?"

Evanstone's jaw tensed and his enormous hands tightened into fists. He loomed menacingly over the shorter man. "Are you suggesting a man would need coercion to marry Lady Sarah, my lord?"

"Certainly not, Simon," Barstow exclaimed. "I would not be so crass. I am merely surprised that Sebastian is so willing to step into the matchmaker's noose. Never got the impression he was in the petticoat line—at least," he amended with a suggestive grin, "not in the *respectable* petticoat line."

"Well, I have recently become so," Sebastian said firmly.

Contemplating Hughes Pride as the gleaming black stallion reared in his paddock, throwing the groom holding his bridle into the dust, Sebastian sighed with satisfaction. "You see, my friends, by marrying Lady Sarah, I will be adding some particularly splendid blood to my own line."

Barstow grimaced. "Really, old man. Not quite the thing to speak of a lady as so much breeding stock."

Evanstone turned away abruptly, his long back stiff with disapproval. Sebastian studied the tall young man curiously, wondering what had put Simon into such a snit. "Careful, Horatio," he murmured. "I think you've offended our friend's sense of propriety."

"Actually, I was not speaking of Lady Sarah. I was speaking of Lord Appleby's racing stock. He recently imported seven horses from Egypt. They're of a new strain, purportedly faster and hardier than our own English type. Probably comes from running in all that sand. At any rate, a betrothal to Lady Sarah was the only way I could wheedle them out of her father. They will be part of her dowry. But enough of that," he finished dismissively. He glanced around again. "What do you suppose is holding up the race?"

"Perhaps the judge is expecting a latecomer," Barstow suggested. "Since he collects his pay out of the stallions' entry fees, it would be worth his while to stall a bit."

Then his dark head bobbed southward. "Ah, yes. I was correct. Look you—here he comes. Big brute, ain't he? By Old Scratch, look at those hindquarters!"

Glancing in the direction his friend indicated, Sebastian's eyes widened as the largest horse he'd ever seen trotted confidently toward the starting line.

"Good God!" he muttered through tight lips. "What a monster! Perhaps I'll take you fellows up on your offer to back another horse, after all. I know Hughes Pride is magnificent and has nearly a hundred years breeding behind his name, but I've never seen such an enormous beast.

"I wonder what breed he is. Look at him: the legs of a thoroughbred and the head of an Arabian. Might have some hunter in him as well. An odd mix, but attractive overall. Can you see the owner? I see no one but the rider."

His two friends did not respond. Barstow continued gaping at the big gray horse. Evanstone appeared to be miles away in thought and didn't look even vaguely interested in the new arrival.

Sebastian watched as the huge gray stallion's rider slipped easily off its back and moved to the entry table.

"Name of entry?" the official demanded.

"I'm Angelo Dell," the boy said. "Stallion's name is Vortex." Dropping a few coins onto the table, he then turned and leapt nimbly back into the saddle.

"Never say that bit of a lad owns the beast himself!" Barstow managed at last.

Sebastian's hawk-eyed gaze ran over the boy's skinny body. Dull black hair stuck out in straight clumps beneath a tattered cap. The boy's face was inordinately pale. "Perhaps the horse belongs to someone who wishes to remain nameless," he proposed. "Rider looks as if he's been ill. I hope he doesn't fall off in mid-race and get himself killed."

"Er . . . quite. Listen, Seb," Barstow said abruptly, "you wouldn't mind if I placed a second bet on that animal, would you? I don't think it could hurt to back both your horse and the boy's—although I shan't if you find the suggestion offensive," he added hurriedly. "It's just that I could stand to win a bit of blunt, whether at your hands or his. I lost quite a large chunk at the gaming tables last week."

"Not at all," Sebastian replied stiffly. Irritation made his flesh prickle as he watched his friend move back to the betting table and place a stake on the newcomer. Surely Barstow didn't actually think the gray had a chance of besting Hughes Pride!

At least Evanstone showed better sense. The tall lord had moved away and stood in the shade of another large oak. To all appearances he had forgotten that there was even going to be a race. But then, Sebastian thought, Simon had never been much of a gambler.

Suddenly the huge gray horse reared. It was quickly brought under control by its rider. Sebastian gazed at the animal thoughtfully. Somehow the beast almost resembled Hughes Pride in structure and form, although the gray was much larger.

Quite abruptly Sebastian decided that, win or lose, he would buy the stallion from the lad—if it truly were the boy's to sell—after the race.

As the starting horn blew he turned to watch the jockeys, their assorted numbers pinned to their shirts, climb aboard their mounts and urge them forward. He had just nodded toward his own rider, who lifted his cap and then looked

Rebecca Robbins

down to tighten his stirrups, when an undeniably whiny voice to his rear made him start.

"Lord Darcy. I trust I find you well."

Sebastian turned, then grimaced with only partially hidden distaste. "Pugsley. Haven't seen you in Town for a while. Been off at one of your estates in Northumberland?"

Sir Corbin Pugsley, baronet, raised a strongly scented lace handkerchief and wiped a few beads of perspiration from his upper lip, inadvertently removing a thin film of red lip-color.

A wide, glassy-smooth scar ran from the dandy's left temple and down his cheek, twisting his mouth into an unholy grimace. Half of his left eyebrow was missing, and his left eye was a hideous milky-white. It constantly slid back and forth, rolling as if loose in its socket. Trying not to stare, Sebastian recalled that, some five or six years earlier, Pugsley had been considered the most attractive man in London—before someone had sliced up his pretty face.

"No," the baronet replied. "As a matter of fact, I have been only a few miles away from here. I have a large estate ten miles to the north." He gestured in that direction with an ornate walking stick of ebony and sterling. "Green Willows. You may have heard of it. I believe it borders a property you inherited two or three years ago."

"I have indeed heard of Green Willows," Sebastian acknowledged. "Though I've not seen it myself, it is reported to be the loveliest estate in this part of the country. As for my own property, do you speak of Windywood Abbey, the place entailed to me by the late earl of Darcy?"

"Yes," the dandy asserted. "Plan to visit it on your way back to London?"

As Sebastian had never liked the baronet above half, he had no desire to continue the conversation. The notorious rumors of odd sexual practices, modeled after the Marquis de Sade's memoirs, that took place in the cellars at Green Willows, made him quite uncomfortable.

"No," he replied repressively. "It is only a small property, and is admirably run by its steward. Please excuse me, Sir Corbin. I must attend my companions."

He turned away, not bothering to add that, along with the property and his title, he had inherited guardianship of a girl child who lived on that estate. As the child was cared for by a doting governess, Miss Tabitha Tritt, with whom Sebastian had corresponded in the past and trusted to keep the child out of trouble, he had found it simplest to stay away and give the girl time to grow old enough to marry off.

Pugsley sniffed daintily. Holding his scented kerchief to his nose as if he smelled something foul, he said quickly, "One moment, my lord. I might be interested in buying Windywood Abbey. As you may be aware, Green Willows surrounds it on three sides. It is bothersome to have that little piece of ground smack in the center of my holdings. I prefer to leave my lands in their natural state, whereas the late earl of Darcy used the Abbey's fields strictly for farming purposes.

"The late earl's father bred thoroughbreds, you must know. His son sold them off when the old man died, and turned the estate into a vegetable farm. At any rate, since it troubles me to have fields of corn and potatoes defacing the middle of my parklands, and, as I am sure you have no wish to play gentleman farmer, I'd give you a good price."

Sebastian bit back an irritated oath as a cloud of the cloyingly sweet perfume drenching the dandy's handkerchief wafted his way. Turning back, he gave the baronet his most disinterested stare. "Quite impossible, I fear," he said in an unmistakably dismissive voice. "It is my ward's ancestral home."

Pugsley's good eye flickered. His mouth dropped open and hung there for a moment. Then, closing it with a snap, he blurted, "Your ward lives at Windywood Abbey? I am sure I do not understand."

Sebastian made to go around the dandy in order to join Barstow and Evanstone. "It is quite simple, really. The estate was left me by the girl's father. When she grows older, I intend it to be part of her dowry. Now, if you will excuse me, Sir Corbin, the race is about to begin and I wish to be at the finish so I might see my stallion cross first."

Instead of moving aside, Pugsley laid one carefully manicured hand on Sebastian's arm, wrinkling the immaculate perfection of the earl's coat. "Please, Lord Darcy, grant me just one moment more of your time."

With difficulty Sebastian kept from planting the impudent fellow a facer. "I trust you have good reason for detaining me, sir?" He glared down at the offending lacquer-nailed fingers until the baronet flushed and removed his hand.

"I was merely enjoying our conversation and wished to extend it. Surely the race will not begin for a few more minutes. So, are you here to enter that black stallion of yours?" Pugsley pressed in a slightly tremulous voice.

"That's right. Hughes Pride."

"Perhaps you'd like to make a friendly wager on the race's outcome. That is," Pugsley added with an uneasy giggle, "unless you think your horse might lose."

Rage shot through Darcy's veins like a spark through tinder.

Apart from his darker reputation, Pugsley was also known throughout racing circles as an inveterate gamester, one who would as soon bet his own mother's tea-money as pour her a cup. But this time, Sebastian assured himself, the baronet was betting unwisely. Hughes Pride was a sure thing, and the baronet severely needed to be taught a lesson in polite behavior.

He nodded. "Shall we say one thousand pounds?"

Sir Corbin coughed. His face flushed with excitement. "Surely we can do better than that, my lord. Perhaps . . . Green Willows against Windywood Abbey? My property is over twice the size of yours. If you lose you have but to," his good eye flickered and he waved his walking stick, "move your ward to another of your many estates. As for her dowry, in the event you should lose I'm sure she won't mind which of your properties you set aside for her."

Sebastian eyed the baronet incredulously. As he had stated earlier, Green Willows was renowned for its beauty. Only a fool or a desperate man would take a chance on losing it. "You would wager an estate worth twice as much as mine, just to own a small piece of property dividing your own?" he demanded. "Knowing nothing at all about how well my horse runs?"

Raising one finger, Pugsley ran it over the scar splitting his face. His good eye had gone flat and cold, like the eye of a corpse. The other still roamed freely, never pausing for a moment. "I would," he declared passionately. "I would risk everything I own to possess Windywood Abbey."

Unable to hide his disdain, Sebastian laughed. He would be foolish to bypass such an easy win. While stopping at Windywood Abbey for the night to give Pugsley time to deliver Green Willows' deed would not get him, Evanstone, and Barstow to Lord Appleby's home by this evening, the wager was too good an opportunity to miss.

He shrugged. "Agreed. If you plan to return to Green Willows this evening, you may call at Windywood Abbey at five. You should reach your estate by four-thirty, and that will give you another half hour to reach the Abbey with the necessary documents."

With that he bowed, forced his way past the baronet, and joined his companions just as the starting pistol cracked and the group of stallions leapt forward.

Chapter Two

The big gray stallion leapt ahead of the pack immediately, but Hughes Pride was close on his heels. In no time the two stallions had left the rest of the horses in the dust.

As he watched, Sebastian could not suppress a small shudder of concern. The gray was a smooth goer and seemed to be taking the obstacles with the grace of a natural athlete, while Hughes Pride, not accustomed to jumping, appeared to be having some difficulty.

He frowned. Could he actually stand to lose Windywood Abbey? He shrugged and swallowed his discomfort.

What did it matter if he lost? If he forfeited the Abbey he would simply move his ward, Lady Angelique Harriette Arundel—her French name a tribute to her Gallic mother, whom he understood to have died giving birth to the girl—to a different estate. The child wouldn't care, and even if she did, he told himself, firmly suppressing a flicker of guilt, it was not up to her to choose her surroundings.

As he watched the closely running horses crest a low

hill and disappear into a glade, Sebastian considered the child and what her future would hold. According to Lady Angelique's governess, Miss Tritt, the girl had been six when her father had died, which made her nine, now. Another eight years—nine at most—and he'd be able to marry Lady Angelique off to some suitable fellow and wash his hands of her.

An unexpected pang of remorse at having neglected the little girl suddenly pricked his conscience. Win or lose this race, it was high time he stopped in to see the chit and discuss her future with Miss Tritt.

He hoped the child was lovely. Rumor had it her mother had been an exquisite, elfin creature, with silver-blond curls and blue eyes the size of sovereigns. If the girl resembled her mother, marrying her off would be an easy task. On the other hand, if she resembled her father, with his flame red, tightly curling hair and masses of freckles, things would be infinitely more difficult.

Again he shrugged. It mattered not. He would see the girl married even if it cost him a fortune. A sizable income should make some man marry her even if she should turn out to be an antidote.

Several minutes later his attention was drawn away from thoughts of his ward as, far in the distance, the two lead horses pounded back toward their owners on the last leg of the race. The rest of the pack was nowhere in sight.

The crowd swarmed forward to get a better view as the animals thundered across a green meadow and leapt a low stone wall. Hughes Pride and the gray stallion sailed as one over the rocks, landing smoothly on the velvety grass beyond. Without warning the black stallion faltered, going to his knees, but recovered in the nick of time.

The stallions' hoofbeats were muffled as they swept over a mossy hill, then echoed again as the horses regained solid ground. Neck and neck, they ran like water, a single length between them, one horse surging ahead only to have the other close the gap and pass his opponent.

Sebastian shaded his eyes against the sun, then drew in his breath with a hiss.

Rather than losing its wind after the first mile, as he'd thought the gray stallion would do, the large horse seemed as energetic as when he'd first begun. Hughes Pride, on the other hand, was wheezing mightily. Sebastian's jockey had pulled out a leather crop and was beating the black sharply about the withers, screaming insults at the animal. The gray's rider bent low over his stallion's back like a small brown burr. His eager cries, rather than a whip, urged his mount on.

Then the horses were upon them. A mighty cheer rose from the crowd as the stallions crossed the finish line. Sebastian slowly let out the breath he hadn't realized he'd been holding. Hughes Pride had lost.

The black stallion stood with head bent, flecks of white slathering his slack lips and nose. His sides heaved, gleaming with sweat. Sebastian's jockey jumped from Hughes Pride's back, slapped the trembling horse sharply across the nose with his crop, and hurried toward the earl.

"I'm sorry, guv'nor," the little man whined. "I tried to make 'im go faster, but 'e just wouldn't go. Stubborn bastard. I'll make sure 'e does better next time."

The big gray, after trotting around in a circle, had rejoined the group of cheering men. His rider grinned happily.

Trembling with rage, Sebastian spared the winners barely a glance. As his jockey drew near, he steeled himself against grasping the man by the throat and squeezing the life out of him. Not trusting himself for the moment, he moved past the jockey to examine the red welts decorating Hughes Pride's withers like broken veins.

Although he had planned to tie the black stallion behind

his carriage on the way to Lord Appleby's and take the entire journey at a trot, he realized now that the horse would have to make the drive at a slow walk. When they did reach Appleby Manor, the wounded stallion would need to remain in the estate stables until well again. God knew how long that would take.

Despite his disgust at the new situation, Sebastian was thankful that Lord Appleby was an expert with horseflesh and lived near enough to make taking Hughes Pride to his estate feasible. Otherwise, Sebastian knew, he'd have been forced to leave the black stallion at an inn, for it was unthinkable that the animal should walk any farther than absolutely necessary. His battered flanks and withers were already swelling.

Without commenting on the ugly cuts, Sebastian turned. The jockey let out a startled yelp as the earl gripped the little man's collar and raised him off the ground so he flailed like a robber in a hangman's noose.

"Mr. Petersneed," Sebastian ground out, "if my horse does not fully recover from your mistreatment, I will take my whip to you and split your worthless hide from your flesh. Your conduct, aside from being cruel and unconscionable, will force me to keep him out of several races in which he needed to run to prepare for the Grand London Gold Cup."

"But guv'nor!" the jockey cried. He'd stopped struggling and now hung from the earl's steely grip like damp laundry. "I 'adn't no choice!"

" 'No choice'?" Sebastian gave the little man a violent shake. The jockey's arms and legs shook like those of a marionette. "What do you mean, 'no choice'? Answer me, damn you!"

Terrified, the jockey whispered brokenly, "I'm s-s-sorry, sir. I thought you'd be wantin' to win no m-m-matter what. Most of the lords I've ridden for in the past felt that way. I'm sorry. T-t-truly."

"You will be sorrier still, Mr. Petersneed," Sebastian assured him. "Not only will you receive no payment for today's antics, but if I ever catch you beating one of my horses again, *I* will beat the life from your scrawny body. If I did not think you'd merely go to work for another man who would not mind how badly you mistreated his animals, I would give you your walking papers at once. However, I assure you that if you ever lay the leather against one of my horses again, you will rue the day you were born."

With that he opened his fingers and the little man sprawled across the ground. "Now, get out of my sight."

Leaping to his feet, the jockey ran like a frightened rabbit.

Behind Sebastian, Evanstone remarked unsteadily, "I thought for a moment you were going to kill him, Darcy."

The earl shook himself. "No," he said slowly, "I wouldn't kill him. It was just seeing someone treat an animal like that . . . I lost control of my temper for a moment." He took a deep, steadying breath. "But come," he finished more brightly, "we must congratulate the winner."

Evanstone's blue eyes widened. "Aren't you upset about losing?"

Sebastian shrugged. "A bit. But I cannot be too disappointed. It was Hughes Pride's first race, after all. I couldn't expect him to win by a landslide, although I did think he would take the field before the gray showed up to give him some competition. That horse surprised me. Big fellow barely broke a sweat. I have decided to buy him."

Barstow, overhearing this remark as he returned to his

friends' sides after collecting his winnings, glanced toward the winner. "Do you think the lad'll sell?"

"He will unless the horse isn't his," Sebastian said confidently. "Every man has his price."

The three of them moved forward as the judge handed the winner a large pouch filled with coins. Smiling, the boy tucked the bag into his coat pocket. Then he jumped lightly from the gray's back.

Leading the horse to the shade of a tree, he rubbed the stallion's nose affectionately. When the big horse nudged his chest, the boy rewarded him with a lump of sugar before proceeding toward a refreshment table. After buying a mug of ale, he returned to the stallion's side and sat down on the grass.

The gray prodded the boy's head. "Sorry, fellow," the lad said with a grin, "I didn't ask for any of your sugar, and I refuse to share my ale."

"Excuse me, my boy," Sebastian said. "I wonder if I might have a word with you."

The lad raised brilliant hazel eyes. For a moment he gazed at the earl, but then replied, "Certainly, my lord. How may I serve you?"

For a few seconds Sebastian stared, startled by the cultured voice so at odds with the tattered clothing. "You and your horse raced magnificently," he said at last. "I was most impressed. Can you tell me what breed your stallion is? I've never seen an animal quite like him."

The lad gulped a bit of ale. "Thoroughbred with a dash of Arabian," he answered in a muffled voice.

"Really? I wouldn't have thought he'd have jumped so well without hunting blood in his veins."

The boy lowered his mug. "I ride him as often as possible," he explained, "and have been exercising him on fences since he was very young. He loves it, and it keeps him in good condition. But his breeding is more for flat stretches than steeple-chasing."

"Well, he is certainly a fine animal. I might try that regimen with Hughes Pride—the black horse you beat so closely. Have you entered your stallion in any big races?"

"Not yet, but I hope to run him in some of the famous ones," the boy said eagerly. "The Grand London Gold Cup, for example. I'm sure Vortex will win."

Sebastian did not reveal the unpleasant sensation the thought of meeting the big gray at the Gold Cup caused in the pit of his stomach. "I see." He cleared his throat. "I say, would you be interested in selling your stallion? I promise I would make it worth your while."

Grinning, the boy shook his head. "He's not for sale."

Sebastian's mouth tightened. "I'll give you five hundred guineas."

Although the boy hesitated, he again refused.

Sebastian raised a brow. "One thousand."

The boy tossed off the last of his ale. He flushed. "No, thank you, sir."

"Five thousand." Sebastian grinned. "Come, lad, I admire your spirit, but I must tell you that I've never paid that much for an animal before—even at Tattersall's—and my stable is filled with the finest horseflesh in the land."

Eyes gleaming like aquamarines, the boy met Sebastian's gaze squarely. "Not meaning any disrespect, milord, as I can understand why you would want to own an animal like Vortex, but I must refuse your generous offer."

"Good God." Sebastian's grin vanished. "Bold chap, aren't you? Perhaps you'd care to name your own price?"

The lad climbed to his feet and brushed off the seat of his worn leather breeches. "I wouldn't sell Vortex for any amount of money, sir."

Sebastian frowned. "Why the devil not?" he demanded shortly.

"Because, my lord. We're friends." With that the boy tugged his cap respectfully, turned, remounted the gray stallion, and trotted away without a backward glance.

Sebastian sighed. "Drat."

Barstow's silver eyes sparkled. "Every man has his price, eh, old man?"

"Shut up."

"Odd, the lad didn't seem even slightly interested in money," Evanstone said musingly, gazing after the gray horse and its rider as they disappeared into the distance. "I mean, considering how poorly he was dressed. Five thousand pounds is a fortune to a peasant boy. To anyone."

Thoughtful, Darcy watched the lad ride away. "Yes," he agreed. "I wonder if there might be more to that pair than meets the eye. I suppose the boy might have stolen the animal, or borrowed it without his master's knowledge. Perhaps I should inquire among the landowners hereabouts. If that is the case, the animal's real owner might be more reasonable."

As he turned to follow his two companions toward their carriage, a voice made him turn.

"Your servant, my lord." Sir Corbin Pugsley bowed. His misshapen mouth was contorted into a parody of a smile. His left eye rolled wildly, while his right, pinned on Sebastian's face, gleamed. He bowed. "As requested, I shall call at Windywood at five."

Chapter Three

Just north of the market village of Pickering and south of the windswept Farndale Moors, a small personage riding an enormous thunder-gray horse drew its mount to a stop in the shade of a beech tree's broad, leafy canopy.

After pulling a handkerchief from her pocket and wiping off a thick layer of lard and rice powder, which it had been necessary to wear in order to hide her freckles, Lady Angelique Harriette Arundel tucked the cloth back into her snug-fitting leather breeches. Then she reached up and pulled a dirty cap and a dingy black wig from her head.

Waist length, tightly curling, carroty red hair sprang free and bounced about her shoulders and past her waist. She shook her head and ran her fingers over her scalp, then tied her long hair back with a bit of string. Tucking the wig and hat into her coat pocket, she urged the gray stallion into a canter.

They moved swiftly along the dirt road leading to Jonas Spindle's little retirement house, Violet Cottage, situated a quarter mile from Windywood Abbey. While Angel's father had been alive, Violet Cottage had been far more of a home to her than the big house, and Jonas, head groom at the Abbey until all the horses had been sold, much more like a father than her own.

Angel's mood was as sunny as the day, thanks to the small bag of silver coins—fifty pounds' worth—jingling merrily in her coat pocket.

Fifty pounds, she thought gleefully, to add to the growing pile hidden in a porcelain teapot on Jonas's fireplace mantel. Only five hundred more and they would be able to purchase Windywood Abbey back from the new earl. At least, she mused with a sudden frown, she *hoped* she would have enough money. The property had been valued at ten thousand pounds when, just after the old earl's death, she'd written to her father's solicitor to inquire.

Her mood darkened momentarily as she remembered learning that her father, who had always held her personally responsible for murdering her mother in childbirth and thus cheating him out of a male heir unless he remarried, had left her nary a cent of the vast Darcy fortune. He had, instead, left everything to the new earl, a distant cousin.

But, Angel consoled herself, despite her father, hers had not been such a bad existence.

For the last year of his life the old earl had lain in his sickbed with the consumption, and Angel had been free to wander the fields and valleys surrounding Windywood Abbey without supervision. Though she had had a nurse while younger, the old earl had felt it a pointless extravagance to hire a governess to keep tabs on his daughter after Angel had outgrown the need for a nurse.

"Of what use would it be to spend good money on teaching Angelique the finer arts?" he had been fond of

saying. *"A chit as ugly as mud need never look to marry. No man in his right mind would have her."*

Once she was of age, he'd frequently told her, he'd planned to send her to a convent to take orders, as he was certain the Good Lord wouldn't mind that her face would stop a coach at fifty paces.

But Angel hadn't minded her lack of a governess. Her nurse had taught her to read and write and do simple arithmetic when she was seven, and thereafter Angel had quickly learned that she far preferred exploring the lovely Yorkshire countryside by herself or in the company of Jonas to sitting over books in a schoolroom.

As she rode down the lane, she thought about Jonas and smiled fondly. The old groom had taken it upon himself to act as her guardian on most of her countryside jaunts, although she couldn't imagine why he'd thought she needed protection. She knew she was far too ugly to attract attention. Her father had been right in that, at least.

The one time Angel had had trouble while wandering the countryside, Jonas had been down with a terrible cold. And she'd come out of that unscathed, which was more than could be said for her attackers.

Still, sometimes she did yearn for a fragment of her mother's loveliness.

How often had she stood in the library gazing up at Lady Harriette's portrait, admiring the silky silver-blond curls framing the perfect face? Too many to count. But she had not been so lucky. Instead, she had been cursed with her father's gruesome countenance.

And *he* had the gall to call *her* ugly!

Her kinky red hair was the same carroty shade as his, her eyes the same mix of blue and green, and she was certain she had not one freckle more than he. But that hadn't mattered to her father. Oh, no. She was a girl and, although no matter what she achieved during her lifetime, she would never be as wonderful as a son would have been. Surely it was not asking too much to expect his daughter to be beautiful.

Angel sighed and shrugged her shoulders to relieve her tension.

Her ugliness didn't matter. She didn't want to marry anyway, and she was fast on her way to achieving what she most wanted from life. Windywood Abbey would soon be hers—*if* she had enough money and *if* the new Lord Darcy could be convinced to sell. But she could not think why he would wish to hold onto a piece of property he had never seen.

Remembering how she had convinced the new earl to stay away from the Abbey, Angel chuckled, making her stallion prick up his ears.

At first, in the months following her father's death, she had waited with trembling limbs for the new Lord Darcy's arrival. Then, when he had merely sent out a new steward (whom Angel had never met, since the man lived in a cottage on a distant part of the estate) to take over the property's management, she had breathed a sigh of relief; it appeared his lordship had fatter fish to fry than worrying about a ward whom he had never even seen.

But just to make certain, Angel had taken certain steps.

Writing as Miss Tabitha Tritt, *six*-year-old Lady Angelique Harriette Arundel's governess, she had sent his lordship a missive inquiring as to his plans for his child ward. The new earl had reacted with the revulsion Angel had expected of a young peer, and had instructed Miss Tritt to do as she saw fit in the upbringing of Lady Angelique, and to keep him informed of the child's progress.

Angel's chuckles deepened.

Really, it *had* been bad of her to continue the game for years now, but what else could she have done? It had taken that long for the tiny gray foal she and Jonas had found in the South Meadow five years earlier to be ready to race, since horses weren't allowed to race until five years of age.

And now she had almost reached her goal. She felt a ripple of pleasure at the thought that she, Jonas, and Vortex had earned the vast sum of nine thousand five hundred pounds—five hundred fifty as of today.

When they had earned ten thousand they would go to the new Lord Darcy with their offer to purchase Windywood.

There was no doubt in Angel's mind that, had Lord Darcy known her true age, he would have bustled her off to London for a Season, so that she might find a husband. Of course, she thought with a wince, as ugly as she was, maybe once he'd seen her he would have realized the futility of such an attempt and run posthaste back to wherever he'd come from.

Shaking her head, she tried to turn her thoughts to less depressing matters.

So what if she had so many freckles it looked as if someone had spilled powdered cinnamon over her cheeks? So what if her tip-tilted nose was impossible, her mouth too wide, her eyes too big for her face, or her red hair so kinky that, if her skin had not been so white, she would have looked exactly like one of the Australian aborigines depicted in the old geography picture book in the nursery?

And at least, she thought with a pang, although her breasts were small and her hips were narrow, they did not let anyone suspect her masquerade during races.

But sometimes, when the moon was a silvery ball in the blue-black sky and the night seemed endless, in her heart of hearts Angel wished she were beautiful. Although it probably wouldn't have made any difference in her father's scathing opinion of her, perhaps if she'd been more physically appealing some gallant gentleman would have wanted her for his own.

As Vortex cantered around the last bend of the road leading to Jonas's cottage, Angel pushed the troublesome thoughts to the back of her mind.

They approached the little house just as a short, wiry man with snow-white curls stepped out of the front door. A brilliant smile creased his leathery face. "Lady Angel!" he exclaimed. "How did the lad run?"

"He won, naturally," Angel said with a satisfied smile.

"And the purse?"

"Not as large as most. Only fifty pounds, but every shilling helps. It won't be long now before the Abbey is ours." Sliding from the gray's back, Angel kissed the stallion on the nose. "Will it, my beauty? And then we shall set about finding you a mare so that you might set up housekeeping. But it could take some time to find a mare as beautiful as you. I won't settle for anything less than perfection."

Turning, she tossed the bag containing the day's winnings to Jonas and proceeded to walk with him around the cottage to a makeshift stable. The huge stallion trailed behind them like an adoring puppy.

Inside the stable Angel reached into a container, drew forth a lump of sugar, and let Vortex lip it gently from her palm. Then, while Jonas rubbed the stallion down, she put one booted foot behind her on the doorjamb, crossed her arms, leaned against the doorway, and chewed on a piece of straw.

"Of course," she added musingly, "it was a little different this time. Vortex only won by a nose."

"What's that?" Jonas looked up, obviously chagrined. "I thought he always won by at least a hundred paces."

"Until today, that was true. But this time there was a group of gentlemen present. Very fashionable. Probably up from London. One of them entered a beautiful black stallion named Hughes Pride. Oh, Jonas," she finished breathlessly, "it was the most beautiful beast I've ever seen—other than Vortex, of course."

She patted her stallion's velvety nose. "The black ran well, although he was quite winded by the end of the race. You should have seen him. When we crossed the finish line he was dripping wet. Naturally Vortex wasn't even puffing, since we have worked with him so often. Still, I'd hate to run across Hughes Pride at another race. I had the impression this was his first competition, and no horse performs ideally, then."

"You're not suggesting that this Hughes Pride could beat Vortex!" Jonas said incredulously.

"I don't know. I honestly don't." Angel tilted her head, shifted the wisp of straw to the other side of her mouth, and considered a large orb-spider's handiwork in the corner of the stable. "The man who owned him tried to buy Vortex after the race," she added in an offhand manner.

"Did he, now?" Jonas raised an eyebrow. "For how much?"

Angel hesitated, not wanting to tell her old friend that, with the five thousand pounds the handsome peer had offered, they could easily have paid for Windywood and had plenty of money left over to buy racing stock for the breeding stable Jonas wished to start. But she had never lied to Jonas, and wasn't about to start now.

She dropped the strand of hay and turned away. "Five thousand pounds."

For a time the old groom said nothing. When Angel turned back she saw that his eyes and mouth were round with astonishment.

"*Five thousand?*" he rasped at last.

"Yes."

"Five thousand bloody *pounds?* For one horse?"

"Yes. Oh Jonas," Angel said brokenly. The backs of her eyes burned with the threat of tears. "I'm sorry. I know I should have accepted his offer."

"Ah, lass," Jonas clucked. He patted her shoulder brusquely. "Don't you fret. I know how you feel about Vortex. How could you feel otherwise with things happening the way they did? First your father deciding to sell all your grandfather's racing stock, knowing how much you loved the animals, and then, just before he did so, the two of us finding Vortex, brand new, wet, and shivering next to his dead mother's body in the South Meadow.

"Why, if it hadn't been for you, the foal would have died, sure as sunshine. As it was, he nearly did even though we built a stable of his own in the far acres to the east and nursed him until he was as grand as he is now. No, lass. I don't blame you for refusing the gentleman's offer. We owe Vortex a great debt for getting us this far. Without him we would never have earned as much money as we have. It would be cruel to sell him simply because he had fulfilled his need. He loves you as much as you love him."

The tears blurring Angel's eyes flowed over onto her cheeks. "Thank you, Jonas," she said tremulously, wiping her face with the back of one hand. "I knew you would understand. You've always been more like a father to me than my own."

"Thank *you*, lass. A greater compliment I couldn't ask for." Jonas brushed furtively at his own eyes, cleared his throat, and tossed a large clump of hay into Vortex's stall. "Now then," he said loudly. "You'd best be getting back home. You've less than an hour before dinner. You know how Cook frets if you aren't there. You don't want her and Mrs. Simpson getting suspicious with us so close to our goal. They might write to the earl and tell him something was up."

"Yes, I guess I'd better."

Turning away, Angel paused in the doorway as, for some unknown reason, the memory of the black stallion's handsome owner flashed through her mind. His eyes had been almost the same ebony shade as his horse's. His hair was nearly as dark, although slightly shot through with silver, and his complexion, faintly tinged blue-black from his shaven whiskers, had been tanned, as if he spent a great deal of time out of doors. His lips had been firm yet full, and more masculine than Angel had ever imagined a person's mouth could be. In all, he had been every bit as beautiful as his black stallion.

And, Angel thought with a flush, the strange tickle she'd felt in the pit of her stomach the first time she'd gazed into his dark eyes had been far different from the nausea she felt whenever her nearest neighbor, Sir Corbin Pugsley, called at the Abbey.

Jonas was the only person who knew what had happened with Pugsley when Angel had been seventeen. The memory made cold shivers run up and down her spine. She could not understand why the baronet continued calling at Windywood, unless he was biding his time for revenge. It might have seemed simpler to turn him away when he called, but it had always seemed safer to abide by the old adage, ''Keep your friends close, and your enemies closer.''

Abruptly, realizing Jonas was gazing at her curiously, Angel smiled reassuringly and hurried out the door. She broke into a trot as she crossed the grassy meadows just southeast of the Abbey.

Chapter Four

Sebastian gazed idly out the carriage window as he, Barstow, and Evanstone neared Windywood Abbey. An uneasy tightness knotted the back of his neck. Although he wasn't sure why, he was quite certain something altogether unexpected was about to happen.

He glanced over at his companions, now lolling comfortably against the carriage's velvet squabs as they slept. Both men had amiably agreed to spend the night at the Abbey before proceeding on to Lord Appleby's, upon reassurance that they might use the services of Sebastian's valet since they had sent their own gentlemen's gentlemen on to Appleby Manor earlier that morning.

Smithby, Sebastian's manservant, had condescended to ride on the top of the carriage with the coachman since the coach, while spacious, was roomy enough only for Sebastian and Barstow to sit across from one another, and Evanstone and his long legs to occupy the other half of the interior compartment. Fortunately for the men riding outside, the day was bright and fine with nary a cloud to mar the brilliant blue sky.

Both Evanstone and Barstow had expressed surprise at Sebastian's sudden *volte-face* where Lady Sarah's invitation and his insistence upon being early for the party were concerned. Sebastian had been unable to bring himself to tell them of his shameful wager. How could he so blithely have gambled away an entire estate? Especially one that, regardless of the legality of the matter, he did not *truly* feel belonged to him?

It was just that Pugsley had made him so angry. He was mortified to have been goaded into such a foolish wager.

He glanced up as his driver tapped on the roof. "Yes, Brownley? What is it?"

"We're almost there, milord. According to the innkeeper's directions, it should be just around this bend."

Shifting to get a better view, Sebastian craned his neck out of the open window. He stared eagerly at the countryside before them. From the back of the carriage, where Hughes Pride was tied, he could hear the stallion's rhythmic hoofbeats clip-clopping against the road.

Then, scolding himself for exhibiting what he considered a plebeian amount of excitement, he sat back abruptly. Why this uncanny sense of expectation? It wasn't as if he was even going to own Windywood Abbey for much longer.

Across from him, Barstow opened his eyes. Rubbing them with his fists, the dark-haired lord nudged Evanstone, who sat on the opposite seat beside Sebastian, with one booted toe. "Wake up, lazybones," he grunted. "You've been snoring for the last twenty minutes," he winked conspiratorially at Sebastian, "and I can't stand another moment of it."

"Sorry," Evanstone replied blearily, opening his eyes

and stretching his lanky body. His sandy hair had fallen over his forehead, and he flipped it negligently away from his face. "Are we almost there?"

"According to the coachman we should arrive any second," Sebastian informed his tall friend in a taciturn voice.

Barstow studied the earl inquisitively. "Aren't you looking forward to your first view of Windywood Abbey, Seb? You don't seem any more interested in the property than if you were picking out a new pair of dancing slippers. I would be wild with excitement, but then I don't own as many estates as you."

Sebastian shrugged and tried to ignore another rush of shame. Realizing he could no longer keep from telling his friends the purpose behind their visit, he stiffly explained about the wager.

"Egad, man!" Evanstone cried when the earl finished. "Never say you plan to stop by as if you were making a social call and coldly inform your ward and her household that you have gambled away their home! What will they say?"

Sebastian answered brusquely. "What *can* they say, Simon? The estate was legally mine to do with as I chose, and I chose to wager it on a race. At any rate, I doubt that Lady Angelique will care one way or the other about where she lives. She's only nine years old, after all."

"Nine?" Barstow grimaced. "I've never been comfortable around young gels. Given to tantrums and such. Most troublesome. What's more, I'll wager you're dead wrong about her not caring that you've wagered away her ancestral estate."

"We shall see," Sebastian responded repressively.

"Indeed," Barstow said with a nod. His frown deepened and his rather bushy black brows drew together. He shifted agitatedly on the carriage seat. "I must say I don't envy your position, old chap. I wish you'd told us about this development before inviting us along. I'd even rather hear about one of Appleby's beetle monologues than watch a child throw a tantrum."

"Horatio, the girl is not going to—"

"Look! There it is!" Evanstone interrupted. "Through the trees!"

Vastly relieved when Barstow forgot their disturbing topic of conversation and, like Evanstone, turned his attention to Windywood Abbey, Sebastian also peered out the window. As he got his first view of the manor house, his mouth tightened and his guilt increased. No wonder Pugsley had wanted the place. And no doubt Barstow was correct; Lady Angelique would *never* understand how the new earl had blithely gambled away such a glorious place.

"It's beautiful," murmured Evanstone, who had scrunched his gangling body into a tight ball in order to crouch beside the carriage window and see past his friends.

"Truly, a sylvan glade!" Barstow agreed enthusiastically. "I say, Seb, perhaps you should buy it back from Pugsley." Then he amended, consideringly, "Or perhaps I should."

Still gazing out the window, Sebastian shook his head. "He wouldn't sell. The baronet wanted Windywood quite badly. But you are right," he admitted. "I sincerely wish I had not been so hasty."

Although, as Barstow had intimated, Sebastian owned numerous estates, the Abbey was quite the most beautiful place he had ever seen. It rose like a jewel from the top of a low hill, its lawns spreading like emerald velvet down to a rippling stream that glittered like a strand of diamonds in the sunlight.

Constructed of deep, red-brown stone, the manor, though not overly large, possessed two stories besides the main floor. Mullioned windows gleamed against white shutters, and red and yellow climbing roses clambered over the high, black, wrought iron fence surrounding the house for a quarter mile on all sides.

A small balcony, nestled just above the doorway like a white crown, held several chairs, as if the house's occupants spent their idle hours gazing toward the east. Glancing in that direction, Sebastian had to admit the view was superb. Rolling green hills scattered with beeches, gleaming silver ponds, and the ever-present stone fences met his interested gaze. It was a restful, pastoral scene. Just looking at it made him forget his troubles for a moment.

His worries surged back like waves on the seashore as the carriage rolled through the main gates and stopped before the doorstep.

An elderly woman rushed out the front door. Her slightly bulging eyes were wide with alarm. "Gracious heaven! I do hope there has not been an accident on the main road!"

Sebastian gave her his most charming smile. "No, no. Do not worry, ma'am. I am the new earl of Darcy. Allow me to present my companions." He gestured toward Simon's tall, gangling figure. "This is Lord Evanstone, and that," he added, waving at Horatio's short, plump figure, "is Lord Barstow."

"Oh!" the lady gasped. Her white cap quivered as she scurried forward. "What a delightful surprise! You must forgive me for assuming there had been trouble. It's just that no one ever comes this far off the main road, and we have had no visitors this age! We didn't expect you, sir, although we have constantly hoped you would deign to visit us.

"But there," she finished in a flustered voice, "I am

rambling like an addle-pate. I am Mrs. Simpson, the housekeeper."

Sebastian bowed politely. "I am sorry to arrive so unexpectedly, Mrs. Simpson," he said smoothly. "But we were in the neighborhood and, along with some business I need to take care of here at the Abbey, I thought it high time I met my ward."

"Oh, yes! Lady Angel will be so pleased. Do come in." The woman motioned them up the steps. "I will send for our groom to care for your horses. He is retired, but does not live far and can be here in a trice."

"Thank you. Would you also ask him to put some salve on my black stallion's wounds? The horse met with some trouble during a race."

"Certainly. It will only take a few minutes for me to prepare your rooms, and I'll instruct Cook to prepare you a light nuncheon. Of course," she added hesitantly, "most of Cook's dishes are country fare, but I'm sure she will be happy to prepare anything you might desire—if she knows how."

"We do not require anything special," Sebastian answered, thinking uneasily of the disruption his announcement about Windywood Abbey's new owner would bring to this obviously well-run household. "As for our staying here tonight, we will be obliged to have rooms, but shall not be staying longer."

Mrs. Simpson nodded. "We don't keep a butler," she said over her shoulder, "since it seems such an extravagance way out here in the country. And we have but a few servants—chambermaids, mostly. Lady Angel doesn't require much. She's a darling, and lives up to her name."

"I'm sure she does. But then," Sebastian said, feeling more discomfitted by the moment, "what child doesn't?"

Mrs. Simpson paused and cast him a questioning glance.

"Er, I suppose that is true enough. Fond of children, are you, my lord?"

"I suppose so. Haven't been around many." Sebastian frowned as the housekeeper began moving again, through the vestibule and into a narrow hall. Why would she ask him such an odd question? Because she wanted him to like Lady Angel? Was there something terribly wrong with the girl?

A long staircase rose toward the north. Rather than turning to climb it, the housekeeper led them into a spacious parlor. "I hope you will be comfortable here while I see to your rooms. Dinner is normally at five and we have a late supper around ten—we have been used to keeping country hours here, my lord, although we would be happy to turn dinner backward if you wish."

Sebastian nodded. "If it isn't too much trouble I believe I would enjoy a light nuncheon immediately, and dinner itself at seven, foregoing supper altogether. My companions and I are rather weary and would like to make an early night."

"I'm sure it will be no trouble at all." The housekeeper turned to him and smiled. "This is your home, after all, my lord, and I am positive the other household members will be every bit as delighted to do your bidding as I am." Then she pointed toward the eastern wall of the parlor. "You will find excellent brandy and port in that side table, my lord. Please excuse me; I will be but a few minutes."

"Thank you. And Mrs. Simpson?" the earl called as she disappeared from the room.

Her white capped head popped back into view. "Yes, my lord?"

"Would you send Lady Angelique to me immediately?"

"Certainly, my lord."

Sebastian cleared his throat and ignored his companions' anxious faces. Suddenly unable to stand the thought of confronting the child by himself, he found he needed Barstow and Evanstone's support, fragile though it might be. However, certain that, if he looked at the two men, they would ask to be excused from this meeting, he avoided meeting either man's gaze altogether.

Shortly, a sound made him glance up. Standing in the doorway was a tall, slender woman with the most amazing hair Sebastian had ever seen. It was precisely the color of opium poppies and curled about her head like windwhipped clouds.

Her eyes were the only really attractive thing about her face. A brilliant mix of azure and green, they sparkled at him with apparent trepidation. For a split second they seemed disturbingly familiar. Then Sebastian shrugged away the fanciful thought and continued his inspection.

The lady was dressed in an out-moded gown of rust kerseymere that had undoubtedly seen a patchwork needle once too often. Sebastian could not help noticing that her figure left a great deal to be desired, unless a man preferred his women shaped like adolescent boys. He did not.

Forcing a smile, he stood respectfully. "You must be Miss Tritt, Lady Angelique's governess. I am Sebastian Hughes, the new earl of Darcy. Allow me to present my companions. This tall gentleman is Lord—"

Without any warning, to Sebastian's astonishment the scant color in the woman's freckled cheeks drained away, leaving her face as pale as a newly opened narcissus blossom. Giving a broken cry, she raised one hand, as if in a gesture of supplication, and then collapsed in a heap just inside the parlor door.

"Egad," stammered Evanstone, obviously impressed. "I know ladies are frequently overwhelmed by your masculine appeal, Seb, but I don't recall one ever actually swooning over you."

Barstow merely stared, his poker-straight black hair hanging over his eyes, and his mouth gaping open like a friendly barmaid's bodice.

Sebastian did not reply.

Rushing forward, he knelt beside the woman. Picking up one of her pale hands, which, he discovered, was astonishingly rough and callused for a lady of such obviously delicate sensibilities, he began chafing it.

Chapter Five

Angel awoke to find the darkest pair of eyes she'd ever seen gazing down at her with a mixture of consternation and concern. Up close they, and the whisker-shadowed cheeks beneath them, were even more outrageously attractive than she'd thought upon her first glimpse of the gentleman at that afternoon's race.

She felt a sudden urge to run her fingertips along his jaw to see if the shadows felt rough. Stopping herself just in time, she shook her head, hard, certain that if she did so her vision would clear and she would realize that the man before her was not the same rakishly handsome peer she'd seen earlier that day, but another, quite different, gentleman.

However, the face remained the same.

She swallowed. Good God. Was she dreaming, or was Hughes Pride's owner *really* the new earl of Darcy?

Slowly she realized that the floor beneath her backside was hard. She also became aware that the dark-eyed gentleman's arm was placed supportively around her shoulders. And that she liked it there. Very much.

Her cheeks flamed. "I am so sorry," she blurted. "I have never fainted before. I do not know what came over me."

The new earl grinned. His teeth were very white in his tanned face. Angel thought he had an altogether marvelous smile.

"It's quite all right," he said reassuringly. "But you did have me worried there for a moment. I thought you had struck your head on the floor when you fell. Fortunately, however, I see I was mistaken, since you shook your head just now, and would certainly have suffered much pain if you had been truly injured.

"Nevertheless, though you do not appear to be in danger, I would be more than happy to carry you to your chamber and send for the local medic, if you think it necessary."

Angel's heart flipped over in her chest as she looked up into his aristocratically fine-boned face. He was almost classically beautiful, but possessed a manliness that could never have been mistaken for femininity. The rich scents of shaving lotion and tobacco rose from his body like the headiest perfume, but did not quite cover the wonderful, warm, masculine scent that, surely, could only be his very own.

Intensely aware of his body close to hers, Angel dropped her gaze from his glittering dark eyes to his neck. His cravat, tied in the manner known as the Mathematical, was snowy white against the deep blue of his coat. Her attention wandered from right to left, following the wide expanse of his muscular shoulders, then rose again to his eyes. Those eyes, rimmed with black, almost obscenely long lashes, crinkled down at her as if he were amused by her examination.

But of course he was amused. Her admiration had to be obvious. The new earl obviously thought her a skittish old maid overwhelmed at being so near to a handsome, eligible male.

Angel's heart plummeted to the pit of her stomach. Flushing, she sat up and pushed the earl's arm off her shoulders. Even then the earl did not move away. Instead he rocked back on his heels, peering into her face.

"Are you certain you are all right, Miss Tritt? Would you like me to call the housekeeper? Perhaps you should go to your room and lie down for a while."

Trying to hide her horror, Angel searched her mind for a way to send the earl about his business without him discovering her dissimulation. But she was not to have the chance.

A movement in the doorway made all of them raise their eyes to the plump figure that rushed into the room. "Lady Angel!" The housekeeper scurried forward. "What has happened? Have you taken ill?"

Angel's cheeks went from warm to flaming, and she wished everyone in the room, save herself, to perdition. Unable to meet what she knew would be Lord Darcy's damning gaze, she murmured brokenly, "I am all right, thank you, Mrs. Simpson. It was the shock of meeting his lordship. I fainted."

Vaguely she heard Lord Darcy's companions' shocked oaths. She watched out of the corner of her eye as the earl rose silently from his position on the floor. He took her by the hand and pulled her, none too gently, to her feet. For a moment tiny black dots, brought on by her standing too quickly, clouded her vision, then faded as she regained her equilibrium.

When the earl spoke it was in the same velvety tones he had used while trying to purchase Vortex after that afternoon's race. "I think perhaps her ladyship and I should speak alone," he murmured. "If you will all excuse us? Mrs. Simpson, are my companions' rooms prepared?"

The housekeeper nodded and accepted the earl's obvious dismissal. "Oh, yes. If you gentlemen will follow me, I will show you upstairs."

The two lords eagerly exited the room with the housekeeper, clearly relieved to be out of the way when the fireworks began.

Stricken with mortification, Angel closed her eyes for a moment. Then she opened them to see the earl cross the room and drape himself comfortably, like a deceptively calm panther that might, at any second, leap to action and strike its victim with a death blow, across an overstuffed Louis XV armchair.

Drawing an unsteady breath, she braced herself for his fury. When it did not come, she said shamefully, "For the first time in my life, I find myself totally at a loss for anything to say."

Lord Darcy said nothing for a long moment, but merely gazed at her with inscrutable ebony eyes. The silence extended into minutes. Finally the earl cleared his throat. To Angel's astonishment, when he did finally speak he sounded amused rather than irate.

"Perhaps you might start by telling me why you thought it necessary to lie to me." His tone was gentle but held an unmistakable undercurrent of steel. "Why did you tell me you were a child? And what of the estimable Miss Tritt, with whom I have corresponded these last few years? I assume you wrote those informative letters about my *young* ward. Was the governess merely a figment of your imagination?"

In the face of such an interested, non-censorious tone, Angel found herself unable to fabricate anything else. She grinned self-consciously, but replied candidly. "Not really. Miss Tritt was my nurse many years ago. And I lied because I was afraid you would insist on my having a London Season and marrying the first man to offer."

The earl inclined his head. "In that you were correct. Marriage, as I am sure you are aware, is a gentlewoman's lot in life. Especially when one is not gifted with a fortune, as your father, if you will forgive me, did not see fit to leave you."

Angel flushed anew. "No, he did not."

"If a lack of funds is why you did not want to go to London, my dear girl," the earl said gently, "I assure you I would have been—and still am—more than willing to supply you with an adequate dowry and a wardrobe suitable for your debut."

He smiled, exposing those impossibly straight, impossibly white teeth again. Angel felt an unfamiliar flurry of feminine confusion cloud her reasoning. Irritated by the sensation, as well as his implication that, no matter how ugly she might be, he could still *buy* her a husband, she shook her head.

"I assure you I did not, and still do not, want a Season," she answered firmly.

The earl, for the moment, did not respond to this statement. Instead, he asked, "Do you not have a governess, Lady Angelique? How is it that you managed to perpetrate this hoax? Or do you have a governess who has aided you in your deception?"

"I do not. After I outgrew my nurse, my father did not see fit to replace her."

Lord Darcy's eyes narrowed disapprovingly. "May I inquire why not?"

Embarrassed, Angel returned his gaze belligerently. "He said that being as ugly as I am I could not possibly hope to attract a husband, so it would be a waste of money to educate me to the finer things that a man might expect of his wife. He preferred to give that money to various charities. So you see, my lord, even if you had insisted I have a Season, it would have been for naught."

The earl's fine mouth tightened. Angel thought she saw a glimmer of sympathy in his eyes.

"Why?" he asked softly.

"For God's sake, my lord, look at me!" she cried, goaded beyond sensibility and thoroughly humiliated at being forced to point out her numerous physical imperfections to this superbly perfect specimen of masculinity. "I am ugly as mud, and I know it, so you may stop being so damned kind!"

Lord Darcy sighed. He rubbed his eyes with the thumb and forefinger of his right hand. His ruby signet ring gleamed. "Lady Angel—may I call you that, since it is so much shorter and simpler than Angelique?"

"Yes."

"Thank you, Lady Angel. You are most considerate."

One corner of his mouth lifted and Angel felt an over-whelming regret that she was not beautiful. If only he would *really* smile at her. At *her*, not at what she might say, or what he might find amusing about her being such an antidote or country mouse who had no ability to flirt and converse easily with gentlemen.

He spoke again and she tried to concentrate on his words instead of his beautiful face. "Lady Angel, will you please come sit nearer to me? I find it unpleasant, and rather irritating, to shout my questions from across the room."

Without answering she moved to a chair directly across from his and sat rigidly. She gazed down at her nail-bitten fingers, clasped in her lap. Her hair seemed to itch the back of her neck, pricking her skin by its sheer scarlet hideousness. Each freckle on her cheeks seemed to burn.

Inwardly she cursed the fates that had made her so ugly. Outwardly, having regained her composure, she remained silent, sitting as straight and stiff as a poker. When Lord Darcy gave an exasperated sigh, she lifted her gaze uncertainly.

"Do you find my presence so distasteful, Lady Angel?"

Her mouth dropped open. "Why, no! Certainly not!" As if any woman could! she added silently.

"Then why do you not speak to me?"

"My father always insisted I be silent until I was spoken to."

The earl frowned, though whether at her behavior or her father's, Angel could not be sure.

"From now on," he said flatly, "as long as you do not interrupt those who are speaking to you, you are to speak whenever you wish. Now then. We must decide what is to be done with you."

Chapter Six

Angel leapt to her feet. "Done with me? You make me sound as if I were an unwanted sow, one you couldn't decide whether to butcher or to sell. Well, my lord, I will have you know I'll not bend my neck quietly to your sword!"

To her astonishment, her guardian shouted with laughter. Angel glared at him through narrowed lids. "My discomfiture amuses you, Lord Darcy?"

"Not at all." He stopped laughing and studied her interestedly. "It is just that I find your outspokenness unexpected—and refreshing. Such candor is a rare commodity in Town. I don't believe I've ever met any debutante—or anyone else, save perhaps my sister—in London who would have dared give me such a set-down."

Not knowing how to respond, Angel didn't reply. After a moment, she asked curtly, "And what do you suggest we 'do' with me, then?"

Lord Darcy sobered. He gazed at her inscrutably. "That depends on your purpose in telling me you were a child.

It seems a rather convoluted and altogether unnecessary story, unless you had something you wanted to accomplish. Or unless you merely wanted to keep me away from here."

"I already told you—"

"I know, you said you lied to keep from being packed off to London. However, for some inexplicable reason I find myself wondering if you had yet another motive." He smiled faintly. "Call it instinct, if you will. Whatever it is, it served me well on the Continent when our armies were battling Napoleon. I learned to trust it then, as it was seldom wrong."

"Well," Angel said a bit too rapidly, "it is mistaken now."

Lord Darcy said nothing. His dark-eyed gaze drifted over her face and Angel wondered if he were counting the freckles spattering her cheeks. Her hot flush deepened. She breathed deeply, trying to calm her unsettled nerves, since she knew blushes only served to make her freckles stand out even more grotesquely—something she desperately wanted to avoid in her handsome guardian's presence.

Oh, why did God have to make her so ugly!

"Perhaps," Lord Darcy murmured finally. "On the other hand, if you had no motive beyond wishing to avoid a London Season, you might just have *told* me you did not want one. I probably would have insisted you go, anyway, but you had no way of knowing that. Therefore, despite your insistence otherwise, I maintain that you must have had another reason for wanting me to stay away from Windywood Abbey and discovering the truth behind your prevarication about your true age."

Unable to maintain her secrecy any longer under the earl's intently scrutinizing gaze, Angel finally sighed and nodded. "You are correct," she admitted. "There was another reason."

"Yes?" he prompted when she did not elucidate.

Thrusting her chin up defiantly, Angel stared at him. "I want to buy Windywood Abbey."

This time it was Lord Darcy's gaze that faltered. His dark eyes shifted in a manner that could only be termed nervously, away from hers. He fiddled with his cravat. "Buy Windywood?" he asked in a strangled voice. "But . . . I thought you had no money."

"Let us just say that I have been saving up."

Lord Darcy's shadowed cheeks reddened. "My dear girl, I fear it would take a very long time to save enough of your pin money to buy this estate. Windywood Abbey is small, it is true, but it is also quite valuable."

Undaunted, Angel pressed on. "I realize that."

"Well, then you can hardly have gathered together enough money to do so."

"Perhaps I have. Two years ago I wrote to my father's old solicitor, your solicitor now, inquiring as to Windywood's value. He told me the estate was worth ten thousand pounds. Was he wrong?"

Lord Darcy shook his head. "I do not know. I have never seen the estate's books. However, from what I have seen while here, I believe I concur with his evaluation."

"Good." Angel breathed a sigh of relief. Suddenly everything in the room seemed brighter. "You see, I have already managed to gather nine thousand, five hundred and fifty pounds. If you will give me time, I promise I will soon have the remaining amount."

"Where in God's name did you find such a fortune?" the earl demanded.

Angel gritted her teeth. If her guardian were going to balk, it would be over her refusal to divulge her monetary source. "That is my concern, my lord."

"Your concern," he replied slowly. Abruptly, his red cheeks darkened even more, and his brows lowered threateningly. "Remember that I am your guardian, Lady Angel. If you have been up to nefarious activities, I have a right to know."

Angel blinked. "Nefarious activities?" she repeated blankly.

"Yes. I must know what you have been doing to earn such a sum. If you are ruined, I must know that before we attempt to find you a husband."

"I have already told you I do not want a husband. I want to buy Windywood."

Standing, the earl paced to the window and glared out at the landscape. "That is impossible."

"Why? Because you think I have been up to 'nefarious activities,' whatever that means? What does it matter what I did to earn the money, as long as I have it?"

Now Lord Darcy's complexion resembled nothing so much as an overripe cherry. "It could matter very much indeed," he snapped furiously, "to prospective husbands!"

As she realized what he was suggesting, Angel's mouth dropped open. "Oh dear. You . . . you think that I . . ." her voice trailed off. Despite the seriousness of the situation, she could not help but laugh at its irony. "Oh, my!" she wheezed through her chuckles. "You actually think that I have been selling my favors? As if anyone would actually find my face or body worth paying for? Worth over nine thousand pounds? Oh, sir," she gasped, "that is rich!"

Lord Darcy stiffened. "If I am mistaken, I apologize. But I cannot think of any other way a penniless young woman could come by such a sum. As to your face and figure, they . . ." he cleared his throat and again tugged uncomfortably at his cravat, "are not all *that* bad."

Angel's laughter broke off as abruptly as if someone

had slapped her in the face. "Not all that bad," she reprised somberly. She studied her handsome guardian, wondering what kind of woman he considered beautiful. She sighed, knowing that she would never fit into that category. "Well, that might be true," she said finally, "but neither are they appealing. And I do not delude myself into thinking otherwise."

Lord Darcy graciously inclined his head. "You still have not answered my question. Where did you get the money?"

Angel stared at him, wondering if he would be more horrified at her dressing in a boy's clothes and entering horse races than he was at the thought of her acting as a whore. She decided he would.

"I cannot divulge that information," she said firmly.

"Lady Angel," Lord Darcy said, returning to his seat and then leaning toward her with his elbows resting on his knees. "You aren't making this easy, you know?"

Angel answered sincerely. "I do not mean to be difficult, my lord. But I cannot tell you where I got the money."

Lord Darcy sighed. "My dear girl, I assure you I have your best interests at heart. I am not asking these outrageous questions simply to embarrass you. But I *must* know all the facts before I make any decisions."

She met his eyes squarely. "I realize you must, sir, but I still will not tell you where I got the money. Suffice it to say that I have it. Now, will you or will you not sell Windywood Abbey to me?"

Lord Darcy went white about the lips. Rising again, he paced the room several times. Finally he folded his hands behind his back, turned, and said gruffly, "I will not."

Angel felt her heart sink to her toes. "But why? If it is because I do not have the entire sum, or . . ." she added, with a catch in her voice, "if you want more for the land, I will pay whatever sum you require as soon as possible!"

The earl seemed to grind his teeth. "You misunderstand. It is not that I *will* not sell Windywood Abbey to you. It is that I *can* not." Then he once again returned to his chair and lowered himself into it. Putting a hand to his forehead, he began massaging his temples.

Angel said nothing. She could not seem to force the necessary words past her lips.

"I cannot sell Windywood to you," the earl explained wearily, "because it is no longer mine. I came here today to tell you that."

Angel felt the blood drain from her face. "What do you mean?"

"There was a horse race not far from here this afternoon. I met an old acquaintance there, and we made a wager." He wiggled restively. "I was certain I could not lose."

"But you did. You bet the Abbey," Angel said in a disbelieving whisper. "And you lost."

"Yes. My stallion, Hughes Pride, has over one hundred years breeding to his pedigree. I was certain he would win. Then this young man rode up with an enormous gray stallion, and . . ." his voice trailed off.

Angel felt unable to breathe. "You lost the Abbey," she repeated, "because the gray horse won the race?"

"That is correct. I am sorry, Lady Angel. But if it is any consolation, I would like to assure you that, had you told me how you felt about the estate, I'd have simply given it to you. It would have been the least I could do, since your own father left you without a shilling to your name."

Slowly, Angel got to her feet. Barely conscious of what she was doing, she moved to stand in the same place by the window that the earl had recently vacated. Staring out the glass and across the velvety lawn, she forced herself to ask one final question. In her heart she already knew the answer.

"And the man to whom you lost?" she said softly. "What was his name?"

"Sir Corbin Pugsley. The man who owns all the land surrounding the Abbey. He should, I regret to say, be arriving here any time to collect the deed."

A slight knock sounded on the parlor door. It opened slowly to admit Mrs. Simpson. Her face was gray with shock.

"I beg your pardon, Lord Darcy," she said tremulously, "but Sir Corbin Pugsley has called and says he is here to collect the paperwork for transference of the Abbey to his possession. Afterward, with your permission, he wishes to address Lady Angel privately."

The earl turned surprised eyes on Angel. "What could Pugsley have to say to you? Never say he wishes your hand in marriage, or that you have been encouraging him! Even though I would like to see you wed, I could not possibly countenance a match with such a reprobate. I do hope you have not been encouraging his friendship."

Despite the sick feeling of despair she felt, as well as her own personal revulsion for her neighbor, Angel was still surprised by this peculiar statement. "I thought you wanted me wed. Surely a baronet is as good as *I* could ever hope to attach."

"It is not that. It is merely that Pugsley's reputation for . . ." Lord Darcy coughed, "odd practices reaches even to London. I assure you, madam, even *you* could do better than Pugsley in Town."

Angel had no time to feel more than a glimmer of pain by this unintended slight. As if called up by the devil himself, Sir Corbin Pugsley, without waiting for a summons, sauntered into the room. Mrs. Simpson, avoiding looking directly at the baronet's misshapen face, hastily departed.

As though oblivious to Angel and Lord Darcy's presence, Pugsley brushed his mauve satin coat sleeve and picked a bit of lint from one apple green clad thigh. When he glanced up he managed a look of surprise. Lifting a gold lorgnette from his chest, he peered through its square lens.

"Ah, Darcy," he said with an oily smile. "I hope you don't mind that I decided to drop by sooner than planned. I know we said five, and it is only four-thirty, but I simply couldn't wait. I was just so excited."

Through the lens, his magnified right eye smiled intimately in Angel's direction, while his left ranged freely about the room. "As for my wishing to speak with Lady Angel, let us just say we have some . . . personal business to attend to."

Lord Darcy rose, seeming to tower over the baronet even though both men were of a similar height. "I am Lady Angel's guardian, Pugsley. It is me with whom you should be dealing, if you have anything personal to say to her."

"Actually," Angel said hastily, "I would prefer to speak to Sir Corbin by myself, my lord, if you would not mind."

A dark query rose in Lord Darcy's ebony eyes. His expression clearly indicated that he assumed Angel had gotten the money with which she had planned to buy the Abbey from Pugsley. This must seem a highly probable scenario to the earl, Angel mused sickly, since Pugsley was so hideous that the baronet could certainly not find her too ugly to bed.

"I believe I understand," the earl said wryly. "Well, I suppose you can do no more harm than you have done already. I do not suppose you want me to send Mrs. Simpson in to chaperone you?"

"No, thank you."

Lord Darcy smiled corrosively. "I thought not. Then we shall speak further after dinner, Lady Angel. Perhaps you will agree to meet me in the library afterward, and we shall continue our discussion." He turned to the baronet. "Your servant, Pugsley."

Sir Corbin, still fingering his lorgnette, merely smiled with the half of his mouth that would rise to the occasion. Lord Darcy, his back stiff with what could only have been disapproval, left the parlor and closed the door behind him.

When the earl had gone, Sir Corbin slithered closer to Angel. His jaw was clenched, making his twisting scar appear stark white against his flushed cheeks.

"My dear girl, you look pale," he said tenderly. "I do hope you aren't too dismayed at learning that I now own this house and its grounds."

Angel stared at him, willing the tears jabbing the backs of her eyes to go away. She blinked rapidly and took a deep breath. "Not at all. I am sure you will be kind enough to sell it to me."

Pugsley's good eye glittered. He dropped the lorgnette back to his chest. "Angel, Angel, Angel," he chided, clicking his tongue. "You must know that you have only one thing that I would value. Yourself. Marry me and I will gladly sign the house over to you as a settlement. I have no interest in your money."

Angel shivered. God knew what Pugsley would do to her if she became his property.

Although British law stated that a husband could only beat his wife with a stick no thicker than his thumb, she made no doubt that Pugsley would happily beat her within an inch of her life each day if she were unfortunate enough to become Lady Pugsley. It was unlikely she would survive a year. She knew, rather than killing her outright, marrying her was the worst thing he could possibly do to her. And that he would cherish tormenting her.

"Never," she said flatly.

Pugsley shrugged and turned away. "I was afraid you would feel that way. In that case I shall pull the house down, stone by stone, until there is nothing here but meadow." He smiled thoughtfully. "Yes, that is precisely what I shall do."

Angel's hand flew to her throat. "Sir Corbin!" she cried, unable to keep silent, even though she knew her agonized outburst would please the baronet immeasurably. "You would not!"

He raised his right eyebrow, looking infinitely bored. "I would."

Closing her eyes, Angel shook her head. Then she looked up, pleadingly. "I beg you, Sir Corbin . . . sell the Abbey to me."

Running a finger over his mangled mouth, Pugsley smiled. "Perhaps if you give me a little kiss, I might consider it."

Angel swallowed the bile that rose in her throat. At the mere thought of embracing the baronet, her stomach roiled. "You jest, sir."

"I have never been more serious in all my life."

Looking into his good eye, Angel knew he meant every word. Swallowing, she nodded. "All right."

"Wise girl."

As Pugsley approached, his white hand glided out to touch her wrist. Sliding his fingers over her skin, he scraped his fingernails softly over her forearm, caressed her inner elbow, and rose to settle at the juncture of her lacy sleeve and more luscious, hidden flesh. His hand was trembling. Squeezing her arm, he pulled her close and settled his mangled lips against hers.

Angel could feel his teeth beneath the slight padding. She swallowed a surge of revulsion. She willed herself to think of nothing, and held completely still.

At last the baronet sighed and, removing his lips from

hers, released her and stepped away. "Dear, dear girl. You are delicious. Even more delicious than I anticipated on the day I nearly possessed your lovely body in your father's meadow and received your vicious refusal."

Angel did not rise to this baiting comment. "You have had your kiss. Now, sir. What price do you ask for the Abbey?"

Pugsley's right eye gazed absently into the corner of the parlor. His left looked as flatly unemotional as if the intimate encounter had never happened. "What were you going to give Darcy?"

"Ten thousand pounds."

"Then I want twenty."

"Twenty!" Angel cried in dismay. "I couldn't possibly raise that much!"

The baronet shrugged. "Take it or leave it, my dear. And, if you accept my terms, you must have the money by the first of August."

"And if I cannot?"

"If you do not deliver twenty thousand pounds to me by midnight of July 31, our agreement is forfeit and Windywood Abbey will be destroyed."

Despite her certainty that she could never raise such a sum by the time specified, Angel nodded wearily. "You'll have your money."

"One moment, my dear, that is not all I want," Pugsley added smoothly.

Angel braced herself. "What else?"

"If you fail to raise the money, you will, of your own free will, spend one night with me and do whatever I request. As you seem so disgusted by my offer of marriage, I shall endeavor to entertain you in a manner you would enjoy more. Or less, as the case may be."

His words were presented tonelessly, but Angel could

hear the malevolence behind them. "I cannot promise that."

Wandering idly toward the mantelpiece, the baronet trailed his lacquered fingertips over a dainty porcelain shepherdess that had belonged to Angel's mother. Suddenly, with a savageness that made Angel step backward, he swept the delicate bauble to the floor where it shattered into a thousand pieces. Then, slowly, his fingers slid to brush a second knickknack, consideringly.

"Please," Angel said, "stop! Those figurines belonged to my mother."

Pugsley blinked. "I beg your pardon, Lady Angel, but everything in this house is mine, now. Unless you accept my terms, that is, in which case everything in the house shall remain untouched until the outcome of our wager is decided."

Angel's heart seemed to sink to her shoes. Loving the Abbey as she did, she could do nothing but accept. "Very well," she whispered. She turned to leave the room, unable to stand another moment in the baronet's evil presence.

Pugsley smiled. "Wonderful. Oh, and Lady Angel?" he added as if in an afterthought.

Angel turned back, dreading his final words, although how they could be any worse than what he had already said was beyond her imagination. She tried not to look at his left eye, which was now rolling back in its socket like a Chinese fishing float on a turbulent sea. "Yes?"

"One word of this to Lord Darcy, and you immediately forfeit the wager. If I hear so much as a whisper that the earl has learned of our agreement, the Abbey comes down, stone by stone."

The bile which Angel had steadfastly repressed now rose in her throat. Clasping a hand to her mouth, she rushed from the room and barely made it to her chamber before losing her breakfast.

When her illness subsided she made her way to the Abbey's front balcony. She sat for some time, gazing out into the emerald distance. But even that restful view did not quiet her jangled nerves. Finally she rested her chin on the railing and, as tears began streaming down her face, let despair wash over her.

Chapter Seven

Dinner was a long and tiresome ordeal. As Sebastian took a few last bites of his caramel crême brulé, he let his gaze slide down the long dining table to flicker between Barstow and Evanstone, who sat across from each other. Both gentlemen looked dashed uncomfortable.

Momentarily both men met his glance, then cast furtive looks toward Lady Angel's bowed head before returning their attention to their plates. It was obvious to Sebastian that they were wishing they had foregone his invitation to stop overnight at Windywood but had, instead, continued on to Lord Appleby's.

From Barstow and Evanstone, Sebastian turned his attention to Lady Angel, who sat opposite him at the far end of the table. Her scarlet tresses, scraped tightly up on the top of her head in what could only be a most painful manner, clashed dreadfully with her frilly, pink silk dinner gown. Exposed above her bodice, her boyish breast was sprinkled with freckles similar to those frosting her cheeks.

Sebastian wished his ward would look up so that he might see her eyes again. The first time he had seen them they had seemed so bright and fiery that he'd had the sensation of being hit on the head with an oak log. He told himself he wanted to see them again simply because he needed to know precisely what, if any, husband-attracting features he would have to work with once he got her to London.

For a moment he wondered absently if she would be more appealing if she smiled. Then, experiencing a flash of self-censure, he hastily discarded this notion. The poor girl had no reason to smile, since he had effectively squashed her life's dream by losing Windywood Abbey on a ridiculous bet.

Momentarily, however, Lady Angel did glance in his direction. Her hazel eyes, while every bit as striking as he'd remembered, were now cold and damning. Guilt seemed to grow in his chest until he could scarcely breathe.

Flushing, Sebastian dropped his attention to his wineglass.

His thoughts turned to Sir Corbin Pugsley's mangled face and perfumed body, and the fact that Lady Angel had almost certainly earned the money to buy Windywood by selling herself to the baronet. What had intrigued the overdressed dandy enough that he had paid a small fortune for Lady Angel's favors? Even a man as hideous as Pugsley could easily afford more attractive bedmates. For that matter, what could have possessed Lady Angel that she would have given herself to a man with the baronet's purportedly outrageous sexual habits?

He rubbed his tired eyes with a thumb and forefinger.

To be sure, any other guardian would have wasted no time in demanding his ward marry the bastard who had ruined her. But, despite Lady Angel's tarnished past,

Sebastian knew he could not in good conscience compel the chit into a union in which she would be forced to succumb to Pugsley's reputedly sadistic lovemaking for the rest of her life, much less look at the dandy's God-awful visage day after day.

But, he thought then, if he did not insist she marry Pugsley, what were the odds he would be able to find a husband for her?

She was hardly what one would term a diamond of the first water, or even mildly pretty. She was truly plain. And, ruined, to boot.

He could only hope that, when he got to know her better, he would discover that she possessed an appealing personality. A sparkling wit, perhaps, that would enable some London gentleman to overlook her lack of desirable physical attributes. Or a sensitive, maternal nature that would appeal to a man with several children and no wife.

He cast her another furtive glance, and again felt a sinking certainty that he would be stuck with her for the rest of her life. Not only stuck with her, but with the white-hot censure that flared in her hazel eyes each time she looked at him. She would never allow him to forget that impulsive moment when he had wagered away her beloved ancestral estate and, with one fell swoop, crushed her fondest dream.

At that moment Lady Angel reached for her wineglass. Her fingers brushed against it, sending it crashing to the table. Red liquid streamed across the embroidered white tablecloth. She uttered an unladylike oath, and then blushed furiously, the freckles on her cheeks seeming even more blotchy than usual.

Sebastian could not help comparing his ward to his future betrothed, Lady Sarah, who was all grace and beauty. A smile lifted his lips as he thought of his promised lady's ebony curls that gleamed like blue-black satin around her milky-white complexion and petal-pink cheeks. The amount of Lady Sarah's skin that he had seen, which was considerable due to the low-cut bodices of which tonnish ladies (bless them) were fond, had nary a blemish over its entire creamy expanse.

Well, he amended suddenly, Lady Sarah *did* have a small mole just over her left breast, but that appealing beauty mark could hardly be termed a defect!

As his thoughts wandered, Sebastian remembered the night he had decided (after Lord Appleby had hinted that the seven coveted Egyptian horses he had brought to England might be added to his daughter's dowry, if that was what it took to procure a countess-ship for her) to make Lady Sarah his bride.

Now, if he closed his eyes he could imagine Lady Sarah sitting where Lady Angel sat now, except that Lady Sarah would be smiling, her flawless face and velvety cleavage enticing in the candlelight, her deep sapphire-blue eyes shining with admiration for something he had said, and her beautiful mouth curving upward as she laughed musically at some jest or other he had told.

However, the thought of her amusement made Sebastian frown suddenly as he recalled how Lady Sarah had responded to a comment he had made in her presence the previous week at a ball.

Although well aware that one usually did not discuss political debates at social functions, Sebastian, truly concerned about a proposed law that was soon to be voted upon, had been unable to hold his tongue when that subject arose among several gentlemen standing nearby. Overhearing their comments, he immediately began pressing his fellow peers to support Sir Robert Peel and Mr. Robert Owen in their attempt to pass the law, which would forbid the employment of children under ten years of age.

He had just commented on how unfortunate it was

that there were so many poor people in London, forcing parents to send their young children—four- and five-year-olds—to work in factories. Many of the children did not survive over a year, the work was so exhausting.

While his friends and acquaintances had agreed that such practices were unfortunate, they had not seemed overwhelmingly in favor of supporting such a law; almost all of them owned part or parcel of the very factories that employed such youthful workers.

Overhearing Sebastian's argument that it was hideously cruel that so many young children suffered such terrible deaths, Lady Sarah had tittered and giggled as though he had made the funniest remark on earth. Oh, Sebastian was certain she had not laughed because she was hardhearted. She simply had not understood a word he'd said.

If one used one's imagination, he reflected now, still gazing absently in Lady Angel's direction, one could almost have imagined seeing a vacancy sign suspended behind Lady Sarah's limpid blue eyes.

Although at the time his shock at Lady Sarah's lack of intellect had been averted by the fact that, as she laughed, her bodice had dropped almost to the point of exposing her delicious pink nipples, now Sebastian could not help but wonder if Lady Sarah might not be a trifle too baconbrained for words.

Then he shook himself. It did not matter. Lady Sarah was not required to be an intellectual genius. Among most of his fellow ton-members, intelligence was not considered an admirable, or even particularly desirable, trait in one's wife.

Which, he mused, suddenly feeling quite gloomy, was just as well, if one was promised to a woman like Lady Sarah.

When Barstow cleared his throat, Sebastian realized with a jolt that he'd been staring at Lady Angel for an extended period of time. Hastily he tried to cover his embarrassment by taking another sip of wine, choked as some of it went down his windpipe, and coughed for several minutes. Some distant part of his mind could not help but notice that, due to the lack of conversation at this dinner party, his coughing sounded disturbingly loud.

When he had recovered, he apologized for the outburst and then redirected his attention, albeit more subtly, back to his ward. Despite Lady Angel's tarnished past, there was still her future to consider and, as a man of honor and responsibility, Sebastian had every intention of seeing her settled.

Somewhere. Somehow. With some poor, unsuspecting devil.

At the same time, he could hardly blame the chit for not wanting to go to London for a Season. She was so plain that, without a fortune, it was highly unlikely she would find anyone to marry her. And he was well aware that, even when a debutante was considered a diamond of the first water, come-outs could be difficult.

Upon consideration, he decided he could even go so far as to forgive her for selling her body to Sir Corbin Pugsley, since she had probably thought she had no other choice.

What she had done, though despicable, had been for a good cause, that being to have sufficient funds to buy her family home. And she had done nothing worse than many less well-bred women in London had done in order to survive.

He could hardly fault her for trying to make her own way in the world. It spoke loudly for her strong spirit that she should even try. But strong spirits were hardly considered appealing attributes amid debutantes. Besides, once any man worth marrying discovered her ruined state, he would balk immediately.

There was only one thing to do.

Sebastian knew he would simply have to keep his knowledge of Lady Angel's lewdness to himself until she had brought several gentlemen to the point. If—*when*, he amended—she accomplished this seemingly impossible feat, he would concern himself with whether or not to inform Lady Angel's potential mate at that time.

Despite her plainness, Sebastian was determined that Lady Angel *would* have suitors, regardless of how much it cost him. And, when she showed a preference to one of them, he would draw the chosen man aside and inform the gentleman about Lady Angel's sordid past. Despite the temptation, it would be unconscionable to marry her off to someone without first informing him of her habits.

But what kind of husband could the chit possibly hope to attract?

Most likely a widower with a large brood to raise— someone on the lookout for a new mother for his children—or a youngest son of a peer. But not too young. And it would have to be a youngest son, as it wouldn't do to allow a marriage between a woman of Lady Angel's habits to wed a gentleman who had the responsibility to secure his title with an heir. A young man, although eager to get his hands on the substantial dowry Sebastian intended to settle on Lady Angel, might not realize until it was too late that his wife was somewhat careless in choosing the father of her children.

Sebastian took a deep gulp from his wineglass.

Sweet heaven. It was bad enough that Lady Angel was plain, he reiterated silently, but ruined as well! Ye gods, what a mess. He would be lucky if he didn't have to put up every penny the late Lord Darcy had bequeathed to him as the chit's dowry—though he would, if that were the only way to fulfill his duty.

He turned his thoughts to the immediate future.

How unlucky he was to find himself saddled with a ward just as Hughes Pride was beginning his racing career. Sebastian was determined to be with Hughes Pride when the stallion ran. It was that simple. And that complicated.

Then the solution to this dilemma struck him as brilliantly and unexpectedly as a shooting star. He had just felt the world lift from his shoulders when Barstow gave a great yawn and stood.

"Well," the dark-haired lord said sleepily, "it is getting late and Evanstone and I must get an early start in the morning. Will you be coming with us tomorrow, Sebastian?"

Sebastian nodded at his pudgy friend. "If all goes as planned."

Evanstone also stood. "Egad, but I'm tired. That last glass of wine has nearly put me out."

Lady Angel jumped to her feet. Her cheeks flamed again. "Oh dear, I have lingered over my dessert too long and doomed you gentlemen to missing your after-dinner brandy, have I not?"

Sebastian gave her a weak smile. "Don't fret about it, my lady. Unless I miss my guess, my friends have no desire to linger downstairs this evening."

"Quite so," agreed Barstow, moving toward the door. "Good night, Lady Angel, and to you, Sebastian. I assure you I want nothing so much as a feather pillow right now."

"And I," added Evanstone, "can't wait to sink into a feather bed." Then, as though mortified at having mentioned sleeping arrangements in front of an unmarried female, the tall lord blushed furiously. His long legs carried him, at a speed only slightly under a lope, out of the room behind Barstow.

Sebastian turned to find Lady Angel's eyes upon him.

"My lord, this afternoon you requested that I attend you in the library. Are you still of that same mind?"

Sebastian nodded, deciding that now was as good a time as any to tell her his plans for her future. "Yes. Shall we go there now?"

"Of course."

Lady Angel stood and moved to the door. Watching her, Sebastian was struck by how gracefully she moved. Like a fine thoroughbred, she seemed almost to glide across the floor rather than walk. When she reached the door and turned her head to see what had detained him, he mentally shook himself and rose. Following, he allowed her to precede him down the hall.

Just outside the library he paused, felt in his coat pockets, and mumbled irritatedly.

"Is something amiss?" Lady Angel inquired.

"Only that I have left my cigarillos in the bedchamber Mrs. Simpson assigned me. But then, it is not proper for a gentleman to smoke around a lady, anyway," he finished with an apologetic grin. "So it is of no matter."

Lady Angel smiled, and Sebastian caught his breath at how the simple act transformed her plain face. Her blue-green eyes sparkled, and a glow of reminiscence softened the planes of her face. "Please, feel free to smoke if you like, my lord," she said sincerely. "My grandfather smoked cigarillos, and I confess I have dearly missed their scent."

Sebastian studied her gentle expression. "You were fond of your grandfather?"

"Oh, yes. I could always talk to him. He never treated me as though I had more hair than wit." Her smile vanished, replaced with a wistful frown. "My own father, God rest his soul, was less conciliatory. But one bears what one must."

Sebastian stared at her for a moment, marveling at how

a frown made her face seem much more forbidding than when she smiled. Then he said, "You are quite certain you will not be bothered by my smoking?"

She smiled again. "Quite."

"Wonderful. Would you be so good as to wait for me here while I go upstairs to fetch my cigarillos? I will be but a moment."

"Certainly."

It was, in fact, nearly twenty minutes before he made his way back to the library. The door was open, and he stood for a moment gazing into the shadowed room. Was she here, or had she given up on him and gone to bed?

He sincerely hoped she had remained, as it would be rather inconvenient to have to hunt her down in the morning in order to tell her his plans before he, Barstow, and Evanstone left for Lady Sarah's birthday party. They simply had to get an early start so that Hughes Pride, tied behind the carriage, would not be forced to trot. The fewer shocks the stallion's legs sustained, the more likely were his chances of taking the prize at the Grand London Gold Cup—and, Sebastian thought determinedly, he *would* have that cup!

Then a slight movement in one corner, near the fireplace where a cheerful fire chattered merrily to itself, caught his attention. Lady Angel had settled into a large armchair near the hearth, and seemed intent upon a book that she held angled toward the fire's dancing flames. Sebastian sighed, relieved.

Then, as he approached and Lady Angel's face fell into view more fully, he came to an abrupt halt and stared.

Chapter Eight

The firelight's golden aura, cascading out into the darkened library, transformed Lady Angel's hair into living flames that sparkled with golden highlights each time she moved or turned another page in the book she held cradled on her lap.

Without making a sound Sebastian moved nearer. The closer he came, he saw with astonishment, the more attractive the girl seemed. He breathed appreciatively. The heat of the fire had apparently stirred up the scent she'd been wearing, for an attractive, spicy aroma tantalized his nose.

Simultaneously he noted that Lady Angel, whose tightly scraped up hair had loosened to allow tendrils to frame her cheek and jaw, had a truly delightful profile. While her features had seemed ordinary from the front, from the side, with her long red-brown lashes and delicate, aquiline nose, she could have been a fine Greek sculpture come to life. Little tendrils framed the side of her face like gentle fingers, adding to the impression of an ancient statue.

Sebastian's fingers twitched with a sudden desire to stroke the mass of silken red hair. He also longed to lean close to her slender neck in order to better appreciate her delicious perfume.

He shook his head sharply, then stepped back and tried to clear his thoughts. Good Lord, was this what had caused Pugsley to shell out almost ten thousand pounds to bed the girl? Was this odd need what had made the baronet give Lady Angel almost enough blunt to purchase Windywood Abbey?

Sebastian moved quietly to stand behind Lady Angel's chair. It was turned slightly away from him, and he leaned over its headrest in order to see the title of the book his ward found so enthralling.

His eyes widened as they fell upon the pages of England's Racing Register. "Are you a fan of the turf, my lady?"

His voice made the girl start wildly. The book flew from her lap. Jumping forward, Sebastian caught it just before it disappeared into the fire and was consumed by the greedily crackling flames.

Lady Angel drew a sharp breath and clasped a hand to her bosom. "Lord Darcy!" she gasped. "You frightened me!"

"I sincerely apologize. It was unintentional." Sinking into the matching armchair beside hers, Sebastian propped the book he had saved from certain immolation up on his knee. "I was unaware that your father was interested in racing," he remarked.

"Oh, he wasn't," Lady Angel said. "He thought gambling sinful. He insisted it was the ruination of many families and their homes."

"And has been," Sebastian remarked, "to those without enough sense to bet only what they could afford to lose."

Feeling another spurt of guilt over losing the Abbey, he

glanced up at the girl's face to see if she had intentionally commented upon his own ruination of what she had foreseen as her future. He was relieved to see no flicker of resentment in her lustrous hazel eyes. She did not appear even to remember the unfortunate incident.

He asked then, "If the late earl was not interested in horses, how does this book come to be in his library?"

"It was my grandfather's book. *He* had a wonderful stable, but my father sold all the horses immediately upon inheriting. The stable was based on the bloodlines of one of the horses my grandfather shipped to Virginia in the spring of 1798, a gray stallion known as Diomed. Perhaps you have heard of him."

"Diomed? Winner of the Epsom Derby in 1780?"

Her eyes lit up as if in approbation of his knowledge. Her lips curved upward, making her plain face appear almost attractive. "That is correct."

Feeling absurdly self-satisfied at having made the girl smile, Sebastian returned her tribute. "What a coincidence," he said amiably. "My own stable-line is based on Diomed's offspring. The black stallion I ran this morning was one of that sire's great grandsons."

"Oh, now I understand!" Lady Angel cried. "That would explain why he ran so well for you, even though it was his first race."

Sebastian's brows shot up. "How did you know it was Hughes Pride's first race?"

Lady Angel's cheeks paled. She caught her breath, then seemed to recover her briefly lost poise. "I believe you mentioned something about it, my lord," she faltered. "Truly, how could I have known otherwise?"

"Quite right." Although Sebastian did not remember mentioning any such thing, it was possible, given his former emotional distraction, he had mentioned the race's particulars and simply did not recall doing so. "At any rate, it is a pity your grandfather's stock was sold. It takes years to build up a suitable breeding unit. I know. With my father's instruction, I've been raising thoroughbreds since I was six. He died not long ago."

"Oh, I am sorry." Then she added, "You have been interested in horses for a very long time, then."

"Not that long," Sebastian retorted, wincing. He suddenly felt quite ancient next to Lady Angel's fresh youthfulness. "I am only thirty-two."

The girl smiled, as if comprehending his discomfort.

Sebastian hurried on to avoid further discussion of the difference in their ages. "At any rate, my father loved horses. I hope someday to fulfill his greatest wish."

"And what was that?"

"He longed to win the Grand London Gold Cup. His stock almost won the race several times, but he died before fulfilling his life's dream."

Lady Angel's eyes widened as her gaze met his. "Then you share his dream."

"Yes." Sebastian closed the racing register, rose, and placed it on a nearby shelf. "But, although horses are fascinating, we have other things to discuss. I thought it best to inform you of my decision concerning your future, as my companions and I are leaving Windywood early in the morning."

"*Your* decision?" Now Lady Angel's eyes seemed to reflect the sparks in the roaring fire. "Am I to have no say in what becomes of me?"

The comraderie he'd felt moments before while discussing horses vanished as Sebastian remembered the licentious nature of the woman he was addressing.

Referring to the illicit affair she had not denied having with Sir Corbin Pugsley, he answered sharply, "I think you have had far too much freedom in making decisions about your life already. I have a duty to see you settled.

Your father assigned your guardianship to me, and I do not intend to betray that trust. Tomorrow afternoon you leave for London."

"London?" she whispered. Her pale rose lips gave the only color to her chalky face.

"Yes. You will be staying with my sister Hilary, Lady Cartwright, who will sponsor you for the Season."

The girl rose to her feet. "But . . ." she said falteringly. "But I do not want a Season! Please, do not make me go to London. I will not go! I *cannot* go!"

Sebastian steeled his will against her pleading gaze. "You can and you will. Furthermore, I fully expect you to be betrothed by the end of the festivities. If, at the end of that time, you have been unable to decide upon a man who suits you, I shall select a husband for you, myself."

The girl's eyes snapped with anger. "You mean you will buy one for me, if I fail to attract one with my infinite delightful attributes."

Sebastian's mouth tightened. He had not wanted to admit this fact, but she had brought it up, herself. "If that is what it takes, I will buy you a husband."

He said nothing more as Lady Angel whirled about and slammed from the library.

As she lay in bed that night, Angel considered Lord Darcy's pronouncement of his plans for her future and tried to decide what action to take to avoid them. It seemed ludicrous to think that, just when she was so close to achieving her goal, everything would go so wrong.

Since Angel had no maid, she and Mrs. Simpson had been up late that evening, packing trunks in preparation for the trip to London. It was the trip that occupied Angel's mind now. Aware that she needed all her mental faculties, she refused to release the storm of tears and rage that warred within her breast, and tried to think clearly.

What were her priorities?

Number one: She must find a way to raise another ten thousand four hundred fifty pounds by the first of August, so that she might purchase Windywood Abbey from Sir Corbin Pugsley.

That meant she must, somehow, continue entering Vortex in races. Other than selling her body, as Lord Darcy had mistakenly insinuated she had already done, there was no other method of obtaining the money. And, she thought dismally, despite Lord Darcy's intimation about Sir Corbin, it was almost certain that, even if her fondest desire was to become a Cyprian, no gentleman would be interested.

Number two: She must keep Lord Darcy from suspecting her actions.

Since, should he discover her clandestine pursuit, the earl would undoubtedly forbid her to have anything more to do with the racing circuit, she must somehow keep him from suspecting anything. Anything beyond the lightest interest in the turf scene was totally unacceptable amid females of the ton and, since his lordship's goal was to get her married off, he would quash any hint of scandal immediately.

With a sick lurch Angel realized that the best way to keep the earl from suspecting anything would be to cede to his desire that she have a London Season.

If he thought she was seriously looking for a husband, the earl wasn't likely to suspect that she was involved in anything else. Even though the thought of opening herself up to such ridicule as would be certain to arise in London circles made her feel queasy, it was still far and away the best method to pacify Lord Darcy. She would simply have to get through the next few months as best she could, and pray his lordship's sister could work a miracle and make her a little less repulsive.

Number three: Since she could not ride Vortex herself in races around the country, she would have to find someone else. The only plausible person was Jonas.

As the hours passed, the Abbey finally fell silent. The little creaks and thumps indicating Mrs. Simpson and the chambermaids were finishing their day's work ceased. Angel had long since heard Lord Darcy's booted feet climb the staircase and make their way down the hall in the direction of his, and his friends', apartments.

Sitting up, she pushed back her coverlet, climbed out of bed, and slipped a wrap over her nightrail. Then, placing slippers on her feet, she tiptoed to her bedchamber door. Opening it a crack, she peered out into the inky hallway, then hurried toward the staircase.

Stepping only on the far right side of the stairs, since the left side had always creaked like an old man's bones, she scurried down the steps and slipped outside.

The night was warm. For a moment Angel hesitated on the steps, gazing up at the stars. One, in particular, had been her friend for as long as she could remember. How oft had she sent her wishes up to it? She smiled wistfully. Too many to count.

Then she shook herself. The time for childish fancy was past. She had to get to Violet Cottage and back before anyone knew she'd been gone.

After glancing up at the face of the house to make sure she was not observed, she set off across the lawns. In no time at all she found herself in front of Jonas Spindle's little house, panting with exertion.

Pounding on the cottage door, she cried, "Jonas! It is Angel. I must speak with you!"

The ex-groom popped out of the house almost immediately. His white curls were ruffled, his cheeks grizzled with new silvery whiskers, and his eyes puffy with sleep.

Rubbing a gnarled hand over his face, he sat down in one of the old chairs he kept outside his door and blinked blearily. "Angel! What are you doing here at this hour?"

Wasting no time with formalities, Angel sank down on the stoop and poured out her heart.

"So I must go to London, and you must ride Vortex," she finished. "I am certain it is the only way we can raise the money to pay the baronet."

Jonas frowned. "What makes you think Pugsley will uphold his end of the wager, and not just take your money and you besides? I've heard naught but ill of him down at the pub. There are terrible stories of the goings-on at Green Willows."

"Such as?" Angel inquired.

Jonas flushed beneath his forest of whiskers. "That's not a young girl's concern."

Angel turned to look back at her home. Bathed in moonlight, the Abbey was just visible behind a distant screen of trees. "You may be right about Sir Corbin trying something unfair, but you must agree that I could not have refused his wager," she said softly. "He threatened to tear the entire house down, stone by stone. I couldn't let that happen." She turned back to face Jonas. "Promise me you will ride Vortex when I am gone."

Jonas nodded grimly. "I'll try, but I know he won't like the idea much. He's never had anyone but you on his back. Perhaps you should explain matters to him."

Although secretly she smiled at his Irish fancies, Angel agreed. Jonas stood, and they walked around the house and into the stable. Going to the sugar bowl, Angel plucked out the largest white lump and dropped it into her pocket.

The old man lit a lamp and hung it on a hook near the

gray stallion's stall. Vortex poked his head out from his stall and whinnied a greeting.

Moving near to her horse, Angel put her arms around his broad neck and pressed her face to his silky hide. The stallion lowered his elegant nose and searched her body for the hidden lump of sugar. After a few moments, not having found the treat, he raised his head once again and studied her with bright, intelligent eyes.

In a self-conscious whisper Angel explained matters to the big stallion. She was amazed when, as she finished with, "Now, you will be a good boy for Jonas, and let him ride you in the races, won't you? If you do, I promise to find you a beautiful bride when the Abbey is finally ours," the gray horse tossed his head as though he understood and agreed.

"You see?" Jonas demanded. "An animal will usually obey if it knows what is expected. Most people treat God's creatures like they have no intelligence. But that is wrong. Animals understand most of what we say, just on a different level."

Angel nodded. "So I see."

Plucking the sugar lump from her pocket, Angel held it out on the flat of her hand. Vortex's velvety nose snuffled her palm; then he fastidiously sucked the sweet into his mouth. "Well," she said as the stallion finished his treat, "I had best return to the Abbey. I am supposed to leave for London first thing in the morning. I must get back before anyone knows I've been gone. If we are going to keep our plans secret, we daren't raise any suspicions now."

As she and Jonas walked back around to the front of the cottage, Angel gazed at him fondly. His white curls, made ice-silver in the moonlight, stuck up in all directions.

They paused at the door and she kissed him on one leathery cheek. "Please be careful, Jonas, during the races," she pleaded. "You are very dear to me. And let me know what is happening. I will write when I reach London so you will know where to direct your letters."

The old man chuckled gruffly. "It is a good thing you taught me to read and write, then." He gazed at her for a long moment as if he could see into her very soul and understood her trepidation about facing Society. "Go with God, child. Try to remember that you're a beautiful person with a beautiful heart. Trust that heart and everything will be fine."

Nodding even though she didn't share his optimistic sentiments, Angel then turned and ran back across the meadow. When she'd almost reached the screen of trees beside the Abbey, she turned and waved. Then she hurried through the trees and crossed Windywood's lawns.

Climbing the front steps quickly, she stepped inside and closed the doors behind her. She stood in the foyer for a moment, listening to the stillness of the old house. A pang of love, so sharp it made her catch her breath, moved through her.

She could not allow Windywood Abbey to be destroyed. She would do anything to keep it safe.

Although certain her first London Season would undoubtedly be horrible beyond measure, she knew she could bear it. For Windywood Abbey's safety, she thought as she climbed the stairs to her bedchamber, she could bear anything.

Sebastian, from the darkness of the balcony, watched his ward sneak back into the house. His lips pressed together fiercely and it was all he could do not to go after the wench and shake her until her teeth fell out. She had obviously been out trysting with one of her paying customers. Old habits, it seemed, died hard even though her hopes of buying the Abbey were no longer pressing.

He sucked in his breath and tried to calm down. No doubt about it. He had to get her married off soon. Before she produced a nine-month wonder and disgraced his entire family.

Still, despite his anger at Lady Angel's wanton behavior, despite his desire to throttle the lust out of her homely body, despite his righteous indignation at her lasciviousness, Sebastian felt something else. A part from a tiny, wholly male part of himself that wished *he* had been her midnight tryster, Sebastian also felt a flicker of disappointment.

In the short time they had conversed in the library he had almost come to like Lady Angel and had wondered if he might have been wrong about his suspicions of her past. She had not behaved like a wanton.

But so much for that. One couldn't make a silk purse out of an old sow's ear any more than one could teach a leopard to change its spots. The sooner Lady Angelique Harriette Arundel was married, and *his* duty fulfilled, the better.

Chapter Nine

The following morning at ten o'clock, Angel climbed into her father's carriage—one he had never used because it had the Darcy crest across its door and he had felt it ungodly to proclaim his social superiority to the countryside. The new Lord Darcy's own entourage had left much earlier, while the rest of the household had been slumbering.

On the seat opposite Angel sat Mrs. Simpson, enlisted by Lord Darcy to act as Angel's companion and chaperone on the journey into Town. The middle-aged housekeeper had already fallen asleep, even though they had not yet crossed the Abbey property line.

With a disheartened sigh, Angel realized, since she had only herself for company, it was going to be an excruciatingly long journey. To occupy her time she pulled out the book she had brought along. Flipping through the pages of her grandfather's racing register, the same book she and Lord Darcy had discussed the previous night, she tried to concentrate on the various pedigrees inscribed on the heavy vellum pages.

Finally, unable to concentrate, she gave up and replaced the book in the carpetbag at her feet. Her mind was too busy flitting from thought to thought to comprehend a single paragraph her eyes had beheld. Was Jonas all right? Did Vortex miss her? Would Sir Corbin Pugsley keep his end of the wager, if she were fortunate enough to come up with twenty thousand pounds?

Where was Lord Darcy? She had not thought to ask why his lordship was not accompanying her to London. Remembering Hughes Pride's wounds, she knew it was unlikely the black would be ready to run again for quite a while, so the earl would most likely not be headed for another race.

Remembering the previous day's race, Angel winced as she recalled seeing Lord Darcy's jockey's riding crop swing past her own head during the race, almost as if the ugly little man had been determined to strike her off her horse if that were what it took to win. Then she recalled the jockey's comment to the earl, after the race: that he'd only been whipping Hughes Pride because he had felt certain Lord Darcy would want to win at any cost.

Although she had not known Lord Darcy's identity at the time, Angel had been greatly impressed by his response. His dark eyes had flashed with outrage, and he had castigated the jockey harshly for treating an animal with such cruelty. Could any man, so concerned with the well-being of a mere horse, be as cruel as Angel had thought he must be to force her to go to London—when it would undoubtedly be horrible for her, since her face was as ugly as a mud fence? Or had the earl merely done what he believed correct?

If the latter was true, it was a new experience for Angel to have a man be genuinely concerned for her welfare. And it was not an altogether unpleasant sensation, at that.

Other than Jonas, she couldn't remember any man being kind to her before.

That is, she amended with another depressed sigh, if sending her to a place where she was sure to be ridiculed for her ugliness could be considered *kind*.

Still, despite her fears and uncertainties about the presentability of her person amid the ton, she could not believe that a man who would be so overwrought at the sight of an animal's suffering would be unfeeling to a fellow human's discomfort. And, despite her nervousness, despite her anger at being packed off to the marriage mart as if she were so much baggage, Angel admitted to herself that she was looking forward to seeing her guardian again.

Since they had been driving at an easy pace, they entered London three days later.

The city teemed with life. From the army of rag pickers and filthy urchins, ladies in silks and plumes (as well as "ladies" in next to nothing), and gentlemen driving sharp black curricles, it was by far the busiest place Angel had ever seen. For a time she was able to put all thought of her dreaded Season out of her mind.

Once the unfamiliar excitement dimmed, however, her head once again began throbbing with anxiety. With each turn of the carriage wheels that brought them closer to the abode of Lord Darcy's sister, Angel's heart pounded more and more violently.

What was Lady Cartwright like? Was she as forceful as her brother—as intent on running other people's lives? Would she be repulsed by Angel's ugliness? Would she turn away in disgust after seeing her new charge?

She would go mad with apprehension if they did not arrive soon!

A few minutes later the carriage slowed to a halt outside

number 105 Dobbins Street, an attractive, but not ostentatious, town house. Of mellow orange brick, Cartwright House had several stories, like the other houses along the street. Unlike the others, it also had a white awning that stretched several feet out from the front door.

The carriage had just pulled to a stop when the town house door opened and a brown-haired woman of average height and weight, dressed in gentian blue muslin, dashed through the door, hurtled down the steps, and waited on the walkway, jumping agitatedly from one foot to the other in a flurry of excitement.

Angel stared, taken aback by the woman's odd behavior. Then she followed obediently as Mrs. Simpson exited the vehicle and greeted the brown-haired lady.

"My Lady Cartwright," the housekeeper-*cum*-chaperone said in a dignified tone. "Allow me to present Lord Darcy's ward, Lady Angelique."

"My dear girl!" the woman in blue cried, ecstatically—and totally *without* dignity—surging forth to grasp Angel's hands in hers. "Welcome to London. I am Lady Cartwright—but you must call me Hilary, and I shall call you Angel, as my brother informed me you prefer to be called. I just know we are going to be great friends. I received my brother's letter yesterday, informing me of your imminent arrival, and have been on pins and needles every since."

Her warm brown eyes sparkled with genuine pleasure. "I cannot tell you how excited I am to be your sponsor. I have always wanted to sponsor my own children, but," her eyes darkened slightly and her smile faltered, "my husband and I have not yet been so blessed."

"I am very pleased to make your acquaintance, my la—Hilary," Angel responded obediently.

Lady Cartwright brightened again. "And I yours, my dear. Of course, I was astounded to think that Seb would have sent you to *me!* He thinks me a terrible rattle-pate. I cannot think why."

Angel laughed and felt her anxiety vanish before Lady Cartwright's sunny disposition and chattery amiability.

"Of course," Lady Cartwright rushed on hopefully, "there is still a chance that my husband and I will have children, although I passed my thirty-eighth birthday two months ago—I am seven years older than Sebastian—so the likelihood lessens with each passing day. But," she said, "I do not mean to bore you. Let me just tell you that I am thrilled to have you here." She clasped her dainty hands to her breast and beamed. "We are going to have such fun!"

Fun?

Angel blinked. Couldn't Lady Cartwright see how ugly Angel was? How hideously unruly were Angel's scarlet curls? Was the Lady blind to the mass of freckles spread over Angel's cheeks? Or the way Angel's over-wide mouth resembled nothing so much as a hungry bullfrog gaping after a plump insect?

Lady Cartwright put an arm around Angel's shoulders and began pulling her toward the house. Too confused to do anything else, Angel followed meekly.

They made their way to a comfortable parlor, where Lord Darcy's sister released Angel and stepped back to take a good look at the girl. Angel closed her eyes and braced herself for Lady Cartwright's damning conviction that anyone as ugly as Angel could not hope to find a husband and might as well go posthaste back to wherever she had come from.

While half of Angel's heart hoped she would be sent away, she found to her amazement that an unfamiliar and traitorous side of her personality had unexpectedly emerged and prayed she would not be found wanting.

As if that were even remotely possible.

Holding her breath, she waited for the gavel to fall. When the expected revulsion did not materialize into horrified gasps, she opened her eyes reluctantly and peered uncertainly at her new mentor. Out of the corner of her eye, she noted that Mrs. Simpson had installed herself on a distant sofa and was examining a half-finished bit of embroidery on an oak tambour near the fireplace.

Lady Cartwright walked all the way around Angel several times, one hand on her chin and the other clutching her opposite elbow, a speculative gleam in her warm brown eyes, which were many shades lighter than Lord Darcy's. "Hmm," the lady murmured as if to herself. "Hmm." Raising one finger, she tapped her cheek thoughtfully, then ran one fingertip over her lower lip. "Well," she said at last, "you certainly are not the type of girl one sees every day."

Angel's heart plummeted. She wondered how she could ever have hoped the earl's sister would have found her acceptable. She must have had a momentary flash of insanity. Briefly, she wondered if that unfortunate malady had run in either her mother or her father's bloodline.

"But," Lady Cartwright continued absently, "that will probably work in your favor. There are far too many milk-and-water misses in London these days. Your coloring is quite unusual. With a few changes, I think you would definitely have promise."

Angel's heart rose again and she bit back relieved, and wholly unexpected, tears.

Lord Darcy's sister spoke again, briskly. "Tomorrow we shall go shopping to buy you an entirely new wardrobe. Mostly blues, greens and yellows, with perhaps two ball gowns, one in gold lamé and one in lavender satin."

"G-gold lamé?" Angel stammered, wondering if her new chaperone intended to smother Angel's ugliness in pomp and circumstance. She was well aware that such tactics would not work, but did not know how to put a stop to Lady Cartwright's rapidly building enthusiasm, which seemed as out of control as a runaway mail coach.

"Yes, lamé." Lady Cartwright took another turn around her young charge. She waved a hand in dismissal as Angel opened her mouth to object. "Oh, I grant you that gold is hardly the usual color for a debutante's garb, but in your case we are going to make an exception. You, my dear, are going to take the ton by storm."

Angel gaped and totally forgot what she had been going to say. She immediately assumed that it was not she, but the earl's sister, who suffered from soft brains.

"The lavender satin," Lady Cartwright continued, unaware of her charge's dismay, "will be for your come-out ball. And we absolutely must have something in a soft mint green for your presentation at Almack's. None of those mealymouthed whites for you, my dear."

"No?" Angel asked, bemused.

"Oh, no," the older woman said sincerely. "You have too much character, too much personality, to wear average, namby-pamby colors."

Suddenly Angel started. "But my lady, we can purchase no new wardrobe, because I have no money to buy clothes. Besides," she added wistfully, deciding that she could only be honest to this woman who, while obviously insane, had already shown her such kindness. "How can you even suggest that a dress of a certain color would make me look more presentable than another? You will never make me more than middling ugly, no matter how hard you try."

Lady Cartwright lowered her brows. "I will have none of that, young lady," she said firmly. "Sebastian mentioned that you were plain, but I am completely bewildered at where he got such a ridiculous idea. Do you not know that people inevitably see you the way you see yourself? We must work on your self-esteem."

The earl's sister missed Angel's horrified gasp.

"Of course you are not classically beautiful," the older woman went on candidly, "but you are undeniably striking and, if you are willing to put forth the effort, might even be considered handsome. As for your wardrobe, Sebastian has already sent me a line of credit on his bank here in London."

Angel tried to suffocate the blaze of hurt and rage she had felt at hearing of Lord Darcy's circumspect opinion of her person. After all, it was not as if he had lied about her appearance. Despite Lady Cartwright's obvious misconception, Angel knew she *was* plain—ugly, in fact. Still, it hurt surprisingly much to hear her own opinion from Lord Darcy's mouth—or pen, as the case may be.

Angel shook her head. "I could not possibly accept such generosity from the earl."

With startling ferocity Lady Cartwright pushed Angel onto a sofa and then sat very close. Speaking softly, apparently so that Mrs. Simpson would not overhear, the older woman hissed, "Cannot accept such *generosity?* You silly girl. Do not try to tell me that you were not upset when my brother inherited your father's entire estate. Sebastian told me the old earl did not leave you a shilling. And you his only child! It is a disgrace the way men treat us women, as if we were chattel!"

Angel flushed and, this time, opened her mouth to denounce Lord Darcy's careless gabbling about her life.

"Please, my dear," Lady Cartwright interjected, this time visibly recognizing Angel's fury at the earl's free speech, "I realize you must be quite furious at my brother for speaking so freely about your situation, but try not to be embarrassed. Men are often like that about women. They speak of us as if we had no more minds than a stick of furniture, while I am sure you will not deny that we are usually far more intelligent than they."

Astonished at hearing such forward-thinking ideas, though she frequently thought them to herself, Angel felt her anger vanish. She blinked and opened her mouth to question the earl's sister, but that estimable lady was already speaking again.

"As for accepting my brother's 'generosity,' you have every right to spend as much of his 'Darcy' inheritance as you wish. That money should by rights have been yours. What your father did to you—leaving you a pauper—was abominable. You know it, I know it, and Sebastian knows it. Furthermore, both Sebastian and I expect you to accept our help, both monetary and otherwise, graciously. To do otherwise would be the height of bad taste."

"Er, quite." Angel couldn't contain the mortified giggle that escaped her lips. She was unable to restrain the question that had been nibbling at her for several minutes. "Women, more intelligent than men? Hilary! Never tell me you are a bluestocking!"

Lady Cartwright grinned, her gentle brown eyes alight with laughter and secrecy. "And why not? Do you doubt for a moment that you are smarter than most men of your acquaintance?"

"Well, no," Angel answered reluctantly.

"Or that you are less of a human being simply because you were born female and not the 'son and heir' your father wanted?"

"No, again."

"Exactly," Lady Cartwright finished with a challenge in her voice. "Yes, my dear girl, I am a bluestocking, and also a staunch believer in women's rights. Mark my words, one day women will have all the rights our husbands do. Probably not in *our* lifetimes, but someday."

"Does Lord Darcy know how you feel?"

"Heavens, no, and you must not tell him or he would sweep you out of my house like a whirlwind! And please do not tell my husband Herbert, either. Like Sebastian, he enjoys believing my brain is to let."

"And that doesn't trouble you?"

Lady Cartwright smiled. "Good heavens, no. Not as long as behaving like a bacon-brain makes him obey my every command. Besides, he would never believe me if I did tell him I was intelligent. He is a charming, adorable, endearing man, and a superb lifemate, but to be perfectly honest, when Herbert goes outside on a spring day, the wind practically whistles between his ears!"

Angel joined her new chaperone in congenial laughter.

"*Do* say you will be my friend, Angel. It will be so nice having another intelligent woman under my roof. I must tell you," the earl's sister added regretfully, "my husband and brother are not far wrong in their opinion of the fairer sex; most of the women of my acquaintance *do* have more hair than wit."

Angel breathed a happy sigh. "I would be honored to be your friend, Hilary." She wished she could tell Lady Cartwright about the wager with Pugsley, but decided that, despite the older woman's seemingly open-minded intelligence, it might be a trifle premature to discuss such weighty matters.

"Good." Lady Cartwright sobered and peered at her curiously. "But tell me, where did you get the idea that you are ugly? You are not, you know. It just appears as though no one has ever taught you how to dress properly, or how to wear your hair in becoming ways."

Angel eyed her new friend skeptically. "I doubt that you will ever make me believe I am not a hag, no matter what you say, Hilary. Since the day I was born everyone has told me I was terribly plain. Especially my father. He used to say to me," here she deepened her voice,

" 'Daughter, you should rent your face out to be used as a paint bucket—then you might gain some color and also hide those abominable freckles.' " She laughed nervously, but noted that Lady Cartwright was not sharing her forced humor.

"How horrid!"

"Yes, it was. But, nonetheless, he was right. I do have too many freckles, and my hair is the most unfortunate shade of red. If I had been born with auburn hair I would have loved it, but this dull scarlet is odious!"

Lady Cartwright scowled. "Men! I swear if your father were here I would take a hot poker to his skull. Listen to me, Angel. I promise that by the time we are finished making you over, you will be quite pleased with your appearance. I have a special cream we can put on your face to fade your freckles somewhat—although I find them quite charming—and I am sure we shall find a rinse for your hair that will turn its rather muddy scarlet to burnished copper. As for your figure, just you wait until you've seen what Madame Sophie, my modiste, can do! I declare, we're going to make you all the crack before we are done, just you see if we do not!"

Angel felt a warm glow rise from someplace near her heart. While she doubted any of Lady Cartwright's miracles would really take place, how could she hurt that sweet lady's feelings by arguing about the futility of the attempt? And maybe, just maybe, all the spun-gold dreams Hilary had woven would really come true. Who could say?

Later that night, after writing an explicit note to Jonas, containing instructions as to where she might be reached as well as a pleading request that he tell her everything about Vortex's latest races, Angel lay down upon a plush feather bed, between fresh silk sheets that smelled of rose water. Her room was the most beautiful chamber she had ever seen, with airy gauze hangings adorning the walls, fine gilt and emerald green mouldings along the ceiling and floor, and a decadently plush viridian-green carpet that fairly swallowed one's bare feet.

She snuggled deeper beneath her coverlet. As a faint breeze swayed the lacy white-cutwork curtains in her window, she gazed out into the night sky. In time her eyes adjusted to the darkness and she noticed a tiny, glittering star—her star—far off in the distance.

Caught back in time, she remembered an old nursery rhyme and repeated it, as she had so many times during her lifetime, like a prayer: "Star light, star bright, beautiful star that I see tonight, give me the wish that my heart holds tight. Please let me win back Windywood Abbey."

Then she whispered, so softly that even she could barely hear the words, "And if it is not too much trouble, please let a wonderful man love me."

She was asleep before the last word slipped through her lips to be caught on the breeze, tossed through the open window, and hurled up into the arms of the glittering star.

Chapter Ten

Angel was awakened the next morning at ten by a dark-haired maid who brought a cup of chocolate and a silver tray of buttered rolls. On the servant's heels came Lady Cartwright, wrapped in a floral-patterned silk negligee in shades of lilac and mauve with a generous fringe of marabou feathers around the neck, sleeves, and hem.

Angel smiled to think that this feminine, frilly woman was secretly an intellectual rebel. "Good morning, Hilary," she said.

"Good morning, darling," crooned Lady Cartwright, perching herself on the edge of Angel's bed. "I hope you are feeling rested. My Herbert came in very late last night and left again early this morning for one of our country estates. So I fear you will not be able to meet him for a bit longer.

"Anyway, I thought we would begin preparing your wardrobe today." She proceeded to launch into preparations, while Angel munched on a buttered, crusty roll. "First we must decide on your Court presentation ensemble, which means we must visit the plumier, Mr. Carberry, and beg him to make you a headdress different from anything he has ever designed. And of course we must also plan your presentation gown."

Angel's breath caught painfully. She had visions of the Regent and his mother balking when they caught sight of her hideous face. "Court?"

"Yes, dear. You cannot be considered 'out' until you have made your bows. Of course, most of the other debutantes have been in Town this age learning to bow gracefully and move backward—so they will be able to back out of the presentation chamber without tripping over their own feet—but I am quite convinced you shall do equally well without all that practice. You possess a grace of movement that I have never seen before."

"Thank you. Heavens. It all sounds overwhelming!"

"One is only overwhelmed by what one allows, my dear."

Angel was not convinced, but did not argue.

"I thought we would have your coming-out ball in three weeks, a sennight after the official Season has begun. I would have liked to have held it sooner, but it will take at least that long to prepare. Oh, and we must take you to Almack's before your ball, so that you might waltz at your come-out."

Lady Cartwright paused suddenly, pinning Angel with a direct stare. "You *must* remember, should we attend any balls before you visit Almack's, you cannot waltz or you will be ruined!"

Angel gave a lopsided grin. "Never fear, Hilary. I do not even know how to waltz. And even if I did, I doubt anyone would ask me." Lady Cartwright frowned and opened her mouth. Before the earl's sister could reprimand Angel for impugning herself, the girl asked quickly, "Is not Almack's also known as the Quality's 'marriage mart'?"

"Yes, indeed," Lady Cartwright asserted. "Once you enter those hallowed portals, the most eligible men in England will be at your feet. Count yourself lucky that both Lady Jersey and Lady Sefton, two of Almack's patronesses, were my bosom bows in our youth and are still close friends, so there should be no problem in acquiring your vouchers. Now then, about your ball. . . ." She nibbled her lower lip, musingly. "We will have to re-do the entire ballroom."

"Oh," Angel protested, "surely not! Think of the expense!"

Lady Cartwright did not reply. She continued staring into space as if gazing into the future. "Given the shortage of time perhaps it would be best if we use Sebastian's ballroom, since its floor was refinished last year, and the one here at Cartwright House is in dire need of a few new tiles. I shall ask him. Maybe I will even manage to convince him the room needs a new coat of paint. Lilac and cream, I think, to set off the lavender gown I plan to purchase today for your ball. And I think we should limit the guest list to a small number. Two or three hundred people should be about right."

"Two or three hundred?" Angel gasped, startled. "If that is your idea of a small gathering, I cringe to think of what you might consider large!"

Lady Cartwright sailed on as if she hadn't heard. "About your Court presentation. I don't suppose you have any jewelry, but you may borrow some of mine. When one attends Royal Drawing Rooms one must be dripping with jewels. Every girl vies to look more magnificent than any other."

Angel frowned, more concerned with drawing as little attention to herself as possible than with looking splendid. "While I confess my ignorance on the matter, a single strand of pearls would seem more suitable for a debutante."

Lady Cartwright's gentle face lit up. "Of course!" she crowed. "My darling, you are brilliant! While everyone else is covered head to toe with ropes of diamonds and emeralds, rubies and sapphires, you shall prove your individuality by wearing only a single strand of pearls, ear drops, and a bracelet."

She gazed off into space and waved one arm expressively. "I can see your gown now: ivory silk, rather than the normal dull white, with only a few seed pearls. Your hoop must not be too massive, and your headdress must have the minimum required seven plumes, as everyone else's is certain to be overdone. We will drape another single rope of pearls over your forehead, amid your curls."

She hugged Angel delightedly. "Child, you are going to take the ton by storm!"

Angel raised a skeptical brow, but had learned by now not to argue with her exuberant chaperone.

Jumping off the bed, Lady Cartwright strode to and fro across the thick viridian-green carpet, her lilac and mauve scarves trailing after her as if she were in the midst of a soft breeze. "After we call upon the proper establishments for your presentation gown, we will visit my favorite modiste, Madame Sophie, whom I mentioned last night and whose shop resides in Leicester Square. We should be able to procure everything else you need for the Season in the Square, as well. If not we shall simply skip over to Mayfair and visit the establishments there."

"Is Madame Sophie French?"

Lady Cartwright laughed, her voice sparkling like newfallen snow on a Christmas morn. "Oh, no, my dear. She is as English as you or I. But everything French is all the rage now that Napoleon has been defeated. Though most of the *beau monde* is quite aware of Madame Sophie's

British antecedents, if the woman openly admitted such a common background she would instantly lose her position as the ton's most expensive modiste."

Angel laughed. "How ridiculous."

"Is it not?" Suddenly Lady Cartwright's expression turned serious. "Now, dear girl, I must ask you some questions and you must answer me truthfully."

"I shall do my best."

"You said you could not waltz. Do you know any other dances?"

Angel's smile faltered. "No. My father never held balls, and even had he done so, I would not have been welcome. He was too ashamed of me."

"No matter. We shall hire a caper merchant immediately. I am sure you will prove a quick learner. Can you play the pianoforte?"

"No." Angel sighed. "Is that also required?"

"Not required, but generally accepted as one of a young woman of Quality's accomplishments. It does not matter. Many debutantes who do play the pianoforte would be better served to keep their hands off the ivories altogether, lest they shame themselves utterly. Do you have a good singing voice?"

Angel shrugged. "I do not know. I enjoy singing, but have only ever done so for myself, when I was alone."

"Then we shall also hire a voice-master. Do you paint?"

"No. I am sorry."

"Do you embroider? Can you sew a fine seam?"

Angel's eyes filled with dismayed tears. "As fine as a sow with a needle in her snout. Honestly, Hilary," she said frantically, "do I stand a chance in Society? From all your questions it would seem I am most ill prepared. Perhaps I should hie myself back to the country before I humiliate us both."

Lady Cartwright smiled gently and patted Angel's hand.

"Don't be a goose. You'll do just fine." Then she shook Angel, lightly. "Now, up with you, child! We have work to do. I want to have you transformed by the time Sebastian returns to London. He has promised to call upon us the moment he gets back in Town."

This news did not brighten Angel's mood. How could she face the earl after learning how unfavorably he had portrayed her to his sister? Though she felt an unfamiliar longing to see Lord Darcy, she also felt nervous about meeting him again.

"Did he say when to expect him?" she inquired. "I should think we'd need a year to make me even passably attractive. I wish we could delay him for that long."

"He did not. But since he is attending a country house party, he should not return for another two days at least."

"Two days! But we can accomplish practically nothing in two days!"

"Yes, we can," the earl's sister stated determinedly. "As for Seb's arrival time, the family giving the party is coming to London for the Season, so the entire group will probably travel here together."

Herewith, Lady Cartwright grasped Angel by the chin, turning her so that their gazes met. "As for your appearance, young lady," she said firmly, "I promise you that by the time this day is ended you will hardly recognize your image in a looking glass. But I must tell you I grow weary of hearing you belittle yourself. As I said already, if you cannot find it in your heart to admire yourself, no one else will, either."

Although unconvinced the promised transformation would ever materialize, Angel allowed the older woman to grasp her hands and pull her from the bed.

One hour later Angel and Lady Cartwright, along with Lady Cartwright's abigail, tooled along Bond Street in a spanking burgundy cabriolet. The attractive carriage was pulled by a snow-white prancer with matching burgundy ribands threaded through its flowing mane and tale.

Within fifteen minutes the trio stopped before "Madame Sophie's Maison de Couture."

Alighting with the help of Hilary's tiger, they entered the small shop, accompanied by the sound of a faraway bell.

Angel gazed around the little room, a bit disappointed. "It is not anything like I had imagined," she confided quietly. "I expected velvet hangings edged in gold braid, thick carpets, champagne and strawberries on ice, and sumptuous chairs, at the very least."

Lady Cartwright nodded and laughed. "I know precisely what you mean. I felt the same on my first visit. But I promise that Madame Sophie's exquisite work more than makes up for her shop's lack of elegance. Although you will find those luxuries at lesser establishments, Madame Sophie has no need for such extravagant lures."

In response to the doorbell, a little woman with hennaed hair emerged from behind a curtained off area. Her eyes widened with delight and she held her arms out from her body. "Ladee Cartwright! Vat a pleazure eet eez to zee you again!"

Angel bit her tongue to keep from laughing aloud at the woman's atrociously false French accent.

"And you, Madame Sophie," Lady Cartwright replied warmly. "I trust business is going well?"

"Ah, *bien sur,* my lady, but of course."

Angel was unable to contain a giggle. Lady Cartwright threw her a warning glance.

"Madame," the earl's sister continued, "I wish you to make a complete wardrobe for my brother's ward, Lady Angelique Harriette Arundel."

"Tiens!" the modiste cried, happily. "Well! So ze mademoiselle is French too, *non? Naturellement* I will prepare

ze most beautiful clothes for her! She vill shine like ze diamond among ze pebbles."

Angel's eyebrows rose, while her spirits fell upon consideration of this unlikely scenario. She focused her attention on Lady Cartwright's reply.

"I want her to look completely different from all the other debutantes, Madame. She must be an Original."

"*Oui, oui,* my lady! She will be exquisite!" The dressmaker made a kissing gesture with her fingers. "Stand up, mademoiselle, *s'il vous plaît.*"

With a premonition of doom, Angel obeyed. As she had done with Hilary, she closed her eyes and braced herself for the modiste's disgust. When she heard Madame Sophie's clucks of disapproval, she wished the floor would open up and swallow her alive. Obviously, while Lady Cartwright had been too polite to be truthful about Angel's features, the modiste felt no such compunction.

"Oh, zis eez *too* bad!" the modiste exclaimed unhappily. "Look at her! Vith that svelte body, those zuperb lines, she should not be dressed zo! In a gown fit only for a svineherd's vife!"

Amazed that the seamstress was decrying her *clothing* as responsible for her ugliness, Angel opened her eyes and peered down at her gown. It *was* ugly, she admitted silently. Of a garish shade of pink, it hung like a sack over her angular hips and scant bosom.

The modiste continued her affronted tirade. "Vith that *très belle* red hair, she must be dressed in bishop's blue, bottle green, jonquille, pistache, or scarlet, but zertainly not pink! Nevair pink! Oh, *c'est terrible!* It is terrible!"

"Of course," Madame Sophie added abruptly, looking askance at Lady Cartwright and suddenly sounding as English as both of their forebears, "you do intend to have her hair styled differently, do you not? Because, otherwise

I must say no gown I design will make her look less like an impoverished country bumpkin than she does now."

Angel flushed hotly.

"Indeed. We are going straight to Monsieur Henri's after we leave here. I thought a hairstyle somewhat pert and flirtatious would suit her admirably. Perhaps cut around her face in little curling wisps and drawn up so that it cascades down her back in a mass of curls. What do you think?"

"It sounds perfect," the modiste continued in unaccented English. "We must design her gowns so that they are very plain, very elegant. No frills and furbelows. She must be one of a kind."

"Precisely my opinion," Lady Cartwright concurred eagerly.

Madame Sophie studied Angel a moment longer. "We must make use of her unusual face and her lithe figure. She must look like a Grecian goddess—but not Venus; everyone wants to look like Venus these days. She must look like . . ." she paused as if searching her memory, "like Artemis, the proud huntress who needs no man and so commands them all."

Then, without skipping a beat, the modiste blithely resumed her counterfeit French accent. *"Bon.* Good. If you vill be zo kind as to step into my dressing chamber, Lady Angelique, we shall begin *immédiatement.* Oh, you are going to be zo beautiful!"

Angel cast a worried glance at Lady Cartwright. "You will come too, won't you?"

"Certainly. I would not miss your transformation for the world, my dear."

Following Angel and Madame Sophie into the fitting room, Lady Cartwright settled herself in a comfortable chair near a table that held a huge pile of fashion magazines, while Madame Sophie instructed Angel to climb onto a low footstool.

From where she stood, Angel could see the titles of a few of the fashion journals Lady Cartwright was intently perusing: *La Belle Assemblee, The Ladies Magazine, Le Beau Monde,* and *Ackermann's Repository of Fashion* were but a few of their names. It occurred to Angel that *she* had never opened a fashion magazine in her entire life.

Madame Sophie clapped her hands and a flock of young women sailed into the rooms, carrying piles of delectable ribands, cards of the finest lace, bolts of exquisite fabric, measuring strings, and large sheafs of glass-headed pins.

Chattering genially, Lady Cartwright and Madame Sophie decided on innumerable patterns to be made up in a multitude of fabrics and shades. Before long, Angel was exhausted, and could barely hide her shock at the earl's sister's extravagance.

Besides her presentation gown Angel was also to have a lovely gown for her coming-out ball, as well as carriage dresses, opera gowns, evening gowns, ball gowns, promenade gowns, two riding habits in chocolate brown and rust, theatre, morning and walking gowns, undergarments and much, much more. In the end, however, Hilary's coveted gold lamé was decided against, as too *outré* even for an unusual girl like Angel.

Angel's legs felt as limp as old noodles from standing for so many hours, and she was certain her body would be marked forever by the army of tiny pinpricks she had withstood. At last, to her surprise and infinite relief, Lady Cartwright arose.

"Now, Madame Sophie," Lady Cartwright said, "do you perchance have anything already sewn up that Lady Angel might take home this afternoon? I had hoped we might be able to go to the opera this evening."

The modiste smiled. "As eet happens, my ladee, I have just ze thing. It vas really made for Lady Delaporte, but what she does not know—how do you English zay eet? Ah yes—vill not hurt her. Besides, I have received nothing on her ladyship's account for over zix months. Marie," she commanded one of the seamstresses, snapping her fingers, "bring me ze emerald zilk opera gown ve finished zis morning."

The girl bobbed a curtsy and rushed from the room. In moments she had returned, carrying the loveliest dress Angel had ever seen.

"Oh, it is beautiful. It will do nicely, Madame," Lady Cartwright said approvingly. "Place it and the rest of the wardrobe on my brother's account. And add something extra for you and the girls. Please, be generous. Lord Darcy can afford it."

"Zank you, my lady." The modiste smiled and curtsied. "I shall have ze first of mademoiselle's gowns delivered tomorrow morning."

Back in the cabriolet, Angel gave a weary sigh. "Thank goodness we are finished. I am so tired I can barely open my lips to speak. I want nothing so much as to lie down upon my bed for an hour."

"Finished?" Lady Cartwright laughed. "Why, my girl, we must still procure wraps, hats, gloves, shoes, and toiletries! And there is your hair to consider! We have not even begun!"

Angel collapsed against the carriage wall. "Oh dear."

The earl's sister smiled. "You *are* tired, aren't you, poor child? Very well. We can finish our shopping later. Just now we need only attend to your hair and gather the items we will need in order for you to be properly dressed for the opera this evening."

"I thought a girl must be presented at Court before appearing in public," Angel protested weakly.

"No, but one is not considered officially 'out' until her visit to the Royal Drawing Room. The next presentation date is in six days, so we have more than enough time to prepare you. Do not worry, darling. All will be well."

Chapter Eleven

That evening, just before dinner, Angel stood before the long cheval glass in her bedchamber. The mirror was covered with lace sheeting so that she could not see her reflection, and her heart thumped with nervous expectation and apprehension.

After she and Lady Cartwright left Madame Sophie's, the earl's sister had shepherded Angel into Monsieur Henri's, where the funny little Frenchman (genuinely Gallic, this time) had snipped and sliced until, looking at the rapidly growing pile of red curls on the shop floor, Angel was certain he planned to leave her bald.

After cutting her hair, Monsieur Henri had instructed Angel to lean backward so that her tresses swam in a sweet-smelling broth of chamomile, lemons, and other herbs Angel could not identify.

When the Frenchman had completed his artistry and Angel's newly coiffed hair was brushed dry, both Monsieur Henri and Lady Cartwright had forbidden Angel to look into a mirror. If it had not been for her companions' thrilled expressions, Angel would have been certain they had performed such a hideous operation on her hair that they were afraid to show the final result.

Back at the town house, Lady Cartwright's maid, Prudie, had presented a porcelain bowl filled with greenish glop that smelled like low-tide slime. The maid had stripped off Angel's clothes, immersed her in a hot bath, and then slathered the sticky mixture over every inch of her body.

Although, at first, Angel's skin had stung everywhere the unction touched, by the time the smelly concoction had been washed off and she touched her cheeks and arms, her flesh felt like the finest velvet.

Her hands were then lotioned and wrapped for an hour, after which her nails were buffed with a piece of kidskin until they shone. Her feet were treated likewise. This tickled almost unbearably, and lightened Angel's mood considerably.

All this time the green silk opera gown lay like a dream across Angel's bed. Every so often she would glance at it, drawing reassurance from its splendid glory. At last, when it seemed that Lady Cartwright and Prudie had forced every beauty treatment they knew onto Angel, it was time to dress.

The silk gown felt like moonbeams rippling over a ferny glen as it rustled past Angel's head and fell in swirling folds about her legs. Prudie's eyes grew wide as she adjusted the gown, but she said nothing as she proceeded to help Angel pull on silk stockings, long white gloves, and green slippers.

The maid dusted sweetly scented ivory powder over Angel's shoulders, bosom, and face. A trace of pink lip-color was applied to Angel's lips, and a bit of the same graced her high cheekbones. Then Prudie dabbed a bit of divine smelling perfume on Angel's wrists, beneath her ears, and in the hollow between her breasts.

A knock on the door heralded the arrival of Lady Cartwright, who had gone to her chambers to dress herself, not wanting to take Prudie away from Angel.

The earl's sister entered Angel's bedchamber wearing a fashionable gown of purple satin, and amethysts. In her hands she held several other pieces of jewelry, studded with glittering green emeralds, which she placed around Angel's neck, wrists, and on her ears. Then she and Prudie stepped back as if admiring a fine painting.

"Oh, Lady Cartwright," the maid murmured. "Have you ever seen the like?"

"Never," her mistress answered confidently, a satisfied gleam in her warm brown eyes. "Prudie, you have earned a large bonus." Taking Angel by the arm, Lady Cartwright then turned the girl gently toward the cheval glass. "You may look now, my dear."

As Prudie lifted the lace covering from the mirror, Angel closed her eyes, whispered a silent prayer, and then held her breath. When she finally gathered the courage to look into the cheval glass, it was all she could do to keep from glancing over her shoulder to see who else was standing in the room.

Surely the elegant creature gazing back at her *must* be a stranger!

The young woman's hair, a gleaming bronze-copper rather than Angel's own dull scarlet tresses, was caught up in Grecian ringlets around her face. Some of the lustrous curls were left loose in back and reached past her hips. They flashed and scintillated like the finest European satin.

The young woman's eyes, fringed with thick blackened lashes, and tilting exotically atop fine, high-boned cheeks colored attractively with the first blush of youth, appeared almost too big for her face. Reflecting the emerald silk gown's rich hue, they looked as deep and mysterious as an Amazon jungle.

And the young woman's face!

Apparently Prudie's astringent salve had done its work extremely well, which the fine ivory powder had completed. Where troops of reddish freckles had marched early that morning, now only the faintest hint brushed the top of Angel's nose and cheeks, giving her a gamine look that was, Angel blushed to admit, undeniably appealing.

Even Angel's mouth, which before had seemed large enough to swallow the Prince Regent and all his court, no longer seemed out-of-reason huge but, instead, looked plump and luscious.

Angel stepped tentatively from side to side, examining herself further.

The emerald ear-bobs, bracelet, and choker borrowed from Lady Cartwright winked and flashed. As expected, the emerald silk gown was simply superb. As Madame Sophie had suggested, Angel knew it made her look like nothing so much as a Grecian goddess.

Turning this way and that, she touched her face, almost afraid she was going to wake up and discover it had all been a tragically wonderful dream. But she did not. And her heart seemed to swell in her chest.

She was torn between a desire to laugh with wildly insane glee or burst out sobbing.

Gracious heaven! The transformation Hilary had promised had truly come to pass! Just look at her!

If only Lord Darcy could see her like this. *Then* he would not call her appearance, "not all that bad." *Then* he would not be so hasty to call her plain!

"Well?" Standing beside Prudie, whose eyes were huge with awe, Lady Cartwright smiled broadly, showing even white teeth that somehow made Angel recall Lord Darcy's rakish, shadowed jawline and roguish grin. "Aren't you magnificent?"

"Hilary," Angel said, turning moist eyes toward her benefactress, "I do not know what to say. Thank you. Thank you so much. And you, too, Prudie."

The maid grinned and nodded.

Lady Cartwright also inclined her head, graciously. "You are most welcome. Now, shall we go down to dinner? Although, as you know, we usually dine at eight, tonight we will be eating at six-thirty so that we might not be late for the opening of the opera."

"Who is performing?" Angel inquired, suddenly very excited with the thought of attending the opera, something she had never in her wildest dreams imagined she would do, and with going out amid the ton, looking as she did now.

"The great Catalini is singing *Semiramide,*" Lady Cartwright explained as they moved out of Angel's chamber and down the hall, leaving Prudie in the room to clean up the cosmetics. "And I, unlike most of my fellow ton-members, go to King's Theater to listen to the music, not gawk and chatter like a confused monkey."

"Signora Catalini!" Angel started, overwhelmed. "The Italian soprano? Why, I heard of her even at Windywood Abbey. My father and his friends used to speak often of her magnificent voice. How thrilling that I shall finally hear her sing!" Then she asked, curiously, "Is she as temperamental as rumor has it?"

"More so," Lady Cartwright admitted. "If the crowd makes too much noise, or does not cheer enough, she refuses to go on. When she began singing at King's Theater I convinced Herbert to purchase a subscription for a box, which, if you can believe it, cost twenty-three hundred pounds."

"Good gracious. Why so much?"

Lady Cartwright waved one purple-gloved hand. "Oh, my dear girl, most of the ton would have been willing to pay twice that. If Herbert hadn't had stock in the theatre company we would never have gotten a box at all.

"Also, I believe you will be pleased to know that we have one of the best boxes in the house, alongside those belonging to Lady Jersey and Lady Sefton. During the intermission I will introduce you. Since, as I previously mentioned, both ladies are patronesses of Almack's, we must procure their good will in order to obtain your vouchers."

Reminding herself that, by some amazing twist of fate (as well as a huge amount of effort and money) she looked quite presentable, and thus needn't worry about her ugliness, Angel nonetheless experienced a nervous shiver.

Lady Cartwright did not notice. She sighed happily. "I just know Sally and Maria are going to love you." Then she frowned. "But listen carefully to what I am about to say, Angel. The only one of the patronesses you must be sure to avoid is Mrs. Drummond-Burrell—a fire-tongued dragon if ever there was one. She'd as soon snap off your head as grant you permission to waltz. On no account are you to go anywhere near her!"

Angel swallowed. "I promise I shan't."

Lady Cartwright smiled again. "Good. Come now, we must make haste if we do not want to be late for Signora Catalini."

Sebastian ran lightly up the steps of his sister's town house and rapped sharply on the door. When his summons was not answered immediately, he scowled and knocked harder.

Where the devil was everybody?

The Appleby party had come to London one day earlier than planned, much to Sebastian's chagrin, since the early departure had meant missing a fox hunt on the Appleby estate. Lady Sarah had preferred leaving for Town to riding to the hounds and, as her future intended, Sebastian had felt compelled to swallow his disappointment. Thus, he had forced a smile and ceded to her wishes, trying not to think of the riders even now leaping hedges and fording streams as they pursued the crafty fox through Quorn country.

Within a few more moments the door was opened by Lord and Lady Cartwright's starchy butler, Fipps. A very tall, very thin man with sparse silver hair, Fipps appeared far more crabby than he was in truth. When he saw Sebastian his dour face cracked into a sunny smile, proving this fact.

"My Lord Darcy!" the butler exclaimed. "What a nice surprise. We were led to understand you would not be calling here until at least tomorrow. Neither my lord nor my lady are here, but I know that, when they return, they will be delighted to see that you are in London already. Will you come in for a glass of spiced wine? 'Tis a chilly evening."

Sebastian frowned.

Hilary was not at home? Impossible. Where would she be, if not at home? She was supposed to be chaperoning Lady Angel, not gallivanting about Town with Herbert. Had she perhaps deemed his ward too lacking in attractive physical attributes to even warrant an attempt at launching the chit?

"No, thank you, Fipps," he said crankily. "I have a bit of a headache tonight, and when I have a headache alcohol makes my brain pound most dreadfully. My sister and brother-in-law are gone, you say? Do you happen to know where they went?"

"Yes, sir. Lord Cartwright has gone to one of his country estates for an unspecified period of time, and Lady Cartwright and Lady Angelique have gone to King's Theater, to hear the great Catalini." He added, rapturously, "The signora is singing *Semiramide.*"

Sebastian's eyebrows drew together. Surely Lady Angel was not yet ready to be foisted onto the world. Or had Hilary, deciding that nothing could be done to improve the chit, leapt into the venture at the earliest possible moment, the better to give the homely girl every opportunity to snag a husband before the end of the Season? "My sister and ward have gone out for the evening? In *public?*" he repeated.

Fipps's austere face creased with pleasure. "Oh, yes, my lord. And what a charming girl Lady Angelique is, if you will pardon my saying so. Your lady sister seems most taken with her. As, if I may be so bold, is the entire staff here at Cartwright House."

"I see," Sebastian replied doubtfully.

"Please, sir, come inside and wait for their return. My Lord Cartwright received a new shipment of French brandy just this afternoon. If you are of a mind, I am certain he would welcome you to sample it."

"I think not. I believe I shall just visit the opera. I find I am suddenly consumed with a desire to hear the great Catalini for myself."

It was the least he could do, Sebastian decided. He glowered as he moved back down the town house steps. Poor Lady Angel must be terrified at being in polite Society, since her plainness and garish hair were sure to be commented upon.

Sebastian climbed back into his carriage. "Home, Brownley," he called to the driver. "Quickly."

He would have missed the first half of the opera, but that didn't matter. Though he had said otherwise to Fipps, it was not truly the great Catalini whom he wanted to observe. He felt he owed it to Angel to be present at her first social excursion, if only to brush aside some of the unkind comments about her person that she was sure to engender.

It took only a few minutes to don evening garb. His valet, scrambling backward as the earl hurried back out to the carriage that again waited in the street, was still fiddling with Sebastian's cravat as his lordship leapt into the vehicle and shouted their destination. Ten minutes later the carriage rolled to a stop before the Royal Italian Opera House, more commonly known as King's Theater.

Sebastian jumped out and waved to the driver. "You may return home, Brownley. I shall ride with my sister, in her carriage." He took the opera house steps three at a time. Intermission had just begun, and the halls were packed with milling bodies.

He passed through the great double doors, then turned to the left and climbed another staircase. He walked swiftly, until he reached the balcony that contained the private boxes. There he ran a hand over his hair and straightened his cravat, then took a deep breath, parted the green and gold velvet curtain leading to his sister's box, and stepped into the small compartment.

The sight that met his dazzled gaze left him completely incapable of movement.

Chapter Twelve

Besides Hilary and Lady Angel, six wealthy, titled gentlemen of Sebastian's acquaintance sat in the luxurious theatre box. His eyes widened as he observed that the men were not speaking solely with his sister, but were also, astonishingly, laughing and flirting quite outrageously with Lady Angel!

And who could blame them?

Gone was the ugly duckling.

Gone was the Plain Jane.

His ward had, as in the most fanciful fairy tale, turned into a veritable swan!

Lady Angel's horrid scarlet tresses had been transformed into piles of tempting red-gold curls tied up with a gilt riband. Her neck, long and white and graceful, emerged from a moderately low cut bodice that made her bosom appear far more amply endowed than he had previously assumed. Her skin resembled white velvet, but was dusted with a sprinkling of freckles that, he noticed with another jolt, was entrancingly sensuous.

Without warning an irrational fury, combined with a bittersweet desire, ripped through his body, making him tremble with feelings he did not understand but instantly decided must be due to the way his ward was flirting with her newfound admirers. To all appearances the chit intended to take up in London where she had left off with Sir Corbin Pugsley! Had she neither shame nor concern for what such actions would do to the family name?

As Sebastian watched, fuming, Lady Angel waved a chicken-skin fan, on which faeries and nymphs cavorted through a woodland glade, before her becomingly flushed cheeks. She batted long, lush lashes as she responded with obvious intelligence and pleasure to her companions' comments. Her eyes, which seemed somehow impossibly transformed from hazel to a vivid, cat-like green, sparkled exquisitely. The gentlemen were obviously not immune to her appeal, either, for they fawned over the girl and gawked like overgrown schoolboys experiencing their first crushes.

Sebastian swallowed an outraged growl. His hands tightened into painful fists at his sides.

How quickly Lady Angel had learned to put her new-found feminine attractions to work! And those poor sots gazing so infatuatedly at her were completely unsuspecting as to what kind of woman they were dealing with! A woman who had sold her favors to one of the vilest, most reprehensible men in the realm!

As Angel swiveled in her seat to smile mischievously up at one of the gentlemen, unbidden lust screamed through Sebastian's loins. The girl's smile seemed to tease his senses like the strongest French liqueur, making his blood boil, and his skin far too tight and hot for certain parts of his anatomy.

Closing his eyes, he gritted his teeth and counted to ten, by which time the sensation had partially abated.

Then he reopened his eyes and glared at his ward just in time to see her raise her pretty fan and flutter it tantalizingly before her huge green eyes as she gave a little, crystalline laugh.

Sebastian sucked in a harsh breath.

How dare she embarrass his sister with such wanton manners? It was bad enough that Lady Angel had behaved so lewdly in the country, but to behave with such conspicuously prurient interest in the gentlemen here in London was the outside of enough.

What in God's name had he done, foisting the fire-haired trollop off on his sister without any thought but that he had gotten his unwanted ward off his own hands for a time?

Finally Sebastian managed to tear his gaze away from Lady Angel. He moved stiffly into the opera chair behind Hilary. Putting his mouth near her ear, he whispered softly, "Hello, Puss. I came as soon as I could."

Lady Cartwright whirled about. Her eyes shone with the pleasure of seeing him. "Seb! You have come home early! I am so glad." She turned toward Angel, pride radiating from her face. "Just look at your ward! Does she not look marvelous? She is such a credit to us both!"

Sebastian glanced darkly in the girl's direction. His jaw clenched again, and he spoke through gritted teeth. "A definite improvement in her looks, at least. But are you sure it is wise to make her so appealing to the gentlemen of the ton?"

His sister laughed. "I thought that was the general idea, darling. You know, get her betrothed to a suitable gentleman? Have I presumed too much?" She added, teasingly, "Have you, perhaps, designs on the girl, yourself?"

Sebastian's face burned. "Do not be absurd," he snapped. "Of course I want nothing better than to get the chit married off. However, the key word in your statement was 'suitable.' "

"My dear brother," Lady Cartwright said uncertainly. "Look around you. These gentlemen are the cream of the *beau monde*. Any one of them would be a triumphant coup for Angel to ensnare."

"Humph," Sebastian muttered. "Triumphant for her, anyway, given the circumstances." He felt a rush of guilt. He must make certain to take Hilary aside and explain Lady Angel's ruination. It would not do to marry the girl off to a man of these gentlemen's caliber. They deserved far better than "damaged goods."

Not to mention, he realized suddenly, that if word got out about the girl's ruined state, it could do no end of harm to Hilary's reputation. People would immediately assume Hilary had known the truth. They would believe she had tried to pull a fast one on their esteemed ranks. She would be completely ostracised from the ton.

"I cannot think why you said Angel was 'plain' in your letter, brother," Lady Cartwright murmured softly, interrupting Sebastian's troubled thoughts. "Just look at her. The girl absolutely sparkles. And the men are positively charmed. I tell you, from the moment we stepped through the theatre door they swarmed around her like bees around a honey-pot."

Tension twisted Sebastian's shoulders. Apparently the men had scented fair, willing game immediately. It would not do to put off his explanation longer. He decided to inform his sister immediately about the true state of affairs. Then she could decide whether or not she wished to keep his ward on as a charge.

"So it would appear," he replied. "Listen, Hil, there is something I think you should know about Lady Angel. For your own safety. When she lived at Windywood she enjoyed a most unsuitable, indelicate arrangement with her neighbor, Sir—"

But Lady Cartwright was not listening. "Angel," she cried, "look who is here! Sebastian! Is that not above all things famous?"

Lady Angel's delectable profile spun about until she faced them. Her cheeks flushed a rosy pink as if she were chagrined at having been caught working her wiles on Sebastian's friends.

"My Lord Darcy!" she burst out. "I understood from Hilary that you were not to return until tomorrow, at the soonest. What are you doing back so soon?"

"My party decided to return early," he replied coolly. He glanced around at her circle of gallants, then bowed. "Glencoe, Harding, Dunheath, Edgecomb, Sinclair. And Rosling, of course. Pleased to see you this evening, gentlemen. I trust I find you all well?"

There was a general, fleeting admission of this fact before the men redirected their attention to Lady Angel. Sebastian's gaze followed and rested on his ward's attractively flushed cheeks for several moments. Then, remembering where he was, he glanced over to see his sister gazing at him curiously.

He cleared his throat. "Ahem. If it meets with your approval, sister, I would beg a ride home in your carriage this evening. I have dismissed my own."

"Certainly. So tell me, Seb, what brings you out tonight? Would it not have been just as well to visit us tomorrow? Not that I am not thrilled to see you here. It is just that you have quite taken me by surprise."

"I did not want to wait until the morrow to visit you. I needed to see how you were faring, and thought to lend my support to my ward."

"How sweet of you. But," Lady Cartwright said softly, glancing at Lady Angel and smiling fondly, "as you can see, the girl is doing very well on her own, do you not agree?"

"Of a certainty." His mouth tightened again as his ward fluttered her lacy fan. He felt like snatching the flirtatious object out of Lady Angel's hands and breaking its delicate ivory sticks over his knee. "I had no idea you could bring about such changes in her. How did you manage it?"

"Oh, you know," his sister replied with a dismissive wave. "Feminine secrets, as well making free with your line of credit." Without further adieu she got to her feet. "Please excuse me for a moment, Seb, but there is something I must attend to."

She raised her voice. "I am sorry, gentlemen, but Lady Angel and I must call upon some of our other friends here tonight." She gazed meaningfully across the way into another theatre box.

Following her glance, Angel paled, but stood and followed obediently.

As the two women moved out of the box, Sebastian opened his mouth and wiggled his jaw to relieve the tension in his neck. It helped only slightly.

He wanted nothing so much as to drag Lady Angel out of the theatre and send her, posthaste, back to Windywood Abbey—and would have done so if it were not for the fact that the Abbey now belonged to Sir Corbin Pugsley. He thought furiously of his other estates, wondering if they would be suitable stashing-places for a misbehaving ward.

Inwardly, he vowed to speak with Hilary as soon as they returned to Cartwright House. His sister *must* know that Angel was not the naive maid the girl seemed bent on portraying. With this decision made, he settled back in his seat and began exchanging tidbits of turf talk with his acquaintances.

Quite a few of the gentlemen present also kept racing

stables. They, as well as those men not particularly interested in the Sport of Kings, hastened to commiserate with Sebastian about Hughes Pride's wounds and resultant withdrawal from the next several races.

After a few minutes Sebastian's attention was diverted to the theatre box to his left, belonging to Lord and Lady Sefton, where a sudden flurry of motion caught his eye. To his chagrin, he saw that Hilary was introducing Lady Angel to Lady Sefton.

The ever-gentle and sweet Maria, Lady Sefton, one of the patronesses of Almack's, smiled and held out one white hand. Sebastian watched Lady Angel curtsy before touching the older woman's fingers with what he considered cunningly demure innocence. Lady Angel's lashes were lowered virtuously, as if she were as pure as her namesake.

Sebastian did not even try to understand why he felt so enraged by his ward's retiring behavior. Instead, searching the enormous, horseshoe-shaped amphitheater with his gaze, he looked around to see if anyone else noticed her treachery. It was as if the chit knew precisely how to behave in order to garner attention from every male within ogling distance. Almost every man Jack in the room was gazing at the girl, their eyes soft and contemplative.

At last Hilary and Angel left Lady Sefton's box and disappeared, once again, into the hall.

Sebastian drew a sigh of relief as he noticed all the men in the theatre turn back to whatever had occupied them before they had spotted his ward. But his relief was short lived, and he repressed a shudder when he saw Angel and Hilary reappear, this time on Sebastian's direct right, in the subscription box belonging to Lord and Lady Jersey. A quick glance proved that his fellow-peers had also noticed the girl's reappearance, and were once more riveted on her figure.

If Sebastian leaned close to the balustrade he could just hear the conversation his sister and ward enjoyed with yet another of Almack's patronesses.

"Sally, dearest," Hilary crooned. "You look exquisite! That rose silk gown makes your skin resemble fresh cream. How are you?"

"Tolerable, although my poor husband's gout has cropped up again." Lady Jersey waved one diamond-encrusted hand. "Grouchy as a money-lender these days, and just as clutch-fisted. He did not like my new gown, at all—said money ran through my fingers like water and this dress was just another example of my extravagance. However, I am glad *you* approve of it. Besides, I refuse to let my husband's opinion trouble me; everyone knows we ladies dress for other women, not gentlemen, at all."

"Is it a Madame Sophie creation?"

"Of course," Lady Jersey said with a blink of surprise. "Who else?"

"True," Lady Cartwright said. "But your poor husband! I am so sorry to hear he is unwell. Please extend my best wishes for his health."

"Thank you, darling, I will."

Finally Lady Cartwright pulled Lady Angel forward. "Allow me to present my brother's ward, Sally dear. This is Lady Angelique Harriette Arundel—Lady Angel, we call her. She hails from Yorkshire. I am sponsoring her come-out this year. Since I would like to take her to Almack's next week in order to obtain permission for her to waltz at her come-out ball shortly thereafter, I do hope I may count upon you for her vouchers?"

"Of course, my dear. I know you would never chaperone anyone who was not totally suited to those hallowed halls." Lady Jersey examined Angel through a diamond-dusted quizzing glass. "Her family comes from Yorkshire, you say?"

"Yes. Her lineage is impeccable," Hilary confided as if Angel were not standing at her side. "Her father was the fifth earl of Darcy—you will remember that my brother Sebastian inherited the title?"

"But of course. And her mother?"

"The daughter of the duke of Branleigh."

"Well," Lady Jersey said in an impressed tone. "Suitable for Almack's, indeed. She is quite lovely, as well as well-bred. Look at those cheekbones. And that luscious mouth. My dear girl," she said, addressing Lady Angel, "I am quite certain you will take the ton by storm. You must call upon me one day soon."

Sebastian strained to hear his ward's reply. When it came it was as soft-spoken and demure as her greeting to Lady Sefton had been. "Thank you ever so much, Lady Jersey. I am truly honored by your invitation. You are every bit as charming as Hilary told me you were. And your gown is a vision."

"Why, thank you, dear girl." Lady Jersey preened.

Hilary and Angel returned to the Cartwright box just as the second half of the opera was about to begin, so Sebastian was forced to clamp his mouth shut instead of tell all to his sister. He fumed until the end of the entertainment.

When the opera finished, Lady Angel's entire male retinue insisted on escorting the ladies to the Cartwright carriage, and Sebastian was once again unable to explain Angel's tarnished past to his sister. However, once the three of them had been installed in the vehicle, he turned flashing eyes on his ward.

"Well," he snarled, "you certainly made a spectacle of yourself tonight, my lady." He watched with satisfaction as Angel's lush, inviting lips parted and her cheeks flamed.

"I beg your pardon, my lord?" she stammered. "What did I do wrong? I do not understand."

"Oh," he said savagely, "I think you do. But do not even think to try your wiles here in London. You are here to get married, not to grant your favors to any man who offers you coin of the realm."

His sister gasped. "Sebastian! How dare you! Angel's first venture into Society went beautifully, and the men were quite taken with her. As were Ladies Sefton and Jersey, I might add. What on earth are you talking about?"

"Her conduct, Hilary. She behaved like the wanton she is."

Lady Cartwright's brows rose. "*I* saw no hint of improper behavior. It is your own conduct, brother, not Angel's, which leaves much to be desired!"

Sebastian threw his sister a quelling glance. "I will readily explain myself, Hilary. As for Lady Angel, she knows quite well why I am angry. Do you not, my lady?"

The girl's wide eyes flashed back and forth between him and Lady Cartwright. "I . . . I—"

"Come now, your innocent chatter and sweet smiles might have charmed my sister, the gentlemen of the *beau monde*, and Ladies Sefton and Jersey into believing in your purity, but you and I know better."

"Sebastian, stop speaking in riddles. You are giving me a headache! What are you talking about?" Lady Cartwright demanded.

"I should not have sent her here," Sebastian continued, too furious with his ward and his own wildly excited response to her new appearance to hold his tongue. "She is nothing but a common trollop, and should have remained in the country. I should have expected her to behave as she did tonight, but wanted to believe she was capable of behaving properly. Apparently I expected too much."

Lady Cartwright stiffened. "I suspect you have imbibed too freely from the brandy bottle this evening, brother. Your behavior is despicable. I trust a good night's rest will bring you back to your senses."

The carriage rolled to a stop and Sebastian glanced out the window to see with surprise that they had reached his town house.

"I will expect you to attend us on the morrow," Lady Cartwright finished frostily. "At which time I shall expect you to proffer a suitable apology to Angel. Good night."

Sebastian felt control of the situation slipping out of his grasp as easily as a buttered eel. "Hilary, if you will just give me a minute to explain. I have every reason for behaving as I—"

"Good night!"

Since his sister looked angry enough to strike him in another moment, Sebastian obediently climbed out onto the road. He saw absently that his butler, Soams, had observed his arrival and was holding the town house door open. Turning stiffly, Sebastian strode angrily up his steps, sailed into the house without speaking to Soams, and made his way to his library.

There, as he had already insisted to Hilary, he had not touched a drop of brandy all evening, he now poured himself a large glass and swallowed it in one fiery gulp. Then he sank into a chair before the hearth and stared gloomily into the crackling flames. His depression deepened as he noted the fiery coals only served to remind him of Angel's red-gold curls.

It was only later, after he'd drunk much more of the potent beverage, that he admitted to himself that Hilary had been right to call his behavior to task. It had not been *Angel,* but rather *he,* who had made a cake of himself. Even though his ward *had* been flirting with her admirers, the chit's behavior had not been out of place. It had, rather, been precisely what was expected from a debutante.

In all truth, he acknowledged hazily, while Angel had looked quite stunning in her emerald green silk gown, with her glistening red curls piled so daintily upon her head, she had done nothing at all to warrant his wrath.

His throat burned with shame. He could only be grateful that he had not castigated his ward in public, but had saved this last inappropriate act for the privacy of his sister's carriage.

Although he would have preferred to lean back in his chair and slide into the sweet oblivion of drunken sleep, rather than examine his motives for taking Angel's behavior to task, as a man who held honesty to one's self as high as one's honor, he could not hide from the truth as his intellect screamed it out to him.

Mentally he reviewed the evening, scrutinizing each moment with agonizing clarity.

There had been nothing to fault about Angel's behavior with Ladies Sefton and Jersey. She had simply smiled and behaved as any other young debutante would have, although, perhaps, Angel had been a bit more poised than a seventeen- or eighteen-year-old girl. What had overset him, he realized now, was her totally unexpected transformation. To see her looking so astonishingly lovely had shocked him to the deepest core of his being. With that first glance, something amazing had happened.

What had disturbed him even more than Angel's transformation, from an antidote into a diamond of the first water, was the abrupt *volte-face* of his feelings toward her.

While she had been interesting to look at in a plain, country maid sort of way in Yorkshire, seeing her as an exquisite London Incomparable had catapulted him head first into infatuation.

He easily recognized the burning need to pull her into his arms and kiss her passionately, to gaze into her green eyes, and to touch her silken curls with his fingertips, as obsession. Further, this realization made him conscious of something else, something far more embarrassing than the way he had behaved.

It was this: when he had experienced that overwhelming lust for her at the opera, he had decided that, like all those men before him—as made obvious by her sneaking into Windywood Abbey in the dead of night after one of her trysts—he wanted to sample her wares, as well.

This appalling realization made him, in his own eyes, appear no better, nay, a thousand times *worse,* since he was Lady Angel's guardian, than that misshapen reprobate, Sir Corbin Pugsley.

Looking back at the way he'd addressed Angel in Hilary's carriage, he admitted that he had lashed out at his ward quite unfairly. She had been all that was charming to everyone at the theatre, and he felt utterly ashamed at having overreacted simply because he'd felt lust for the girl. Somehow, it seemed, his rage had burst into life because he had inwardly recognized the inappropriateness of his hunger for Lady Angel and had struck out at her through his own frustration.

Thus, while he still intended to inform Hilary of Angel's fall from grace in the country, just because it should be Hilary's decision whether or not she wished to continue sponsoring a ruined girl, it was *his* behavior that evening that had been quite beyond the pale.

Early on the morrow he would apologize to both his ward and his sister. Then he would tell Hilary all the damning details of Lady Angel's misbehavior and subsequent ruination. And under no circumstances would he allow himself to feel anything more than dutiful toward the girl, ever again.

He would see the chit married off, and marry his own exquisite promised fiancée, Lady Sarah. Then he would never, ever again lay eyes upon Lady Angel's damnably beautiful red hair and seductive green eyes.

Chapter Thirteen

Angel and Lady Cartwright visited a number of Hilary's acquaintances the following afternoon, including the duchess of Harcourt, in whose drawing room they now sat. The visit was meant to be a chance to introduce Angel to more members of the ton.

Earlier, when she and Lady Cartwright had arrived at the appointed "at home" hour, they had been the only ones in the room. Since then, however, some twenty more people had arrived and were conversing in little knots here and there throughout the exquisite ivory and rose chamber.

Since she knew no one but Hilary, it was not long before Angel's thoughts drifted back to Sebastian and the visit he had made to the Cartwright town house earlier that morning.

The earl had insisted she call him by his Christian name, probably in order to prove she accepted his proffered apology and friendship. Really, he was a most difficult man to understand! One minute bellowing at her like a raging bull, and the next as polite and charming as a Frenchman. She shook her head bemusedly.

"Lady Angel? Did you attend my question? I am waiting for a reply."

The gruff inquiry was posed by the marchioness of Dunkley, a frightful-looking woman in a puce gown and a clashing purple turban with gold braid trim. Lady Dunkley was possessed of triplet daughters, all equally homely and all coming out this Season.

Angel, who had not been attending the conversation shared between her, Lady Cartwright, and the marchioness, cast a pleading glance at Hilary.

"I think perhaps Angel is feeling a trifle tired, my lady, and, thus, that her mind was wandering," Lady Cartwright interjected quickly. "She is only recently come to London, you must know, and I have kept her very busy shopping and preparing for her come-out since her arrival."

Angel smiled gratefully.

"What her ladyship was asking, my dear," Lady Cartwright informed Angel, "was whether you enjoyed the opera last night."

"Oh, yes," Angel replied fervently. "Very much. Signora Catalini has a most extraordinary voice."

The marchioness tossed her head, nearly dislodging her garish turban. It tilted over one eyebrow, or, rather, where the lady's eyebrow would have been, had Lady Dunkley not plucked out every hair and replaced the natural feature with a thin charcoal line. This line now smeared, marring the gold braid on the edge of the turban. Angel tried not to stare.

"Of course she has, you silly booby," the marchioness cried. "That is why Catalini is so well compensated for each performance! Do you think the board members of the King's Theater, of which my husband is head, would be so generous to performers who were unworthy of such munificence? Do you mean to slight my husband's intelligence, miss?"

"Oh, no, ma'am! Not at all. I beg your forgiveness." Angel flushed and looked about wildly, trying to think of a way to join one of the other groups of people scattered around the drawing room.

Although she knew no one else in the room save Hilary, the duchess, and now the marchioness, Angel could not help wishing she could escape Lady Dunkley's caustic tongue. From the moment they had been introduced the marchioness had seemed determined to find fault with Angel, and it was a most disconcerting feeling to be so obviously disliked and not have an inkling as to why.

Finally, to Angel's relief, Lady Cartwright stood. "Lady Dunkley," she said cordially, "it has been our pleasure to see you today, but now we must greet our other friends. I hope to see you and your daughters at Court one week from today, as well as at Angel's come-out ball. You will, naturally, be receiving an invitation."

Angel could have groaned aloud at this prospect. She could just imagine the marchioness moving about Lord Darcy—Sebastian's—ballroom like an enormous spider, telling everyone who would listen how Lady Angel had ignorantly insulted Lord Dunkley by inferring that he and all the other board members of the King's Theater were lame-brained imbeciles.

However, to Angel's surprise, although the marchioness had clearly taken her in dislike, Lady Dunkley was just as obviously unwilling to bypass an opportunity to marry off her three daughters.

The marchioness smiled creakily (as if she had not done so in years, Angel thought grimly) and nodded her acceptance. "Thank you, Lady Cartwright. We shall be pleased to attend. It has been . . ." her narrow mouth turned downward sharply, "interesting making your acquaintance, Lady Angel."

"And yours, my lady," Angel replied with a weak smile. When they had moved out of earshot she leaned over and murmured in Lady Cartwright's ear, "What an awful woman, Hilary. I do hope she does not come to my ball. If we happen to serve strawberries with cream, she will surely curdle the stuff."

Lady Cartwright grinned and linked arms with Angel, propelling her about the room. "You needn't worry. Lady Dunkley never accompanies her daughters on their excursions. They have a poor relation who lives with them and fills the post of duenna."

They paused to greet three more of Hilary's acquaintances, then moved on.

"Are Lady Dunkley's daughters as horrid as their mother?" Angel asked when they had moved out of earshot of their most recent companions.

"Oh, not at all. They are quiet, of course, having such an outspoken gorgon for a mother, but are well-mannered and likeable. In all they are very dear girls, although unfortunately plain. I believe that is why the marchioness did not take a shine to you. I am sure that, with you in the same room with them, her daughters will get little or no male attention."

Angel came to an abrupt halt. She stared at Sebastian's sister with disbelief. "I? How absurd. Whyever would you say that?"

Smiling, Lady Cartwright urged Angel forward again. "You short-change yourself, child. In that new morning dress you are a veritable picture."

Angel glanced down at the fern-sprigged muslin that had been delivered from Madame Sophie's early that morning and shook her head. "To think that mere clothes can change a woman from ugly to appealing. I should never have thought it possible."

Hilary paused beside a sweet-smelling potted gardenia. She lowered her dark head to sniff a bloom, then straightened and resumed their progress about the chamber. "And you would have been correct."

"I do not understand."

"Do not think your new clothes are what makes you different, Angel. Or your new hairstyle, or cosmetics, or anything else, for that matter." Lady Cartwright chuckled softly at Angel's obvious doubt. "You have a certain sparkle which, although not so shiny when you took no care for your appearance, was nevertheless still present. You were rather like a diamond in the rough which, with a little polishing, has taken on a sparkle all its own."

Angel felt herself flush. "I declare, Hilary, you are going to make my head as big as the Tower of London. Thank you. Even if your words are not true, they seem to lend me a confidence I have never had before."

"You are welcome, child."

"But if, as you say, Lady Dunkley's daughters will get little attention in the same room with me, why would she want them to come to my ball?"

Lady Cartwright smiled again. "Because there are many rooms in a house, my dear, and *you* cannot be in all of them at once."

Angel laughed. "I was right before. You are absurd."

"Perhaps a bit. But tell me," the older woman continued. "What did Sebastian say to you when he called this morning and I was still in my chambers? From my window, I saw him arrive, but knew he would want to speak to you privately. I trust he apologized for his behavior last night." She scowled, her warm brown eyes darkening. "If he offended you further I shall chastise him most severely."

"Oh, no," Angel said swiftly. "He did apologize, and very prettily, too. He insisted I, also, call him by his Christian name."

Lady Cartwright came to an abrupt halt. "Did he, indeed?" she asked curiously.

"Yes," Angel said.

A faint smile played about Hilary's lips. "How interesting. I declare, Sebastian never fails to surprise me."

"I confess," Angel added slowly, as they resumed their march, "I don't know what to make of him. He is a most confusing man. Last night he considered me not quite . . . quite . . . *nice*, yet this morning he was as charming as a pipe-playing Indian with a cobra."

"Well, as long as he apologized. Even that much is difficult for a man as proud as my brother. His behavior was reprehensible." Then, distracted by a group of newcomers entering the duchess of Harcourt's drawing room, Lady Cartwright dropped the subject and said softly, "Look over there. Do you see that very beautiful young woman in blue muslin?"

Angel obeyed. "The one with deep blue eyes and black ringlets?"

"Yes. Although it is not yet common knowledge— so you will understand when I ask you to keep this to yourself—she and Sebastian have come to an understanding."

Angel caught her breath, both from surprise and from a curious, sharp pain that struck somewhere near her heart. She stared in dismay at the exquisite newcomer. "She is betrothed to the earl?"

"Not quite yet. But as good as." Lady Cartwright narrowed her eyes, thoughtfully. "Perhaps Sebastian is overcome by the whole affair; that could explain his snappish behavior toward you last night."

"What do you mean, 'not quite yet'? I thought one was either betrothed, or they were not."

"They have come to an understanding. However, the girl, Lady Sarah Moreton, who is the daughter of Lord and Lady Appleby, wishes to keep their plans a secret until the end of the Season."

"For heaven's sake, why?" Angel demanded. "I should think that if one is in love, especially with a man as handsome as Sebastian, and he returns her regard, one would want to shout her good fortune to the stars!"

For a moment Lady Cartwright stared at Angel uncertainly. Then she shook her head and her expression turned cynical.

"*If* one is in love, that may be true, my dear," the earl's sister admitted. "But marriages amid the ton are seldom for such a humble reason as love. As you get older and wiser you will find that it is better to feel secure in one's home and hearth than to wed for love and watch your love die as a result of penny-pinching just to have enough meat on your table."

"Oh, of course, I know that is the usual way of things," Angel agreed morosely. "But never tell me Sebastian plans to marry that poor girl just to ensure the earldom. They shall never be happy if that is the case." She shook her head regretfully. "I believe that if one cannot marry for love, one is better off never marrying at all. Just look at you, Hilary. You married for love and have never regretted it."

Lady Cartwright replied slowly. "Herbert and I were lucky, it is true, because we fell in love with people of our own station. Many are not so fortunate. As for Sebastian and Lady Sarah, not being privy to my brother's heart, I cannot say if theirs is a love match or not. But I rather doubt it. He does not behave like a man in the throes of passion."

Angel sighed, attributing the heaviness in her chest for sympathy for the betrothed couple. "Poor Sebastian. As for his intended, she does not look as happy as she should, either."

Lady Cartwright shrugged. "I shouldn't worry. Both she and Sebastian are adults and know their own minds. At any rate, would you care to meet Lady Sarah?"

Angel nodded. The least she could do for her guardian was to find out if the girl really loved him, or if Lady Sarah was just marrying the earl for his fortune. Surely Sebastian would appreciate such knowledge. While his behavior seemed oddly inconsistent in regard to *her*, his reaction to seeing his black stallion, Hughes Pride, beaten by his jockey, showed him to be a truly gentle man who deserved more than a cold, loveless marriage.

She followed Lady Cartwright across the tiled floor toward the newcomers, who were standing near the duchess.

Hilary touched the young woman's arm, causing the dark-haired girl to turn deep blue eyes upon them. "Lady Cartwright," she exclaimed. "What a pleasure to see you here today."

"Indeed. Lady Sarah, may I present my brother's ward, Lady Angel?"

The girl's blue eyes widened. "Oh, by all means, Lady Cartwright! Lord Darcy mentioned at my birthday fete that he had a ward who was coming out this Season." She gazed curiously at Angel. "But he never told me you were so beautiful, Lady Angel. Is this your first Season?"

Angel drew a relieved breath. Surely this charming girl would never consent to marry where her heart was not engaged.

"Thank you for the compliment, Lady Sarah," she said with a dubious grin. "And yes, this is my first Season."

"You are going to enjoy it. This is my second." The

dark-haired girl turned toward Hilary. "Will you excuse us, Lady Cartwright?" she inquired politely. "I would so like to know Lady Angel better. We appear to be of an age, and I am sure we will be great friends."

Involved in a conversation with Lady Sarah's mother, Hilary waved a hand in dismissal.

Angel's heart lightened at the thought of having a friend here in London, especially one who knew how to go on in Town. She allowed Lady Sarah to pull her toward a low marble bench, then sat beside the beautiful girl. As Lady Sarah had implied, within a very short time they were bosom bows.

Lady Sarah kept up a near-constant flow of chatter, allowing Angel to sit and absorb, which suited both women very well, although to Angel's mind it seemed that Lady Sarah had a disturbing tendency to blurt out everything that chanced upon her tongue.

It was this tendency, perhaps, which made Lady Sarah blurt out, "Oh, Lady Angel. You seem so kind. I must tell you of my plight."

Angel frowned. "Certainly, but please, call me Angel."

The dark-haired girl smiled. "And you must call me Sarah." Then she, too, frowned. "May I tell you of my troubles?"

Angel was dumbfounded, and did not know what to say. However, though in her mind their friendship seemed a bit newborn to pour out one's heart as Lady Sarah seemed intent on doing, she nodded reassuringly.

"Thank goodness. Given your relationship to Lady Cartwright and her brother, I feel certain you will understand."

"I shall try," Angel assured her new friend, sincerely.

Pulling a fine lawn handkerchief from one lacy sleeve, Lady Sarah twisted the shred of cloth in her hands. "I simply cannot stand it. It is just too, too dreadful. You cannot know what I have to bear." Lady Sarah's voice caught on a sob. "My heart is near to breaking."

Angel grasped her new friend's hands gently. "What has overset you?"

Lady Sarah sighed dramatically. "My father is determined I wed a man whom I do not love," she said tremulously, "while the man I *do* love is too shy to speak his heart! So I am doomed. And to me, if one cannot marry where one's heart is engaged, one should never marry at all."

Angel, who had only moments before proffered those identical sentiments to Hilary, now paused, dumbstruck. Tilting her head to one side, she asked hesitantly, "Forgive me, Sarah, but . . . are you not to marry my guardian, Lord Darcy?"

"Yes." Lady Sarah's voice broke again. "Forgive *me*, Angel, but I must tell you that he is horrid! He wants nothing from our marriage but a bunch of dirty old horses! They are all he talks about! Horses and horse racing. The horses, you see, are a part of my dowry, and are the only reason he wants to marry me!"

Although her friendship with Sebastian was only a bit older than her friendship with Lady Sarah, Angel suddenly felt quite indignant at Lady Sarah's opinion of the earl of Darcy.

On the other hand, for some reason the discovery that Sebastian wanted the exquisite Lady Sarah Moreton's hand in wedlock for such an unromantic reason as to obtain fine horseflesh made Angel feel like she could walk on air. She almost laughed, giddily, but caught herself before such an unseemly response could escape her lips.

On further consideration, though, she dismissed her new friend's fears and felt her newfound happiness vanish.

"Never tell me Lord Darcy is not in love with you,

Sarah," she said flatly. "You are so beautiful. How could he help but love you?"

"The *only* thing Lord Darcy loves are horses," Lady Sarah answered firmly. "And I loathe them. Nasty, smelly things. They should all be made into glue!"

Angel drew back, aghast. Before she could retort angrily, the dark-haired girl leaned closer as if afraid to be overheard.

"To tell you the truth," Lady Sarah whispered, "I am absolutely petrified of horses. I cannot bear them. I break out in hives each time one comes near me, and I get sick to my stomach every time I have to ride behind them in a carriage."

Despite her love for the animals, Angel's heart contracted with sympathy. "Oh, you poor girl. You know," she added considerately, "everyone has something they fear. I feel that way about rats. They scare me to death."

"I knew you would understand," Lady Sarah breathed. "Do you know, I practically forced my father to leave our Yorkshire estate a day early just to avoid riding in a fox hunt. I know Lord Darcy was disappointed," she finished with a shudder, "but I knew I would just die if I had to ride. And it would have been expected, since the hunt was being held in honor of *my* birthday!"

Angel nodded compassionately. "That is true. But, Sarah, surely if you feel that way about horses, you *must not* marry Lord Darcy. His stable is the most important thing in the world to him. Why, you would never be happy."

Lady Sarah's lovely blue eyes filled with tears, somehow making her appear even more ethereal than before. "I know. But what can I do? My parents are delighted with the match. And I am not so spirited as you, Angel, to go against their wishes. I fear I shall have to marry him." She sighed and dabbed at her eyes with her handkerchief. "But at least I have one final Season as a maid."

"What of this man you love?" Angel demanded. "Who is he?" She glanced around to ascertain their privacy before whispering, "Why does he not simply sweep you away to Scotland? You could elope."

Lady Sarah's cheeks flushed at this shocking suggestion, but her eyes gleamed longingly. "Oh, if only we could! But I fear I have not told you the worst. My darling is Simon Radcliffe, Lord Evanstone. He is one of Lord Darcy's closest friends. And, although I know Simon loves me, he will never tell me so, now that Lord Darcy and I have an understanding."

Angel agreed, disheartened. "Certainly not. Men are so ridiculously honorable about their friends' interests."

Lady Sarah sniffed. Her lovely face threatened to crumple. "I do so love Simon. He is everything to me. Without him I might as well die." She stifled a whimper. "Or marry Lord Darcy."

Lady Sarah's pronouncement left Angel filled with dread. Despite what might happen to Lady Sarah and Lord Evanstone in the future, Angel knew she could not allow Sebastian to marry a woman to whom life as his wife seemed a fate worse than death.

"Do not fret, Sarah," she said without thinking. "*I* shall speak to Lord Evanstone, so that we might find out his feelings on the matter." She finished decisively, determined to do her part in saving two people—nay, three— from making such a drastic mess of their lives, by saying, "Everything will be fine."

Chapter Fourteen

One week later Sebastian sat at his sister's breakfast table, having spent the night there after being chased from his own town house due to a horrendous leak in his roof. The leak had marred both the ceiling and paper in his bedchamber, and the southern wall in the ballroom (an incident that had pleased Hilary mightily for some reason).

Choosing to have both rooms repainted in more modern colors, jade green for his bedchamber and a soft lilac that Hilary had suggested for the ballroom, Sebastian had escaped to Cartwright House in order to avoid inhaling the noxious paint fumes.

Thus, after breaking his fast that morning with kidneys and eggs, he sipped a cup of coffee and relaxed as he glanced at the racing news in the *Times*.

Hughes Pride's jockey-inflicted wounds had healed nicely, thanks to Lord Appleby's superior head groom. Thus, as Sebastian had given Lord Appleby leave to enter the black stallion in a local race, so that the horse might be more conditioned for the Grand London Gold Cup, it was possible the horse would be mentioned in today's paper.

Sebastian scanned the times and placements of various horses that had raced the day before. Just as he had nearly decided he was wasting his time and that Lord Appleby had decided to give Hughes Pride an extra week to recover, he turned the page and his gaze fell upon a headline in bold black letters:

Big Gray Newcomer Beats Expected Gold Cup Winner!

"Bloody hell," he burst out. He folded the paper and peered more closely at the miniscule type. He was so engrossed in the article that at first he did not see Lord Evanstone enter the breakfast room.

"What ho, Seb?" the tall, sandy-haired lord said heartily. For some reason his cheer did not seem to reach his eyes. "Stopped by your town house this morning and your butler told me you were here at Cartwright House. He asked me to inform you that the painters should be finished by this afternoon, and, as he plans to leave all the windows open, the place should be aired out by tonight if you wish to return."

"Ah. Excellent." Sebastian quirked a brow. "Did you stop here merely to pass along that bit of information, or is there another reason I have been blessed by your company on this fine morning?"

"Actually," Evanstone grinned abashedly, "my chef, Pierre, is refusing to cook again because he didn't think I acted suitably impressed by a chocolate soufflé he made last night. Man knows I hate chocolate. At any rate, I got up this morning to cold sardines and knockwurst."

Sebastian cast a disgusted glance at his friend and shuddered. "So why don't you turn him off and find yourself a more congenial replacement?"

"Turn him off? I couldn't do that. When he does cook, Pierre is the finest chef in London."

Sebastian grunted. "Then suffer the consequences and enjoy your knockwurst." He returned his attention to the *Times.*

Evanstone was undaunted by this obvious dismissal. "So anyway," he said hopefully, "I thought I'd drop by to deliver the news about the rapidly drying paint in your town house and see what *you're* having for breakfast. Mind if I have some eggs?"

Sebastian shrugged. "Suit yourself. You can have anything you want as long as you don't expect me to play the polite host and serve you. I'm not in the mood."

"No, I can see that." Evanstone regarded him doubtfully. "You're in a right foul humor this morning. Did the brandy bottle trap you last night?"

"No." Sebastian tossed the paper toward the younger man. "On second thought, I will serve you. That way you can sit down and read this article about Hughes Pride."

While Evanstone studied the column, Sebastian, well aware of his friend's enormous appetite, piled a china plate high with bacon, eggs, kidneys, and rolls. When he finished he plunked the plate down on the table.

Evanstone raised sympathetic blue eyes when he'd completed the article. "I say, that is too bad. Was it the same gray horse that beat Hughes Pride before, do you think?"

Sebastian grimaced. "If there is a God there can be only one horse like that." He sat down wearily and warmed his own coffee with a few hot drops from the pot. "Eat up. Your eggs are getting cold."

Needing no further encouragement, Evanstone dug into

his breakfast. "Mm. Good bacon. Ye gods, but I was famished."

Despite his discouragement at having lost the race, Sebastian glanced at his friend's lanky build and laughed ruefully. "You look it," he agreed, then said, "Seriously, Simon. Why don't you just turn your chef out and find another? I know he's an excellent cook, but there are plenty of others who I am certain equal Pierre's accomplishments."

Evanstone laughed. "If you ever tell another soul what I'm about to divulge," he joked, "it'll be grass for two and breakfast for one between us, Sebastian. I do not turn the man off because I'm quite desperately afraid of him. The servants tell me whenever he gets angry he goes after them with a butcher knife."

Sebastian choked on a sip of coffee. "You jest!"

"No, I'm quite serious. Who knows but that, if I got him too angry, he wouldn't poison me before he left? I'd rather suffer cold sardines than warm eggs Benedict with arsenic."

"I don't blame you."

There was a sudden flurry of movement in the dining room doorway. Both men looked up as Angel entered the room. The gentlemen stood, politely.

Angel smiled sunnily. "Oh, please, sit down. I do not mean to interrupt your conversation. Will it cramp your style if I eat here, or would you prefer I take a tray in my room? If you are discussing important matters I would be happy to make myself scarce."

Evanstone grinned, while Sebastian returned Angel's smile weakly and shook his head.

"No, no," the earl said. "Please stay. You can join Simon in laughing at my misfortune."

Evanstone's head popped up as he went to take another

bite of eggs. His blue eyes flashed. "I never laughed! Egad, man, I'm not such a flat as all that!"

"Just joking. I have to put some humor into this, somehow," Sebastian said mournfully. "I apologize for my remark. It was uncalled for."

Evanstone shrugged. "That's all right. I'd be upset, too."

"Upset about what?" Angel asked, choosing a selection of edibles from the sideboard and then taking a seat.

Sebastian reclaimed the newspaper from Evanstone and pushed it toward her. "See for yourself." He leaned back in his chair and watched as his ward took the *Times,* scanned the article, and then, to his utter dismay and total mortification, crowed with delight.

"He won! He won! Oh, and there was a one hundred pound purse, too! How wonderful!"

Evanstone cleared his throat uncomfortably. "I say, Lady Angel. I don't think you've read correctly. Sebastian's horse lost."

"What was that?" Angel's coppery head jerked up. Her lustrous hazel eyes stared at Evanstone blankly for a moment. "Oh," she said then, flushing. "So he did. I am sorry."

Sebastian studied her pink cheeks thoughtfully. Her behavior seemed dashed odd. He'd not have thought her the type to misread a newspaper article; she was remarkably intelligent—for a female.

"Perhaps Angel placed a bet on the gray," he said lightly, not quite realizing what he was saying.

Evanstone gave a scandalized cough. "Really, Seb, you know it ain't the thing for women to have any business with the turf."

Still peering at Angel, who had turned startled blue-green eyes upon him and was gaping as if his hair had turned to snakes, Sebastian sipped his coffee and tried to figure out what his intuition, prickling like an angry hedgehog, was trying to tell him.

"Quite right," he agreed, not taking his attention off the girl. "Forgive me, Angel. It seems all I am able to do this morn is offend and then apologize."

Angel's gaze dropped. "Accepted, my lord. And I hope you will accept my apologies as well, for making such a stupid mistake." She remained quiet throughout the rest of her breakfast and, although she had piled food upon her plate, ate scarcely a bite. Her lighthearted mood seemed to have suffered a complete turnabout.

"Ahem. What activities do you have planned for today, Sebastian?" Evanstone asked after completing a second plate of kidneys.

Sebastian allowed his attention to slip from Angel to Simon. "Nothing entertaining, I fear. I must see my solicitor in three quarters of an hour, and later I am meeting with two of my estate agents. Something about my cattle in Sussex suffering from hoof-rot."

"I hope it is not too serious."

"As do I."

"Will it take most of the day?"

"Probably. It's my experience that the worse the news, the longer it takes to discuss."

"Mm-hmn. Too bad," Evanstone continued. "I was hoping you would be free to visit Tattersall's with me."

"I wish to God I were."

Suddenly Evanstone brightened. "Say, I have an idea. Why don't I take Lady Angel out for a drive this morning? Get her out in the fresh air."

To Sebastian's disconcertion, Evanstone looked quite enthused with this notion. "What about it, Angel?" he inquired. "Care to go for a spin with Simon?"

Although Angel blushed, she seemed genuinely

delighted. In fact, her beautiful eyes were sparkling in a manner that seemed disturbingly speculative.

Seeing this, Sebastian frowned. He wondered if the girl had designs on Simon. That simply could not be allowed.

"We could take a turn about Hyde Park," Evanstone suggested. "What say you, Lady Angel?"

"Oh, yes, please. I will just dash upstairs and change into something more suitable. I will only be a moment." Jumping up, she hurried out of the room, while Evanstone moved to pick at the bacon platter on the sideboard. He was smiling.

Suddenly suspicious, Sebastian wondered if his friend and his ward might not have been showing more warmth for each other than he'd noticed. After a moment's reflection he decided that was impossible. To the best of his knowledge, aside from the time spent at Windywood Abbey, Angel and Evanstone had never been together. Still, he kept a watchful eye on Simon's countenance, which had brightened considerably since his arrival, when the tall lord had seemed in a dreadful brown-study.

When Angel re-entered the breakfast room, she had changed into a buttercup yellow walking dress and was carrying a matching parasol. A little chip-straw bonnet decorated with lace daisies sat pertly on her gleaming copper curls, and dainty white gloves adorned her small hands. Green silk leaves scattered amid the flowers on her hat emphasized the same shade in her sparkling, expressive eyes.

A flicker not unlike those heated feelings he had felt for Angel at the King's Theater suddenly rose in Sebastian's belly, but was ruthlessly doused. He cursed himself, irritated at feeling so damned disapproving of his ward's fine looks. Did he expect the chit to go out looking like a guttersnipe? He'd never get her married off that way.

He shook his head sharply to clear his confused thoughts.

Blue eyes crinkling, Evanstone gazed at the girl admiringly. "By Jove! You look charming, Lady Angel."

Neither of them gave Sebastian a backward glance as they walked out of the dining room. He remained seated until he heard the front door close behind them. To his surprise he found that he almost resented Angel's delight in the prospect of driving out with a long-shanks like Evanstone.

Would she have been as pleased at the thought of taking a turn about Hyde Park with *him*?

Then he shook himself a second time. It would be a good thing when he got the hoyden married off. She was simply not good for his peace of mind.

As the curricle rolled smoothly along the road leading to Hyde Park, Angel tilted her head slightly and peeked up at Lord Evanstone. He was not nearly so handsome as Sebastian, she decided, but then, her opinion was of little import. What mattered was that Lady Sarah believed herself madly in love with the tall young man.

Angel had already decided that whatever it took to keep Sarah from marrying Sebastian—thus making both them and poor Evanstone, who supposedly returned Sarah's affections, from making a botch of their lives—she would gladly do.

But where to start?

Pinning a smile to her lips, she looked at Evanstone more directly. "It is so kind of you to bring me here this morning, my lord. I know you must have had more important matters to which to attend. You are a truly chivalrous gentleman."

Evanstone looked surprised. "Not at all, Lady Angel.

I assure you this is entirely my pleasure. I am delighted
that you agreed to a ride. It is a beautiful day, and you
are a lovely woman."

Angel bit her lower lip.

This was not at all what she had anticipated. It would
be dreadful if Evanstone fancied himself in love with *her*.
Searching her mind, she said hesitantly, "But not so lovely
as Lady Sarah Moreton. Do you agree, my lord?"

To her delight, the young lord flushed a vivid scarlet.
"Well . . ." he stammered. "Well . . . you are as lovely
in your own way as Lady Sarah is in hers, Lady Angel.
It is my experience that every woman has her own special
beauty. It would not be fair to compare two attractive
ladies to each other when both are equally appealing, just
in different ways."

Angel grinned inwardly, though she kept her outward
expression sober. "Hmm. I suppose you're right. It's just
that, when I first saw her, I was so struck by Lady Sarah's
beautiful blue eyes. And her shiny black curls."

Her tall companion said nothing, and Angel fumed
silently. How to get the man to proclaim his love? She
pressed, determinedly, "Do you not think Lady Sarah has
lovely hair, Lord Evanstone? And that her eyes are the
most remarkable, exquisite color?"

Evanstone's hot flush deepened. He cleared his throat
loudly and tugged at his snowy cravat. "Ahem. Indeed,
her eyes are very attractive. As are your own, Lady Angel."

Afraid that he might think she was merely fishing for
compliments by forcing him to compare her loveliness
to that of Lady Sarah, Angel once more bit her lip. She
tried again. "I think Sarah finds *you* quite attractive, as
well, my lord."

Evanstone now turned quite purple. "She does?" he
asked eagerly. His blue eyes searched Angel's face
intently. Then, as if noticing her triumphant grin, he

returned his gaze to the road. "Er, that is," he repeated more cautiously, "does she really?"

"Oh, yes. She told me so when last we talked. Sarah and I are the best of friends, you must know."

"No, I did not. Has she, then, told you of her . . ." the tall lord's voice trailed off. He looked miserable.

"Her understanding with Sebastian?" Angel inquired innocently. "Oh, she mentioned that they might wed."

Evanstone sighed heavily. His blue eyes seemed to lose their shine. "It is true. Seb told me as much, too."

"I am not convinced the match is a wise one. Sarah suggested to me that her heart was otherwise engaged. She was," Angel remarked pointedly, "quite insistent on that fact, my lord."

Disregarding the other traffic behind his curricle, Lord Evanstone drew his horses to a stop in the middle of the road. Swiveling on the seat, he pinned Angel with a direct gaze. "I fear I do not understand why you are telling me this, Lady Angel."

She frowned. Good Lord, if he did not understand, how could she make him see what she was trying to say without embarrassing them both? "Do you not?" she asked with a sigh. "How disappointing."

He raised one sandy-colored brow. "Disappointing?"

"Yes." Angel realized there was nothing for it but to be completely honest. "What I was trying to say was that Sarah hoped, if the love she felt for the gentleman in question was returned, that the gentleman would find it in himself to sweep her off her feet and carry her off to Scotland."

"What! For God's sake, Lady Angel," Evanstone cursed. He gave up his pretense of ignorance. "You must see that I cannot do anything of the sort. The engagement papers between Sebastian and Sarah are as good as signed.

'Twould be the height of dishonor to speak of my feelings at this late date. It is quite impossible."

Angel smiled and patted his hand, kindly. "Pray, Lord Evanstone. Please do not be angry with me. Sarah was afraid you'd feel that way. But I had to try to help. It is so very sad that you should love each other and be forever separated because *you* did not want to explain matters to Sebastian. I assure you, he would understand. If he is as good a friend to you as I believe he is, he would not deliberately steal the woman you love."

Stiff with embarrassment, Evanstone jerked his attention back to the road. He snapped the reins over his horses' withers, making the curricle jerk into motion. "Thank you, Lady Angel," he said stiffly, "but I believe I can handle my own affairs. Anyway, I would not expect a mere woman to understand why it is impossible for me to do anything about matters at this late date."

"Oh, dear. You *are* angry." Angel shook her head, sadly. "I am so sorry. That is not at all what I intended. But really," she added, "you cannot handle your own affairs, you know, any better than any other man. You all need a woman's hand to guide you. The right woman's hand."

Without warning, Evanstone threw his head back and laughed. "Do we, by George? Egad, but you're a spunky chit. Poor Sebastian's got his hands full with you, I'll warrant." He narrowed his eyelids and glanced at her. "You know, since we are trading opinions about each other's love lives, it is my impression that you would make Sebastian a far better wife than would my Sarah."

Angel's mouth popped open. A slow warmth filled her cheeks, and a ridiculous happiness swelled through her midsection. Dropping her gaze to her hands, she said in a muffled voice, "I have never heard anything so ridiculous."

Evanstone shook his head. "It is not ridiculous at all.

Sarah is far too emotional and sensitive for a fellow like Sebastian."

"Oh!" Angel cried, unable to keep from laughing. "And *I* am not? Really, my lord, I should be most offended by that remark. I take back everything I said about your being chivalrous!"

"It is not something to be offended by. It is mere fact." Evanstone chuckled. "You see, I am quite certain you have more spunk in your little finger than Sarah—no matter how much I love her—has in her entire body. Of course, I am not a spunky person either, so Sarah would have suited me just fine if I'd had the forethought to approach her sooner than Sebastian."

"Well then?" Angel demanded.

He sighed, humor disappearing. "Well, nothing. It is true, theirs is an unfortunate match. I do agree with you that their feelings for each other and their reasons for planning to marry are hardly what I'd call a firm basis for matrimony."

"Oh, Lord Evanstone," Angel said earnestly, "if you love Sarah you *must not* let another man, who does not even care for her, steal her away. It would be criminal for the two of you to live the rest of your lives pining for each other. And how can you even think of allowing Sarah to ache for you for the next fifty or sixty years? Does she not deserve more? Does not Sebastian? And you?"

"Sebastian is my friend. And the marriage has been arranged and agreed upon by all concerned parties." Evanstone added with an air of finality, "There is nothing I can do."

Angel felt angry and helpless at the same time. "Even if it means that all three of you will be miserable for the remainder of your lives?" she demanded ruthlessly.

He inclined his head. "Even then."

"That's the craziest thing I've ever heard."

"Perhaps we should turn back, Lady Angel." Evanstone's voice was regretful, but resolute. "I believe this ride—and this conversation—has gone on quite long enough."

Angel glared mutinously at the road ahead. "As you wish, my lord."

During the return trip she was very quiet as she tried to comprehend the differences between men and women. Why, if she were in love with her best friend's fiancé, and knew that her friend felt nothing for him, she would not hesitate to state her devotion. She knew without a doubt that, were she to do so, a true friend would gladly step aside.

What was it that made men so different? Why could they not approach one another with as much honesty as women did?

As Lord Evanstone drew the curricle to a stop before Cartwright House, Angel turned to look at him. She smiled faintly. "My lord, if you are certain you will not rethink this madness, I hope we can still be friends. Please do not dislike me forever because I tried to stop this misadventure."

Evanstone smiled with an obvious mixture of relief and pleasure. "I would be honored to call myself your friend, my lady."

"Thank you. And, please, call me Angel."

Evanstone leapt to the street, walked around to her side of the curricle, and helped her down. "Then you must call me Simon."

They both grinned, pleased that, even though the problem of the unfortunate engagement had not been solved, they were not parting enemies.

*   *   *

Neither appeared to have noticed, as they strolled up the walkway toward the Cartwright town house, that Sebastian stood behind the lacy curtains of a nearby window. He frowned as Angel tilted her head and smiled sweetly. His frown deepened when he saw Evanstone return her smile.

Seeing their pleasure, Sebastian felt strangely despondent. He blamed his depressed mood on his ward, and the grave responsibility he'd had thrust upon him when he'd realized she'd been older than previously believed—and ruined, to boot. He should never have allowed her to ride out with one of his best friends without telling Simon to watch himself because the chit was no better than she should be.

Was everyone blind, or just taken in by Angel's pretended innocence? And why, he thought, grinding his teeth in sudden fury, was he suddenly wishing beyond anything that she really *was* innocent, that she *was* pure, and that she would look at *him* like she was looking at *Simon?*

Faith, why was he suddenly thinking that, even if she were not as pure as her name, it did not really matter?

Not one to hide from his feelings, he was well aware of what was happening to him, although it was not something he could ever have foreseen. He had mapped out his life so carefully, and to one purpose: to win the Grand London Gold Cup.

That was his life's dream, as it had been his father's before him. He had no time for romantic nonsense, which was why he had decided to marry Lady Sarah. That good lady knew exactly what she would be getting and would not spend hours moping when he didn't spend every moment with her. He did not love her, and she knew it, just as he knew she was not enamored of him.

And yet, something about Angel, though she would never be as exquisitely beautiful as Lady Sarah, made him feel absurdly giddy. Just looking at her made him want to burst out in joyful laughter—unless he happened to look at her when she was smiling at another man.

She made his heart light and heavy all at the same time. She made his blood tingle as if it had been replaced by champagne. He knew now, without a doubt, that he was obsessed with her. But, thank the Good Lord, he knew he was not in love with her, because he knew he could never feel love for a woman who had allowed herself to be ruined at the hands of anyone as repulsive as Sir Corbin Pugsley.

But no matter whether he felt love or obsession, he simply could not afford any such romantical imaginings. He had neither the time nor the inclination. He had to concentrate on winning the Grand London Gold Cup.

He *would not* allow his physical attraction for Lady Angel to grow any stronger.

And yet, out of nowhere came the discovery that he wished that, even though he would lose those prime bloods, Lady Sarah would reject his suit and leave him free. He did not really want to marry her, not even for Lord Appleby's prime racing stock. He wished intensely that he had never offered for her.

If he were free, he thought with a pang of longing, he would . . . he would . . .

He didn't know what he would do.

But he did know that watching his best friend and his ward laughing together, seeing Angel flirt up at Evanstone

with her huge blue-green eyes, made his heart feel like
a lump of cold cheese, and the blood, that had fizzed so
delightfully moments before, settle in his stomach like
cold bread pudding.

Chapter Fifteen

Angel stood in the line of noisy, chattering females, all intent on adjusting their headdresses and pinning and re-pinning their jewels. While she felt somewhat under-dressed for her Court presentation, she also thought everyone else terribly overdone. Never in her life had she seen so many feathers, bobbing and swaying like a sea of exotic white birds, while multicolor gems flashed like rainbows over a misty sea.

The heat of so many close-pressed bodies was nearly unbearable. As she fanned herself desperately with her dainty cream silk and seed pearl fan, Angel was not surprised to see several girls succumb to the stress and discomfort of the occasion. These unfortunate creatures swooned, sweeping to the floor in heaps of white satin like exhausted doves.

Actually, though uncomfortable in her numerous stays, her powdered hair, and the strange, malformed hoops that pointed front and back rather than side to side that Angel knew must make her body look like a broad-beamed ship, she found the entire episode rather ridiculous and altogether absurd.

Turning to glance at Lady Cartwright, who was chatting calmly with another chaperone, Angel gave Sebastian's sister a soft nudge. "Hilary, this is ridiculous," she whispered with a muffled giggle. "We debutantes look like remnants of another age! And these awful hoops! It looks like we've all put them on backward."

Lady Cartwright threw her a warning glance. "This is a very somber occasion, Angel. Do not let anyone hear you mocking it. You would be flung out of polite Society. Young women of good breeding have been presented to their monarchs for hundreds of years."

Angel stifled her laughter and nodded, but couldn't restrain a grin as a tall woman herded the line of girls toward the door leading to the throne room. One by one the debutantes went into the room and were presented to the Prince Regent and his mother. Then the girls curtsied before backing out of the room through the same door through which they had entered.

Finally it was Angel's turn.

Holding her head high, a smile playing about her lips, she moved confidently forward. As her name was read, she smiled brilliantly before sweeping into a deep, graceful curtsy. Then she straightened to receive her tribute from the Queen, a light and impersonal embrace on her forehead. As Angel began backing respectfully away, however, a majestic murmur made her pause and glance up at the Regent.

"Hmm."

The prince pressed one plump finger aside his nose as if in deep contemplation. He gazed down at her through myopic blue eyes. "Lady Angelique Arundel . . . I say, you wouldn't happen to be old Chas Arundel's granddaughter, would you?"

Angel felt overwhelmed. She did not know how to respond. No one had told her to expect a direct address from the Regent of all England.

In a quandary, she straightened and answered with a friendly smile. "Why, yes, Highness. Charles Arundel, the fourth earl of Darcy, was my grandfather. And I believe he was known by his friends as Chas."

The prince beamed and poked his mother sharply in the leg through her stiff gold brocade gown. She returned this attention with a frown of maternal disapproval.

"You see, Madam?" he crowed triumphantly, slapping his plump thigh. "I told you when she came in the gel looked familiar. Did I not? Just as she came through the door, I told you that. Did I not?"

Her majesty rolled her royal eyes in a manner that would have looked ridiculous had anyone else made the gesture. "That could have been because her name was just read aloud to the entire room, George," she replied curtly.

"No," he contested. "I assure you, I did recognize her. She is the picture-image of her grandfather."

Redirecting his attention to Angel, he raised his eyebrows. Even though his waistcoat appeared several sizes too small and his stays creaked abominably, he managed to appear quite regal. No one, Angel realized, could have doubted for an instant that he was the current head of all Britain.

He leaned forward so that his next words were hushed. "My lady," he said softly, a sparkle in his blue eyes, "I know it is not quite the thing to discuss with a gentlewoman, but I hope you will not be offended if I tell you that, when your late pater sold your grandfather's racing stock, I bought every last horse. A true genius when it came to breeding prize animals, old Chas was. We were very good friends, despite the disparity in our ages."

Angel gasped, then smiled brilliantly. "Oh, Your Highness!" she cried, forgetting to keep her own voice down. "I assure you I am not offended. I have always wondered what became of the horses. I am so happy to hear they are with you. I loved them all, you see. Your kindness to your livestock is renowned throughout all England. It is indeed an honor to know, after all my years of worrying about them, that they are in your stables."

The Regent beamed. "Why, thank you, my dear."

"You are most welcome, Highness," Angel replied sincerely.

Then the prince quirked a brow. "I say, perhaps you would like to visit my stable before the Season ends, to see the animals? It is such a pleasure to meet someone who seems as much in love with horses as I."

Angel hesitated. "I would love to, Highness, but is it not forbidden for ladies to involve themselves in the racing scene?"

"To be sure, you are correct," the prince answered with a little frown. Then he brightened. "But, just as surely, no one would dare suggest that I would do anything that was socially unacceptable. No, my dear, I say it will be quite all right for you to see my horses, and so it will." He turned to the Queen. "Is that not right, Mother?"

The Queen shrugged disinterestedly. "You do not seem to have worried about common opinion in the past, my son. I do not think you will allow such a simple thing as societal rules curb your behavior." Then, glancing at Angel and apparently noting the girl's worried expression, she added more gently, "And to be sure no one would dare ostracise Lady Angelique for obeying a direct command from her Regent."

Angel smiled, relieved. "Oh, thank you, Your Majesty!"

"Yes, thank you, Mother." The prince kissed the Queen's cheek, then said to Angel, "I have also recently purchased some prime bloods on which I would love to receive your opinion. Any granddaughter of Chas Arundel's must surely know her stock. You may also, naturally, bring your duenna. We shall take tea, as well."

Cognizant of the great honor being bestowed upon her, and also utterly thrilled at the prince's invitation, Angel sparkled up at him. All she could manage was a breathless, "Oh, yes, sir! Yes, please!"

The Regent leaned back in his chair. "I shall have my man see to it. I believe it will be some weeks before I am free enough from State business to follow through with this invitation, but when I am available I shall be honored to reintroduce you to the animals, personally. My dear girl, I am so pleased I was here today. I am not often at these hen-sessions, and am delighted I was present today so I might make your acquaintance."

With this he inclined his royal head and his mother did likewise.

"Thank you, Your Highness, Your Majesty." Bubbling with excitement, Angel curtsied again and then backed out of the royal presence. Outside the royal chamber, the waiting room was abuzz with chatter. Everyone whispered and pointed at Angel.

Angel was worried that, despite the Queen's approval of the Regent's invitation, the ton was already gossiping about the impropriety of the prospective visit. She was greatly relieved when she arrived at Lady Cartwright's side and saw that Hilary was beside herself with delight.

"Angel, darling!" the older woman cried. "The Regent himself spoke to you, and for such a long time! And the Queen! Oh, my dear, you are *made!* What did they say?"

"The Regent is the one who purchased my grandfather's racing stock, when my father sold them. The prince is going to show them to me. As well as his new animals."

Hilary's smile faltered. "The prince spoke to you of *racing?*" she asked in a scandalized tone.

"Yes. And the Queen said it would be all right. So you and I are to visit him and take tea in a few weeks, as well as see his horses. Oh, Hil, he is the nicest man. And the Queen is charming."

Lady Cartwright stared, openmouthed. Finally she laughed and shook her head. "Well, I suppose if the Prince Regent wishes to show you horses and talk of racing, his mother is correct in assuming such is his royal right. And you thought him nice? Only you, Angel, would refer to the crown prince as 'the nicest man,' and be more excited to see a stable filled with horses than speak to the next king."

During the next week Angel discovered she was an apt pupil at dancing, singing, and painting watercolors. Also during that next sennight, she was delighted to hear from Jonas that Vortex had run in and won another three races— all of which had also contained Sebastian's black stallion, Hughes Pride, although the black nosed nearer and nearer to a win with each successive event.

While Sebastian's temper had become fouler with each race lost, Angel could scarcely contain her joy as she thought of the large purses, three hundred, three hundred fifty, and five hundred pounds, being added to the coffers at Violet Cottage and bringing her ever closer to winning the wager with the repulsive Sir Corbin Pugsley.

Oh, if only her dream of owning Windywood Abbey could come true!

While her heart was troubled by Sebastian's unhappiness, her discomfort did not extend to purposely forfeiting the races which she desperately needed to win. She had, after all, no choice but to want Vortex to take the prizes if she did not want Sir Corbin to destroy her family home.

Her acute longing to gather the money was particularly fierce that afternoon, since a footman had, just after breakfast, handed her a note from Sir Corbin. The single sheet of parchment had contained instructions that she meet the baronet at three A.M. beside the Roman fountain in Lady Cartwright's tiny garden, late on the night she was to make her first appearance at Almack's.

Though petrified at the thought of being alone with the baronet, she dared not disobey out of fear that he would do something drastic to the Abbey, or that another of her mother's precious figurines would suffer at Sir Corbin's sadistic hands.

The day before her first visit to Almack's, Angel sat in Lady Cartwright's parlor surrounded by her beaus. She still shook herself often, astonished even now by the change in her circumstances and the way she had gone from hideously plain to, according to her admirers, a "diamond of the first water."

The gentlemen present today included the six peers she'd met at the opera, as well as Simon, Lord Evanstone, who had become an everyday caller, a good friend, and who frequently took her driving in Hyde Park.

Happily regaling the group with the news that her booklet of vouchers for Almack's had been delivered that afternoon, Angel remarked that she was to enter the building's hallowed halls for the first time the next night, and that she hoped they would all be present so she should not be left a wallflower.

That her visit to Almack's should come a week before her come-out ball was, as Lady Cartwright had previously told her, of particular good fortune, since she hoped one of the patronesses would grant her permission to waltz. It would be a terrible shame, Hilary pointed out, if Angel were forbidden to waltz during her own ball.

The gentlemen seconded this opinion noisily, each man begging to partner her once at least, and twice if she would allow it. Each also pleaded to be allowed one of the more intimate waltzes, when the patronesses gave their permission. Superbly happy, Angel smiled and gave her solemn promise that she would give them each as many dances as propriety would allow.

Sebastian and Lord Barstow had called at Cartwright House before continuing on to Manton's Shooting Gallery, to ask Hilary if she required anything else for Angel's upcoming ball. The Cartwright butler ushered them into the front parlor.

Sebastian battled down a burst of annoyance as he noticed the crowd of masculine admirers clustered around Lady Angel like rays about the sun.

After assuring Sebastian and Lord Barstow that all necessary arrangements for the ball were taken care of, Hilary invited them to pay their respects to Angel, who had smiled at them momentarily when she saw them enter the room.

The moment Barstow, who had not yet seen Angel since his first introduction at Windywood Abbey, noticed the changes wrought in the girl, the little man edged his way through the crowd to stand very near the girl's chair. To Sebastian's disgust, Horatio, the confirmed bachelor, soon showed every sign of being as completely smitten as the rest of the group.

Feeling testy and unwilling to fight for a spot near his ward, Sebastian found himself seated away from the rest of the group on a rather hard chaise longue. He rested his chin in the palm of one hand and wished unreasonably that Angel would suddenly take sick. He could hardly stand watching the other men mooning over her.

The recollection that he was expected to escort Angel and Hilary to Almack's the next night made his head ache. What would it be like, watching Angel swirl about the room in other men's arms? How would he be able to keep from calling out anyone who so much as laid a finger on her? Despite her ruined status, he thought sternly, he would not allow any man to be less than completely proper with her.

He shifted uncomfortably on the chaise longue, hoping glumly that his infatuation would soon burn itself out. He glared at her admirers, especially put out with Barstow.

When Angel laughed, his gaze was drawn to her face. Her smile seemed to brighten the entire room, and her laughter was like music, or a mountain spring burbling over smooth boulders as it danced its way to the sea.

So much for his thinking that the only man she'd be able to land was an elderly widower with a brood to raise. And it didn't look like she'd need a penny of his fortune for a dowry, as all her current beaus were very plump in the pocket. It would be no surprise to him if she were to receive offers from all of them. And Barstow and Evanstone as well, damn their eyes. What a surprise, to find his homely ward the center of attention and the belle of the Season. And what a disaster.

As if taking pity on him sitting all alone, Hilary rose from her chair on the sidelines of Angel's entourage and came to sit on the chaise longue beside him. Not at all grateful, Sebastian glared at her, too.

Hilary tilted her head to one side and inquired, "Is something bothering you, Seb? You don't look at all well. You are very pale. Do you have a headache? I could ask my maid, Prudie, to mix you one of her restorative powders."

Sebastian shuddered. "No, thank you. I am quite well, just in a bit of a brown-study. I cannot fathom why."

Hilary laughed. "Neither can I. You should be delighted. Angel is a huge success. I suppose you have heard of her triumph with Prinny?"

"Yes," he replied glumly.

"You hardly seem pleased." When he did not answer, she continued. "Anyway, I had been meaning to speak with you about Angel. Since she has so many admirers, and will obviously be able to have almost anyone she chooses, perhaps it is time for you to make a list of acceptable suitors so that I may start weeding out the unsuitable characters."

Sebastian blinked, dismayed. His throat felt tight. "Surely that would be a bit premature."

Hilary's warm brown eyes widened. "Why, Seb, I was under the impression that you wanted the girl settled as soon as possible, to get her off your hands."

"And so I do," he agreed half-heartedly. "But I had expected the choice to be simple. I did not expect these hordes of applicants." Then he groaned and ran a hand over tired eyes. "Can you not just pick the most likely candidate, Hil?"

"Certainly not," she said sharply. "That is your duty as Angel's guardian. You know you are in more of a position to decide which of them will make her the best husband. I have seen only their best sides at my 'at homes,' while you have undoubtedly seen them at their worst, at your clubs."

"True," he agreed. "But none of these gentlemen have any dire failings."

"Well, that is a relief. We can discuss which would suit best, now, if you like."

Sebastian didn't answer, but sank his chin further into his palm. His chest ached with unfamiliar pangs that were not wholly a physical pain.

Taking his silence for acquiescence, his sister turned toward the group and nodded at one of the men. "What of Roslings? He is quite wealthy and, although only a viscount, comes from a good line."

"Roslings?" Sebastian retorted. "He is twice her age!"

Hilary nodded. "Well then, what about Dunheath? He is younger."

"That's for certain. I doubt he has even seen nineteen summers. He is much *too* young."

"Glencoe? He has numerous holdings in Scotland, and cannot take his eyes off Angel."

Sebastian sneered. "Too many freckles. Can't you just imagine their children? Horrid little red-headed goblins covered with spots?"

Hilary arched one aristocratic brow. "You are a hard man to please for one who wants nothing more than to wash your hands of the girl, brother."

Sebastian merely growled.

"Not Glencoe, then. What of Edgecomb? He is a nice man."

Sebastian shuddered. "*Too* nice. He'd bore her to tears within a fortnight."

Hilary's other brow flew to her hairline. "I do not recall unending excitement as a requirement for matrimony."

Sebastian shifted on the chaise longue, avoiding his sister's sharp gaze. "Perhaps not, but at least one shouldn't be bored to death."

Hilary sighed, exasperated. "Well, besides your two friends, Lord Evanstone and Lord Barstow, that leaves only one candidate: Lord Sinclair." Her mouth quirked wryly. "I can hardly wait to hear what deadly fault he possesses."

"You speak as if I am being completely unreasonable, which is ridiculous." Sebastian gave her an affronted glare. "Can I help it if Sinclair wears too much cologne? The man is a dandy. A macaroni. Angel's digestion could not help but be disturbed by his smell."

Hilary gazed over at the group crowded around the girl. "Evanstone, then?"

"Impossible. I could not allow him to marry her."

Hilary frowned. "Whyever not? Angel is a charming girl, and she and Simon seem to be good friends already."

Sebastian looked at Angel. Although he had intended to inform Hilary about his ward's impure status long before now, for some reason he could not bring himself to speak the words. "He—he is too tall. Angel would get a crick in her neck every time they danced."

Hilary laughed aloud, causing several of the gentlemen to turn toward her for a split second before returning their attention to the object of their desire. "Too tall?" She shook her head. "Now I have heard everything. The next thing I know you'll be telling me Barstow is too short. Or has hair too straight."

"Well," Sebastian retorted, "you must admit they would make an odd couple, with her towering over Barstow by a head."

Hilary's lips twitched. "Well, in light of all this new information, I suppose we had best wait for more prospects to show up."

"Quite right."

"Since Angel's first visit to Almack's is tomorrow night," Hilary continued as she looked toward the laughing girl whose copper curls gleamed in the sunlight streaming through the parlor window, "we should have another dozen or so by the time the evening is over."

"Almack's," Sebastian repeated somberly. His heart crowded into his throat.

"Yes." Hilary glanced at him sharply. "You have not forgotten you are to accompany us, have you?"

His lips tightened. "No."

"Good. And of course there is her ball next week, as well. I hope you have remembered to send to your estate hothouses for fresh orchids and delphinia, to match the ballroom's new lilac paint, as well as Angel's gown."

Sebastian sighed gustily. "I have not forgotten. The flowers should be here the morning of the 'big day.' "

"Good." Hilary smiled happily. "Once Angel is seen by everyone, she should have no dearth of swains. I am positive she will be engaged by mid-Season, and married by the end of it." She looked at her brother uncertainly. "That news should make you happy. I know how much you resented having the responsibility of her future foisted upon you."

When he said nothing, she demanded sharply, "Sebastian, is there something you have not told me? Something I ought to know?"

The earl laughed almost maniacally, causing the party on the other side of the room to look up again. Was there anything Hilary should know? That her charge had served time as mistress to one of the lowest men in the land?

Or, worse, that he, himself, was fast falling heels over head with the chit in spite of his ward's tarnished past?

"No," he muttered. "There is nothing."

Hilary gazed at him long and hard. At last she nodded slowly and a little smile curved the corners of her mouth. Her brown eyes sparkled. "Ah . . . I see."

Fortunately, Sebastian was spared the trouble of a reply. Barstow had gotten to his feet and, after kissing Angel's hand, sauntered toward them. "Congratulate me, Sebastian. I have the honor of driving your ward through Hyde Park one week from today." He added in an aside, "It was the only day she had free."

The short lord then glanced back toward Angel. "Perhaps I should have made several appointments with her," he suggested suddenly. "All of her time was booked up solid until then, and I would not want her to be unable to fit me into her schedule in the future."

Sebastian grimaced. "I am sure she will make time for an old friend, Horatio. Now that you've done the pretty, shall we go practice our marksmanship at Manton's? I hope our reserved time has not completely elapsed."

"Oh," Barstow said, looking chagrined. "Sorry, old man. I forgot. Time just seems to get away from a man when he's in the company of a woman like Lady Angel. She is truly an Original. Truth is," he said quietly, "if I weren't determined to remain a bachelor all my life, I'd toss my hat over the windmill for her, myself! Who knows, I might, anyway. Well, come along, Seb."

As his heart gave a pained throb, Sebastian stood and followed his friend from the room.

Chapter Sixteen

Later that evening a knock sounded on Angel's bed-chamber door. Moving to stand beside the door, she said softly, "Who is it?"

"Hilary, child. Let me in."

Smiling, Angel pulled the door open as her chaperone entered the room. Then she frowned as she noticed the harried expression on her friend's face. "What is it? Is something wrong?"

"Oh, I should say! That is, I think so. I mean . . ." Lady Cartwright threw up her hands. "Oh Angel, I don't know."

Concerned, Angel led the older woman to the bed. Then, perching beside Lady Cartwright on the mattress, she asked, "What is it? Is it something to do with my ball? Has something been left undone? Is my gown not going to be ready on time? Or have my vouchers for Almack's been withdrawn?"

Lady Cartwright smiled at Angel fondly. "Oh, no, dear, nothing like that. Sebastian has agreed to hold the ball in his newly painted ballroom, the flowers to decorate it are on their way, and your vouchers are safe in my jewel box."

"What is it, then? Have I forgotten something I should have done? Only tell me what it is and I shall rectify the situation immediately. Not for the world would I see you so overwrought."

"You have done nothing wrong, darling. In fact, you have behaved admirably. In only two weeks you have learned to dance very well, sing a pretty tune, and paint a surprisingly good watercolor. In short, you are a charming girl. Everyone who meets you seems utterly enchanted. Perhaps," she said slowly, gazing at Angel's face, "that is the problem."

Angel waited.

"Something completely unforeseen has happened, my dear," Lady Cartwright blurted. "I do not know what to do. I am at my wits' end. You know that my brother is to marry Lady Sarah Moreton."

"Of course."

"Well, I do not know if I can allow it, now."

Angel's heart began pounding. "Why?" she asked, trying not to sound as delighted as she felt. Again she asked, "What is wrong?"

Lady Cartwright gazed at Angel. She said after a few tantalizing moments of silence, "I don't know that I say there is anything 'wrong,' precisely."

"Hilary!"

"I know, I am acting as addlepated as an old maid with a new beau." Lady Cartwright smiled faintly. "I cannot allow my brother to marry Lady Sarah because I care too much for him." She wrung her hands. "He is my little brother, and my only sibling, and his happiness is quite possibly more important to me than my own. I cannot stand by and watch while he marries one woman, but loves another. Which he does, I assure you, although . . ." she finished hesitantly, "I doubt he quite realizes it, yet."

"Loves another?" Angel returned. Her heart seemed ready to rattle right out of her chest. Momentary flashes of the impossible, that Sebastian loved her as she was quickly coming to love him, flitted through her mind. Although she had many beaus, she could not seem to drum up any enthusiasm for a single suitor. Each day she prayed no one would make her an offer, since she did not want to hurt any of the sweet gentlemen. All of them paled when set up beside her guardian.

She said quietly, "But I have seen Sebastian show no preference."

"Perhaps because you have not been attending, my dear. Or perhaps because you have been so busy lately that you have not spent much time with him." Lady Cartwright's smile deepened and her eyes shone. "Yet, I assure you his preference was completely obvious this afternoon."

"This afternoon?" Angel shook her head bemusedly. "Hilary, you must be mistaken. There was no woman present other than you and myself. So how could he have shown a preference for her?"

"Quite easily, I am afraid."

Angel exhaled gustily. She thought she would go mad in a moment. "You speak in riddles. Just tell me: who is this mystery woman Sebastian loves?"

Lady Cartwright rose from the bed and walked to the door. Turning, she answered softly, "Why you, Angel, of course."

Although somewhat deflated by the plain brickwork exterior and somber Ionic columns of Almack's Assembly Rooms, Angel gave no indication of her disappointment as Sebastian's crested carriage drew to a stop along the curb of King Street, St. James's, at fifteen minutes to eleven.

When a footman lowered the carriage steps Sebastian climbed out and proffered his hand to his sister and ward. Momentarily the hem of Angel's mint-green beaded silk evening gown, the color of which Hilary had insisted upon even though it was customary for debutantes to wear only white, caught on the carriage door.

As she reached down, Angel's gloved fingers brushed Sebastian's, as he had also moved to release her. The earl seemed to draw in his breath, and their hands seemed to touch for an endless moment. Then he pulled sharply away.

Still shaken, confused, and utterly delighted by Lady Cartwright's confidence of the night before, Angel could not bring herself to meet her guardian's dark-eyed gaze.

Instead, she looked up at the austere building they would soon enter. To her dismay, the assembly rooms' only claim to beauty was the six arched windows in the second story, which shone brilliantly white against the ebony sky. Now and then she caught glimpses of ladies and gentlemen moving past these windows as they waited for the evening's festivities to commence.

As their small group climbed the steps and entered Almack's hallowed portals, however, Angel found her eyes drifting again and again to the devastatingly handsome figure of Sebastian, Lord Darcy, in full evening dress. Her heart, as it so often did these days, beat tumultuously in her breast.

The earl, wearing pale satin knee breeches, stockings, a midnight blue coat of Bath superfine, and buckled dancing slippers, was the perfect cosmopolitan gentleman.

A single sapphire in his snowy cravat—which was tied intricately without appearing frilly—reflected the light from the candles lining the walls, adding to Lord Darcy's air of debonair sophistication. He had removed his ruby signet ring, but on his left hand rested a sapphire similar to that in his neckcloth. The gem was embedded in a lump of heavy gold in the shape of a horse's head, with the jewel portraying the animal's eye.

After handing their wraps to a waiting footman and their vouchers to Mr. Willis, the lease owner of the building, the trio continued up a flight of stairs to the ballroom.

Again Angel paused, gazing around with dumbfounded surprise. Rather than the spacious, glittering room the six arched windows had led her to expect, the ballroom was a hideous chamber with an extremely battered floor—though none of its other occupants seemed to notice its shortcomings.

But, Angel told herself, none of that mattered. Almack's lack of elegance had nothing to do with her. She was not here to be entertained, or, as so many other young women were and as her own companions expected of Angel herself, to find a husband. She was merely here to bide her time until Jonas and Vortex had won enough money for her to take back possession of the Abbey.

At the thought of the baronet, an icy chill seemed to ripple down her spine. Her heart gave a shudder and she remembered his note instructing her to meet him that night. Then she thrust the thought from her mind, determined to enjoy the evening until then. She would not allow Sir Corbin to ruin her first night at Almack's.

For several minutes she, Lady Cartwright, and Sebastian wandered about the room, with both Sebastian and his sister making Angel known to their various acquaintances. Then, as the clock struck eleven, a small band of musicians launched unenthusiastically into a minuet. This, Lady Cartwright told Angel softly, was the way the weekly entertainments at Almack's always began.

"Sebastian," Lady Cartwright commanded then, "dance with Angel."

Caught up in mutual amusement at Hilary's imperiousness, Angel and Sebastian forgot their mutual discomfort in each other's company.

Grinning, Sebastian bowed gallantly. "I would have asked even if my dear sister had not beaten me to the task. Lady Angel, will you do me the honor of standing up with me?"

"With pleasure, my lord."

Angel sucked in her breath as the earl took her hand and led her to the center of the floor. She suddenly remembered Lady Cartwright's startling revelation of the night before, and felt painfully aware of both Sebastian's closeness and her own devastating response to him. Without warning all memory of the dance steps fled her mind and she could only think of his touch, his eyes, his smile, and the strong masculine scent of soap and cologne that emanated from his muscular form.

Tipping her chin, she gazed up into his dark face—and was transfixed.

Why had she never noticed how black his hair was? It seemed almost blue in the candlelight. Or how devilishly appealing were his dark brown eyes, as they returned her inspection?

When Sebastian grinned rakishly, obviously taking pleasure in her attention, she flushed hotly and tore her gaze away from his face.

After watching the other dancers for a moment, she recalled enough dance steps to begin. After that her feet seemed to move of their own accord, and she was free to dwell upon the unfamiliar, disturbing sensations participating with her guardian in the mild dance wrought in her breast.

When she realized, too late, that he had spoken to her,

she flushed and cleared her throat. "I beg your pardon, my lord," she muttered. "I was concentrating on my steps and fear I did not hear what you asked."

"I merely said that I hoped you were not being so quiet because my company was boring you."

"Oh, no!" Unable to think of anything else to say, Angel was glad when the dance forced them apart. She felt terribly gauche and immature, and cursed her inability to come up with witty, entertaining conversation.

As she and the earl came together again she proffered inanely, "The music is nice, is it not?" As the words left her mouth she bit down on her tongue, embarrassed at having sounded so jejeune.

Sebastian's smile grew wider and he inclined his head. Pressing her fingers, he replied easily, "If you deem it so, Angel, then as a gentleman I must agree. Although I believe I've heard better in Covent Garden. Aside from the Scotch violinist, Neil Gow, who leads the orchestra here at Almack's, I believe the rest could likely be replaced with monkeys and no one would notice the difference."

The feel of his fingers holding hers, ever so gently, was almost more than Angel could bear. When she felt him press her hand she murmured, "Oh my, yes!" in response more to the exquisite pleasure of his touch than in agreement with his opinion.

Silence fell for a few more moments.

"You are enjoying the dance?" Sebastian finally offered. He seemed disgracefully pleased by her obviously nervous response to his touch.

The roguish arch to his black brows made Angel's heart trip erratically. A slow, sweet ache filled her body. The earl's dark, brooding eyes glittered with reflected candlelight. She could almost imagine him sitting on a throne in the netherworld, the candlelight replaced with the roaring flames of Hades.

Strange, she thought wildly, how she had never before recognized that hell might be more appealing than heaven. "Very much, my lord," she managed weakly.

His well-formed mouth curled upward. "I am glad. I am enjoying it, as well."

Angel felt as if she could not breathe. Why had she not realized how utterly splendid dancing with him would be? Even this simple minuet was like flying. Like soaring above the clouds on gossamer wings, or sailing the high seas on a splendid schooner. She allowed herself to be carried away by the music and the lights and the sheer joy of dancing with Sebastian.

When the last strains of music drifted away, she sighed, sorry the dance had ended.

She did not have much time to spend brooding, however, for the moment the earl led her back to Hilary's side Angel was surrounded with admirers. Her dance card was filled within seconds. For the remainder of the evening she was swept into the crowd of twirling bodies again and again in contredanses, cotillions, more minuets, and country dances of all kinds until she thought the bottoms of her thin, mint-green silk slippers would burn away.

The only time she was allowed to rest was when the orchestra launched into one of the grand, winging waltzes. The music was like nothing else she had ever heard; it made her want to sway to and fro like a a willow in the breeze. She hoped one of the patronesses would grant her permission to really participate very soon.

During one of these respites she stood, fanning herself rapidly with an ivory-handled fan of mint-green silk, beside Lady Cartwright. "Oh, Hil," she said contentedly, "I am exhausted. But this is such great fun!"

Lady Cartwright laughed and nodded. She beckoned to Sebastian, who stood nearby speaking to an acquaintance—though Angel was quite delightfully certain the earl had not taken his attention off of her for the entire evening. "Just wait 'til you try the waltz, my dear. You've not danced 'til you have waltzed."

Angel sighed. "I have not yet been granted permission by one of the patronesses."

"It is customary for the first half of the evening to pass before the ladies begin giving their consent."

When Sebastian approached, Hilary leaned toward his ear. "Take Angel over to Countess Lieven and beg her consent to waltz. My dear friends Lady Sefton and Lady Jersey are not present tonight, but I am somewhat acquainted with the countess and am sure she will grant her leave."

Sebastian lowered his dark brows. "I beg your pardon, sister, but I am not totally without connections in London, despite my frequent absences." Offering Angel his arm, he led her across the ballroom.

Since Angel was too stunned at the feel of Sebastian's hard-muscled forearm to notice where they were going, she almost gave a dismayed cry as they paused before the most terrifying of Almack's Society dames, Mrs. Drummond-Burrell.

Sebastian did not seem awed in the least by the large woman's beak-like nose and hostile demeanor. "My dear Mrs. Drummond-Burrell," he said smoothly, "permit me to introduce my ward, Lady Angelique."

Angel's legs trembled. What was Sebastian thinking of? Why would he bring her to the most fearsome of the patronesses?

Did he not know that Mrs. Drummond-Burrell's favorite pastime, according to Hilary, was refusing to allow debutantes to waltz? Did he not know that her disdain could lead to Angel's social downfall?

Then the imposing woman spoke. "Darcy, how

delightful to see you here this evening. You should come more often. Lady Angelique, how nice to meet you. Allow me to compliment you on your gown. That color is lovely and suits your red hair to perfection. Extend my compliments to Lady Cartwright on choosing such an individual shade rather than the usual boring white."

"Th-thank you, ma'am," Angel managed shakily.

"Are you enjoying your visit to Almack's?" the older woman inquired, obviously expecting a positive response to her question. "I hear you made quite an impression on the Regent. It is all anyone is talking of. Is it true he invited you to see his stables?"

Scarcely conscious of her reply, Angel replied, "Yes, ma'am."

"Well," the older woman remarked sympathetically, "I suppose you must go, although heaven knows what Prinny was thinking of, discussing such a topic with a young lady."

Angel hastily suppressed an hysterical giggle. What would Mrs. Drummond-Burrell think if she knew Angel had not only been in a stable, but had actually ridden her own horse in a race? For money?

"You'll be all right with him," Mrs. Drummond-Burrell finished comfortingly. "Although His Highness is fond of dallying with older ladies, there has never been a breath of scandal about him behaving improperly with innocents."

Then Sebastian inclined his head and murmured into the grande-dame's ear. The woman nodded graciously. Before Angel could blink the earl had taken her arm again and they were moving away from the terrifying patroness.

"Oh dear," Angel whispered weakly. "Did I embarrass myself utterly? I don't even remember what I said."

Sebastian grinned. "I'm tempted to say that you told her she had a figure like a battleship and a nose like

Napoleon's—which she does. But you said nothing unto-
ward. Not at all. You were quiet, but totally acceptable.

"I have never understood why everyone considers Mrs.
Drummond-Burrell to be such a gorgon. She has always
been most pleasant to me." He stopped and Angel realized
they stood in the exact center of the ballroom. "Now then,
my dear. I trust the caper merchant my sister hired, at
great expense to me, has taught you the steps to the
waltz?"

As if on cue the orchestra struck up a tantalizing melody.
With her heart in her mouth, Angel nodded. Sebastian's
hand wrapped around her waist drew her against the solid
mass of his chest.

Angel swallowed hard. Licking her lips, which suddenly seemed parched, she placed her right hand in his
left, and let him ease her into the dance.

The music swelled above them like a rosy cloud, enveloping them in breathtaking waves of harmony. Never in
her life had Angel felt so light. It was as if she were
walking on air, sailing like a gull over a golden beach.

Still, she was unable to lift her gaze beyond the sapphire
in Sebastian's pristine cravat. The waltz seemed so personal, bringing the two of them together in such an intimate fashion that mere inches separated their bodies. She
could feel the heat of the earl's chest penetrating the thin
stuff of her bodice, his warmth caressing her breasts.

She tried to move back slightly but was caught off
guard when his arms tightened about her and her nipples
grazed his chest. Her gaze flew to his and found him
staring down at her with an oddly intent expression.
Cheeks burning, Angel dropped her gaze to his neck, but
found that the slight blue-black shading of his shaven
skin was almost as sensually devastating as the fire in his
eyes.

Her breath, coming in little gasps, made the lace at his throat flutter slightly as if caught in a breeze.

What would it feel like to touch the shadows beneath his chin? Rough, or soft? Would the whiskers be sharp? And what would it feel like if she brushed his neck with her lips? At this thought, an unexpected blaze of heat swirled through her lower body, making her legs tremble.

Suddenly Sebastian stiffened and pushed Angel away so that their bodies no longer touched. Lifting her gaze, Angel saw that his attention had left her. She stumbled, but the earl held her firmly in his strong arms, and did not let her fall.

Sebastian's attention was riveted on a group of newcomers standing at the head of the stairs. Lady Sarah Moreton, along with her parents Lord and Lady Appleby, and several other young people including Lord Evanstone, had joined the select throng crowded in Almack's ballroom. And then, behind the small gathering, but obviously not one of their party, another face swirled into view.

Angel cried out in dismay as her gaze locked with the single clear eye of Sir Corbin Pugsley. The baronet grinned, his twisted mouth making a mockery of the smile, and bowed.

Chapter Seventeen

The waltz ended with a loud flourish just as Angel cried out, so no one save Sebastian heard her exclamation. His gaze spun away from Pugsley and came to rest on her flushed face. The warmth he'd felt while dancing with his ward a moment before vanished. He took her immediately to Hilary's side and, without another word, walked away to join Lady Sarah's party.

Though, outwardly, he managed to smile and converse wittily with his intended bride, inwardly he gritted his teeth so hard he thought his jawbone would crack.

How dare Angel so obviously show her delight at seeing Pugsley? Didn't she know the man's reputation? Of course she did, he amended with a snarl.

She shared it.

Thrusting the pair of them ruthlessly from his thoughts, he participated in the requisite two dances with Lady Sarah and spent the next hour squiring her about the room. He was not, however, able to keep his gaze from drifting back to Angel's lithe, silk-clad body each time the opportunity presented itself. Neither did he miss the fact that Sir Corbin Pugsley's one good eye followed Angel wherever she went.

Although the baronet never approached her, seeming content to lean negligently against a column, his gaze (at least that in his right eye; his blind left one dipped and swooped with careless abandon) never left Angel's body. Sebastian did not once see Pugsley's attention rise beyond her bodice.

Finally Sebastian's patience reached its limit. Determined to do something about the baronet's behavior, he practically thrust Lady Sarah into Lord Evanstone's arms. Although startled, Evanstone smiled brilliantly and seemed more than willing to accept the burden.

Striding purposefully toward Hilary, Sebastian snarled, "We are leaving. At once."

Hilary gaped at him. "Leaving? But Sebastian, Angel is such a success! The evening's entertainment is only half over!"

Sebastian shot back furiously, "It is over when I say it is over."

Hilary looked too stunned to reply.

When Angel's most recent partner returned her to Hilary's side, Sebastian informed his ward coldly, "We are returning home, immediately."

"Home?" Angel's eyes widened. "Why? My dance card is filled. Will not the gentlemen be offended if I leave them partnerless?"

Sebastian laughed a trifle wildly. "I don't give a hang if they are so desolate they blow out their brains, my lady."

Hilary glanced about worriedly. "Really, brother, must you be so loud? People are staring. You are making a scene. And at *Almack's!*" she finished in a mortified tone.

Sebastian glanced from side to side, noting immediately

that his sister was correct. He felt a flash of shame at embarrassing her, and lowered his voice. "I'm sorry. But we cannot remain here any longer."

Hilary shook her head, but said, "All right. At least we have accomplished what we came for: obtaining the patronesses' permission for Angel to waltz at her coming-out ball."

Angel's eyes flashed green and blue fire. To Sebastian's gaze she looked tormentingly lovely.

"Well, it is not all right with me. I would like to know why it is suddenly so vital that we go home. I was having a perfectly wonderful time." She turned her outraged gaze on Sebastian's face. "I demand to know my guardian's reasoning."

Goaded infinitely beyond sagacious behavior, Sebastian snarled, "Gladly. If you will excuse us, Hilary, my ward and I have something to discuss."

Taking Angel tightly by the arm, he pushed her before him, across the room, and down the stairs, opening and shutting doors until he found a deserted chamber. He forced his ward into the room. Slamming the door behind them, he released her arm, walked halfway across the room, turned back, and glared at her balefully. His blood raced in his veins like hot acid, burning him until he wanted nothing more than to drag Angel to the floor and take what she had sold to that bastard Pugsley.

"What in God's name is wrong with you, Sebastian?" Angel demanded. "Will you please tell me what this is all about? This is the second time you've flown off the handle for no reason. The first, as I'm sure you recall, was after the opera, in Hilary's carriage."

A tingle of outraged excitement made Sebastian shiver. "For no reason?" he retorted softly.

"That is correct."

Seeing Angel standing there, looking so demure and

innocent in her mint-green gown, a few strands of her coppery hair framing her face like that of the madonna at Whitechurch, he was nearly driven out of his mind with hunger and rage and confusion at why he wanted her so desperately.

"Sebastian, have you brought me down here merely to glower?" Angel challenged angrily. "What is this all about?"

The flames dancing in Sebastian's head roared out to consume his entire body. Without further adieu, he closed the gap between them, seized Angel around the waist, and pulled her toward him so roughly their bodies collided. "This," he ground out.

Claiming her mouth with his, he kissed her brutally, as though he could kiss away the depravity she had shared with Pugsley.

For a few seconds Angel tried to push him away. Then, gradually, her arms snaked around his neck and she pressed herself against his chest. When her cries of outrage changed to moans of pleasure, Sebastian eased his grip. A fierce throbbing in his lower half matched the quickened tempo of his heart.

Teasing Angel's lips with his tongue, he urged her to open herself more deeply to his kiss.

She obliged.

Groaning, he plunged his tongue into her softness. His hands released her to sweep across her slim ribs and come to rest beneath her soft bosom. When she cried out and moved, lowering her breasts so that they pressed into his fingers, he stifled a groan. Clasping her gently, he ran his thumbs over her nipples so that they hardened to sharp points beneath the thin fabric shield of her bodice.

Raising his head briefly, he threw a desperate glance around the chamber.

There was an old armchair in the shadows. He pulled

her toward it, sank down, and settled her on his lap. One of his hands dipped below her skirts, raising them swiftly. Above her silk stockings, her thighs were velvety smooth, tantalizing.

Sebastian longed to feel their softness beneath his tongue. Instead, his lips traced her face, then rose to follow the curve of her ear. He took the soft lobe between his teeth and bit gently.

When she cried out he moved up to capture her lips with his. Plundering ruthlessly, he forced her mouth open, kissing her again and again until she was limp and willing and eager in his arms.

At that moment, a soft knock sounded on the antechamber door.

Sebastian gasped as the intruder entered the room. Thrusting Angel off of his lap, he tried to steady his breath. He crossed his legs, hoping to hide his straining manhood, then, recognizing the newcomer, he sighed with relief only faintly tinged with shame.

Hilary's shocked expression made it clear she knew precisely what had happened. Moving toward Angel, she put an arm around the girl's trembling shoulders and led her to the door. There, Hilary turned back.

"I think you should find your own way home tonight, Sebastian," she said softly. "Angel and I will be leaving immediately."

And they were gone.

Sebastian put his forehead in his hands. Dear God. What had he done?

What, in the name of all the blessed saints, had he done? Without a doubt he had betrayed not only his ward, his sister, and his promised betrothed, but his own honor as well. He was no better than Pugsley.

Indeed, as he had thought once before, he was far, far worse.

He rose much later to return home. It was later still when he realized he had spared only the barest thought all evening for his betrothed, and had not even said good-bye to Lady Sarah upon leaving Almack's. He hoped Evanstone had taken care of the girl, and had seen her home safely.

Truly, he was fortunate to have such faithful, trustworthy friends.

Despite her desire, out of sheer emotional exhaustion, to take to her bed, Angel forced herself to go to keep her appointment with Sir Corbin at three A.M. in Lady Cartwright's garden.

Hilary had said nothing about what had happened at Almack's, but Angel knew the earl's sister had been deeply mortified. Lady Cartwright had disappeared to her bed-chamber immediately upon their return home, without a word to Angel. Still, Angel did not get the impression that Hilary was angry, but simply bewildered about how to mend the situation.

Still dressed in her evening gown, Angel sat stiffly on a chair in her bedchamber until the meeting time arrived. Then she grabbed a thin wrapper and, making certain no one else was about, dashed down the stairs and out a side door as the clock chimed thrice.

Tiny hairs on her arms stood up straight from a combination of the chilly night air and abject terror. Moving swiftly, she hurried along the gravel path toward the Roman fountain, hoping beyond anything that Pugsley had been unable to keep their appointment. In moments she had reached her destination.

Although she'd purposely avoided thinking about the baronet during the last few hours, now she cringed to think what he might want to say to her. If only she had dared tell someone where she was going, or had thought to bring a knife or revolver! But she had not, for fear Pugsley would discover her weapon and take his reprisal out on Windywood Abbey.

Casting her gaze in the darkness, she tried to make out Pugsley's shape amid the shifting shadows.

Although the moon gleamed, it was still a very dark night. She glanced toward the fountain where, silhouetted against the sky, King Neptune had pierced a large fish with his triton. Water streamed from the dying fish's mouth, splashing in the pool below.

She did not see the baronet.

Her legs trembled as she turned this way and that, listening for Pugsley's footfalls over the din made by the showering water hitting the pool. She circled the fountain three times. Then, just as she finally allowed her pounding heart to relax, just when she finally decided that Pugsley would not come, he strode through a thick stand of holly-hocks.

Angel's heart dropped into her satin slippers.

Stepping close, he placed one hand on her bare forearm. "Angel, my love, how good it is to see you."

Noticing the way his white eye seemed to glow like a second moon, Angel shuddered. The baronet's misshapen face seemed even more repulsive than ever, and he reeked of cologne and spirits. When he spoke, it became even clearer that he had imbibed heavily before coming to the garden.

"How pretty you looked at Almack's this evening," he said hungrily. His voice was slurred. "As, I see, you do now. I am so glad you did not change out of your ball gown. Did you remain dressed so fine just to please me?"

A wave of disgust shook Angel's entire body. "I would do nothing to please you, Sir Corbin," she hissed, afraid if she spoke louder someone from the house would overhear their conversation. "Had I known you would be at Almack's, I should have stayed home."

Raising the hand that was not grasping her, Pugsley shook a finger slowly in front of her nose. "Ah-ah-ah, my dear. You really ought to be nicer to me. I can still turn Windywood Abbey to a pile of rubble if I become so inclined."

"And risk forfeiting our wager? I think not." Trying to look scornful, Angel then demanded coldly, "What do you want?"

Caressing her arm with his long fingernails, Pugsley replied sorrowfully, "Oh, Angel, I am wounded. Is that any way to greet me? As though the only reason I would wish to see you was that I wanted something? I am hurt.

"I missed you, my darling girl. I just wanted to see you so that I might relish the thought of taking up where I and my friends left off so many years ago. You remember, I am sure. But of course you do. How could you forget? You are reminded each time we meet—just as I am each time I look into a mirror."

"I remember only that you were a cad and that you and your two friends should have been hanged or deported for your attempted rape."

The baronet sneered. "You were asking for our attentions, girl. Walking through that field, picking daisies. We'd been riding past and you smiled up at us with more invitation in your eyes than a Mayfair streetwalker. And then, after my friends kindly agreed to let me have you first, and you picked up that branch and hit me when I wasn't looking."

"I had no choice," Angel replied, voice trembling. "But I was not aiming for your face. I did not mean to cut you so badly, Sir Corbin. As for your 'friends,' they laughed at your misfortune. Had they not been rolling on the ground with laughter, I would never have escaped."

Pugsley grinned faintly. "And you will not escape this time. Not after I claim my prize on August the first."

"That will never happen." Angel wrenched her arm free and stepped back. "I will win this wager. And when I do I will never, ever see you again." Despite her best efforts, her voice quavered.

The baronet's cockeyed grin mocked her. "We'll just see about that, won't we?"

Before Angel could turn and run back up the path toward the house, he leaped forward and seized her wrists between viselike fingers. Still fearful of awakening the house, she sank her teeth into her lower lip to keep from screaming as her delicate bones threatened to crack in the baronet's agonizing grip. Only when she whimpered with pain did Pugsley lighten his grasp.

"Oh my dear," he said, his voice heavy with passion, "you are so white and soft. Your cries of pain when I claim you will only make my taking you all the sweeter." His nostrils flared as his good eye roved eagerly over her body. "Surely you cannot begrudge me just one kiss before then. Just to tide me over, so to speak?"

Jerking her toward him, he lowered his lips to hers.

Angel could feel his teeth on the crumpled left side of his mouth, dry against her lips. Her stomach roiled violently and she fought to keep from vomiting. As his exposed teeth sliced her lower lip, she tasted blood.

Then, from somewhere deep within, a surge of strength rose inside her. Opening her mouth, she latched onto his tongue and bit as hard as she could. He shoved her violently away.

The baronet put his hand to his mouth and drew fingers away dark with blood. "You little bitch!" he snarled. "You already had a lot coming to you, but by God you will pay for that."

Angel lay sprawled against the dew-soaked earth where

the baronet had thrown her. Wiping the sour, old-wine taste of him off her lips, she scrabbled to her feet as he lunged forward. His fingers tore the hem of her evening dress as she dashed past him and ran as hard as she could for the house.

His scratchy, low calls chased after her. "I'll have you in the end, Angel. And when I do you will never escape me. I'll see you dead first. I'll see you skinned alive and bleeding like a dying roe. I'll drink your blood while you watch me! Better yet, I'll see you look exactly like me!"

Chapter Eighteen

Angel wrenched open the side door and slipped inside. Closing and bolting it behind her, she leaned back against the solid wood. She gasped for breath as she tried to calm herself enough so that her wildly quaking limbs would carry her back upstairs to her chamber.

Only after her breathing finally slowed did she realize tears were streaming down her face. Her beautiful ball gown, slathered with mud from her fall and torn by Pugsley's grasping fingers, was quite ruined. Even if it had not been, she thought violently, she would have burned it after having seen it held in the baronet's evil clasp.

Wiping her face with her hands, she moved forward and dragged herself up the grand staircase. In her room she removed the filthy gown, prodded the smouldering ashes in the fireplace into raging flames, and thrust the garment into the blaze. The smell of burning silk was nearly overpowering. She opened her window as wide as it would go, then returned to the fire. Soon, nothing remained of the gown but a pile of blackened ash.

Then she climbed into bed.

She lay gazing out her window, staring up at the star upon which she'd made so many wishes. Forcing her thoughts away from Pugsley, she remembered Hilary's words of Sebastian's love for her, and his behavior that evening.

It seemed obvious that he desired, if not loved, her. And God above knew she loved him beyond anything in her life. But it was no good. Too many obstacles stood in the way of their happiness.

Why had she assumed that, simply because she was female, it would be any easier for *her* to approach Sarah about her love for Sarah's promised spouse than it would be for *Simon* to approach Sebastian? Truly, she had been gravely in error.

What was to be done?

To allow Sarah and Simon to be kept apart simply because neither wished to offend Sebastian seemed absurd in the extreme—especially when Sebastian supposedly loved *her*. Still, Sebastian had never told Angel he loved her and, despite his passionate lovemaking (here her heart gave an aching throb), he might never do so.

Perhaps the agonies Lady Cartwright had informed Angel he'd suffered during the afternoon "at home," which Hilary had suggested had been due to love for Angel, had actually been due to indigestion rather than matters of the heart.

Rolling over, Angel pummeled her pillow. Oh, why could she not simply put these things from her mind and go to sleep!

Instead, a pair of infinitely fine dark eyes beneath a shock of thick black hair seemed to gaze at her each time she closed her eyes.

Should she tell Sebastian that Sarah loved Simon? Or would that infuriate Sebastian's masculinity to the point where he insisted upon marrying Sarah even though he did not love her, just to keep from being thrown over by his best friend? In the worse scenario, it was possible that he would do precisely that, and lose his best friend in the bargain.

Men were so horribly obtuse at times. Particularly in matters of the heart.

So what, then, was the answer to the dilemma? Was there any answer at all?

Finally Angel gave up trying to sleep and rolled onto her back. Pushing aside the coverlet, she climbed out of bed and padded over to the open window. The garden below was dark in the light of the waning gibbous moon; only the shadows of trees, shrubs, and the Roman fountain on the black velvet lawn were visible.

Leaning her elbows on the sill, Angel rested her chin in her hands.

The question foremost in her mind was, Was there any chance Sebastian would *ever* tell her he loved her even if he did?

Given what he believed about her background, it was doubtful. What man would want a fallen woman for his wife? She could not simply tell him he was wrong about her, that she had never prostituted herself to Pugsley, because then he would demand an explanation for where she had gotten the money to attempt to buy Windywood Abbey.

And if she told him of her venture into the masculine world of the turf, he would undoubtedly forbid her to enter her horse in any more races, since it was a completely unacceptable thing for a woman to do.

Not only was it socially unacceptable, she realized, but, considering how much angrier Sebastian became each time Vortex beat Hughes Pride, the earl would probably be infuriated to know it had been Angel's horse that might very well snatch the Grand London Gold Cup out of his grasp.

If he found out she was to blame for his losses, would he ever forgive her?

She could not risk Sebastian's pulling Vortex out of the races, as, being her guardian, he could legally do. Vortex *must* race in as many contests as remained before the Gold Cup. Even then, if he won every race, it was still possible that he would not have won the entire required twenty thousand pounds by August first.

The wager weighed heavily on her mind as she gazed out into the night.

As far as the Grand London Gold Cup went, if it seemed that Vortex *would* take the cup away from Sebastian and Hughes Pride, Angel just didn't know what she would do. She sighed again. It all seemed so hopeless.

Shortly before dawn she returned to her bed and, despite thinking it was impossible, fell asleep instantly.

The first thing that greeted Sebastian when he sat down to his breakfast in his newly refurbished town house the following morning was news of yet another loss by Hughes Pride to the gray stallion, Vortex. The purse had been one thousand pounds. The Prince Regent, an acknowledged fan of the turf, the article read further, had offered to buy the gray at any price if the stallion's mysterious, unknown possessor would just step forward.

By this time Sebastian was not even mildly surprised at Hughes Pride's loss of this most recent race; he was rapidly becoming accustomed to it. It seemed doubtful that his greatest wish would ever be fulfilled. Gloom settled over him like a rain-heavy cloud. He would not win the Gold Cup this year, at any rate.

Pushing both the paper and his disappointment aside,

he poured himself a cup of coffee and sipped it, pondering, sick at heart, what he had seen the night before.

Unable to simply return home after holding his sweet Angel in his arms, he had instructed his coachman to drive past Cartwright House in the off-chance he might see his darling silhouetted against her bedchamber window. Instead, to his horror, he'd seen his beloved rushing into the side door of Hilary's town house, her beautiful green gown covered with mud, a long rip up the right side, starting at the hem.

He had no doubt as to how the tear had gotten there.

A razor-sharp shaft of pain twisted his heart. His fingers, icy cold, trembled so violently he nearly dropped his coffee.

Why did Angel persist in her clandestine meetings? With which lucky suitor had she been rendezvousing? What kind of animal had the bastard been, that he had ripped Angel's gown so badly in his lustful eagerness to possess her?

Was that what Angel required? Violence?

He had heard of women like that, as well as men, but couldn't for the life of him believe that a girl as seemingly gentle as Angel would be so coarse. And yet the evidence of her base nature had cropped up yet again. Hard, irrefutable evidence.

He shook his head, irritated with himself for caring so deeply.

How long would he moon over the chit? How many times did he have to see her sneaking in after a late night tryst, before he could accept that, despite his longing she be otherwise, she was truly no better than she should be? Hadn't she proven exactly that in his own arms tonight, the way she had clung to him with her lips and breasts and hips pressed against his body almost as close as his own skin?

He sighed so deeply that his shoulders rose and fell three inches.

Running his fingers over tired eyes that had not been closed more than an hour all night, he tried to order his thoughts. Disregarding the fact that he was heels over head in love with her—he freely admitted this now—he was the girl's guardian, for God's sake. He had to do something about her midnight rendezvous before she ruined both herself and his family name.

If he were free of his duty to Lady Sarah he would marry Angel himself, just to give a name to any brat one of her lovers might have already sired. He would wed her willingly, even though it would kill him each time she shook the bedsprings with her most recent lover.

No, he amended ruefully, he would wed her even if she continued with her crude behavior. And love her despite it.

In societal reasoning, it was a pity she was wellborn. Had she been a cit's daughter, no one would have batted an eye. She could have had a whole slew of keepers and everyone would have congratulated her on her success. Innumerable Cyprians had gained fame and fortune for exactly that behavior.

Rather than reviling these exotic creatures, the public seemed to delight in each new exploit.

But Angel was an earl's daughter. The granddaughter of a duke. She was his ward. And yes, he loved her more than life itself. And yes, he would marry her even though he owed more respect to his position as the sixth earl of Darcy.

He knew that, if Angel stayed in London, it would be a miracle if he could keep from ravishing her. He had never felt such a yearning need in his life. It would be dangerous even to attend her coming-out ball that evening; he was well aware that all he needed to do was look into her exquisite blue-green eyes and he would, again, be lost to all sense of propriety.

How would he be able to dance with her and keep from spiriting her away as soon as he got the chance, to finish what they had begun the evening before? He knew she would be willing. God knew she seemed to be willing with anyone who offered an invitation.

The only solution, however painful—and by all the saints in heaven, it was painful—was clear.

One of them had to leave London, and it could not be he, since the Grand London Gold Cup was in a mere three weeks. But how could he possibly send her away? Not only had he promised her a Season so she might snag a suitable husband, but exiling her would be like banishing his own heart.

What was he to do?

From her position beside her aunt, standing at the top of a large staircase descending toward Sebastian's ballroom floor, Angel gazed about during a lull in the arrival of her guests.

Watching the most recent arrivals spread out amid the other exquisitely garbed members of the ton, she wondered where Sebastian could have gotten to. He was supposed to be standing in the welcoming line with her and Lady Cartwright.

Thus far he was nowhere to be seen.

As Hilary had commanded the ballroom's new shades of lavenders, lilacs, mauves, and pearl whites matched Angel's new gown to perfection. Enormous bouquets of flowers—delphiniums, pale violet and dusty pink orchids, lilacs, phlox, and irises—marched like sentries in narrow recesses against the walls and twined around the wrought iron balustrade on each side of the staircase and the four silver marble pillars standing at attention in the corners of the large room.

The flowers added their heady scent to the multitude of costly perfumes worn by the women, who resembled nothing so much as even more gaudy blooms as they moved about the ballroom floor.

Although it was a warm, bordering on hot, evening, the chamber remained cool due to the fresh breeze that blew through two large sets of French windows that opened out onto a tiled terrace overlooking the gardens. It was just after ten o'clock, and was already dark outside except for a brilliant moon.

As another group of guests was admitted by Sebastian's supercilious butler, Angel pasted a smile on her face, although she honestly felt like bursting into tears.

Despite the gloriousness of the ballroom and all her guests, she knew the evening would be dull as clay to her if Sebastian did not make an appearance. Nevertheless, she exchanged meaningless pleasantries and expressed flattering pleasure as each male in the new party took her dance card, picked up the tiny silver pencil attached to its side, and scrawled his name beside one of the listed capers.

Where was Sebastian?

If he did not come soon he would be unable to obtain a dance. She could not keep the opening and closing waltzes free forever. Already Hilary was looking at her strangely each time she begged—ever so prettily—that any man requesting one of those dances choose another. It would look extremely odd if the girl of the evening did not take part in the opening festivities.

Then the newest flock of guests moved down the staircase into the crowded ballroom, and Angel and Lady Cartwright stood alone once again.

Angel let the polite smile fall from her lips and slide

back into the pit of her stomach from whence she had dragged it. Opening her lilac fan of Brussels lace, she flitted it before her cheeks to hide the sudden moistness stinging the backs of her eyelids. She cleared her throat to dislodge a miserable lump, then turned as the earl's sister spoke.

"I wonder what is keeping Sebastian. It isn't like him to be so late. I am sure he knew he was supposed to stand with us this evening." Lady Cartwright eyed Angel sympathetically. "I do hope your evening will not be ruined if he does not come, my dear. At least he remembered your flowers."

Angel nodded, but could not speak around the lump in her throat.

Flicking a glance down toward the deep purple riband surrounding the high waist of her lavender silk gown, she gazed at Sebastian's tiny bouquet of violets, pinned just below her breasts. Each time she moved a delightful cloud of their sweet scent caressed her face. "They are lovely, are they not?"

"Yes. I was surprised to see he had sent violets—they are such a simple flower, not fancy at all. But now I realize he chose those because there were none among the flowers decorating the ballroom.

"He must have scoured England to find so many shades of purple. I instructed my workers to find the delphiniums and lilacs, but the rest must have come from his hothouses. And your violets are exactly the color of your waist band. Of course, it is a pity the only jewels we had to match were those chunky amethysts of my great grandmama's you are wearing."

"On the contrary, sister," remarked a voice from behind them. "Our *grandmere's* jewels look beautiful on Angel, as would mere chunks of coal. But I do hope my ward will honor me, by replacing them with these."

Angel spun about. He had come! He had not stayed away!

"My lord!" she cried. "I was beginning to think you had forgotten."

He smiled crookedly, looking rakishly handsome with his shadowed jaw and curving lips. His dark eyes gleamed. "Forgotten?" he repeated huskily. "As if God himself could forget one of his Angels."

Then he straightened and spoke louder. "Do not be ridiculous. Do you really think I could have forgotten this evening's entertainment with so many workmen in and out of the house at all hours of the day, carrying bouquets of flowers and small tables and a veritable army of chairs? Hardly.

"But come, if you would be so kind as to step over there," he pointed to a little alcove, "I would like to present you with your coming-out gift. Sister," he added, "if you will excuse us momentarily?"

Hilary's eyebrows rose with an unspoken warning, but she nodded. "Have her back here in one minute, Sebastian. It would be most awkward if more guests arrived and she were absent. And mind your manners."

Sebastian inclined his head. He smiled again, though even more mournfully than when he had questioned the sincerity of Angel's insistence that he had forgotten her ball. "Of course."

As he held out one black-clad arm, Angel laid her fingers upon it and allowed him to lead her toward the alcove.

Chapter Nineteen

Once out of view of his sister, Sebastian turned his head and smiled down at Angel. His arm suddenly felt like a live coal, and she jerked her hand away as though she'd been burned. A combined flicker of regret and chagrin flashed in the earl's dark eyes.

"I promise I will not put you to the blush again, Angel," he said gruffly. "My behavior the other night was despicable and I assure you I have no intention of repeating the mistake."

Angel felt her cheeks warm and then go icy as the full meaning of his words registered on her ears. She dropped her gaze to the single diamond glittering in his snowy cravat.

Mistake? Was that what he'd thought of their embraces? Of course, she realized hastily, he could hardly have meant the lovemaking to happen, since he was betrothed to Sarah, and was infinitely honorable.

"I know you will not, my lord," she replied with a catch in her voice.

Sebastian reached into the inner pocket of his superbly tailored evening coat of black superfine, worn over a silver satin vest and light gray pantaloons. He extracted a square, gray velvet box.

Angel stared at the box, but was far more aware of the bearer than the gift.

"I hope you will accept this," he said. " 'Tis the reason I am late. I had instructed the jeweler to have it delivered to my house this afternoon. Since I expected him to comply with my wishes, I was under the impression it was waiting on my desk in the library." He laughed self-consciously. "When I discovered the jeweler had not had it delivered at all, I went to his home, dragged him from his bed, and 'asked' him to accompany me to his shop so that I might fetch it myself."

His words jolted Angel out of her saddened reverie, and she held out a hand for the box he now proffered. The container, covered in silk, felt cool and smooth.

Turning slightly so that the light from one crystal lamp hung on the wall fell on the box, Angel opened the lid. Then her mouth fell open and she gasped with delight and astonishment.

"I designed them myself. I hope you like them . . . although they can easily be returned if you'd prefer something else," he finished tentatively.

"I love them," Angel murmured. Raising her lashes, she gazed up at the earl, awed. "You designed these pieces yourself? Sebastian! They're the most beautiful things I've ever seen in my life."

He looked at her for a long moment. "Not in mine," he said then, pointedly, before flushing as if he'd said something unforgivable. Which, Angel knew, given his honorable bent, he had.

Feeling her cheeks heat again, she looked back down at the jewels nestled on their ivory satin pillow. A necklace of deep purple Brazilian amethysts and glittering green Colombian emeralds, set in platinum and shaped like tiny violets with diamond centers, winked up at her in the candlelight. The flowerets were repeated in a set of earrings and a delicate bracelet.

She swallowed, feeling absurdly close to tears. "I must put them on."

Moving across the room, she leaned toward a looking glass hung on one gilt- and fleur-de-lis-painted wall. After removing Hilary's borrowed jewels, she raised the necklet toward her throat.

At first she could not get the ends together and felt a mounting frustration as her fingers fumbled with the tricky clasp. Sebastian stepped toward her and raised his hands. She released the necklace into his fingers. He seemed to take an eternity joining the ends together. His fingertips seemed to scorch the nape of her neck as they lingered, brushing against her skin as though loath to complete their task and be forced, by propriety, to move away.

Then the clasp snapped together securely. Sebastian sighed, audibly. He picked up the ear-bobs and set one, then the other, on her lobes.

Angel caught her breath and somehow managed to keep from leaning into his warm palm as he adjusted her right earring. A deep, near-painful ache settled low in her belly as she looked up at him.

The earl's beautiful, dark eyes were filled with emotion. His fine mouth was a tight white line against his tanned face. Obviously avoiding her gaze, he picked up the bracelet and settled it over her wrist, his thumb rubbing her flesh slightly so that the ache in her belly deepened to excruciating agony.

Finally, clearing his throat, he picked up Hilary's discarded jewels, dropped them into his pocket, and backed away. "We'd best get back before Hilary comes looking for you," he said softly. "I will return her jewelry to the family vault."

Angel sucked in her breath. "Yes," she managed at last. Then, removing her dance card from her wrist, she dangled it, hopefully, from its silken cord. "I hope you will be so kind as to take the first and last dances on my card. I thought it proper to save them for you, since you are not only my guardian, but my host."

Sebastian's lips arched into a sardonic smile. His eyes seemed to glitter with an inner fire.

Reaching out carefully so that he did not touch her, the earl accepted the proffered booklet. "Proper?" he murmured plaintively. "My dear girl, I have become unswervingly convinced that nothing between us is proper. I . . ." he hesitated.

Angel stiffened, certain he was going to refuse. When he laughed softly and signed his name in the two blank spaces, she released her breath in a relieved sigh.

". . . would be honored." He laughed, but it sounded not amused, but somehow bitter. "It appears it is fortunate you saved these dances for me. I see your card is completely filled, otherwise."

He said nothing more, but returned the booklet, again without touching her, to her wrist. Then he held out his arm and led her from the alcove in time for Angel to see Hilary deserting her place at the top of the stairs to come looking for them. Although Lady Cartwright flashed both of them a searching look, she did not remark on anything but Angel's lovely new jewelry.

"Violets!" she exclaimed. "Oh, how beautiful! Now I understand why you sent fresh violets for Angel's bouquet, Sebastian. I commend you. As always, your taste is superb."

"Thank you, sister."

Hilary turned to Angel. "I think we might leave our

post now, dear. If there are any latecomers the butler may show them in. I will instruct the musicians to begin playing."

She moved away and Angel lifted her gaze to Sebastian's face. He returned her inspection silently for a moment before raising one eyebrow and gesturing toward the center of the floor. The music from the player's box flowed like sweet honey, rippling over the ballroom and enticing everyone to dance. Then the earl's hand was at Angel's waist, and she let herself melt into his arms, filled with the sensation of being home at last.

Sebastian tried to pretend they were alone in the ballroom.

When Angel laughed up at him as he swirled her about in a graceful turn, he nearly lowered his head to kiss her sweet lips, but stopped himself just in time. Actually, the thing which prevented him was catching a sudden glimpse of his promised fiancée, Lady Sarah Moreton, sailing past in Lord Evanstone's arms.

Lady Sarah was smiling up at Evanstone, something she never did when she danced with *him*, Sebastian realized with a sense of shock.

The revelation nearly stopped him cold in his tracks. Then he noticed Simon's shy, answering grin, and Sebastian did stumble. Apologizing hastily to Angel, he scrupulously returned his concentration to the steps of the waltz.

Apparently Angel had also noticed the passing couple, for she, too, was gazing concernedly at their faces. In an effort to remove her frown, Sebastian whirled about so that Angel's back was to Lady Sarah and Evanstone.

When Angel tipped her chin up to glare at him with exasperated eyes, he laughed aloud. "My dear girl," he said, "unless both of us concentrate on the dance instead of the other dancers, we are surely headed for disaster."

"I'm sorry, my lord," Angel apologized. "You are right. But Sarah and Simon just seem to look so . . . so *right* together, somehow. Do you not agree?"

She colored brightly, and Sebastian wondered if she were troubled by the attention Evanstone was showing Lady Sarah. The thought made his smile vanish. Was Angel jealous because she wanted Simon's attentions for herself?

"They are both simply accomplished dancers," he said brusquely. "I am sure that even we would look 'made for each other' if we concentrated on our steps. The notion that two people could look as if they had been created for each other is absurdly romantic."

"I think," Angel retorted sharply, "that unless two people are truly meant for one another they could never look more than adequate together. No matter what they were doing."

She said nothing more, a fact for which Sebastian was grateful. He, too, had noted the "rightness" of Evanstone and Lady Sarah, and could not help but notice the corresponding affinity he felt while holding Angel in his arms. And, he acknowledged with a flush, though he had dutifully kissed Lady Sarah's lips after requesting her hand in marriage, he had certainly never experienced such burning passion with his promised bride as he had when kissing Angel.

Abruptly, he paled.

Of course, he had not felt passion from his promised betrothed simply because Lady Sarah was pure as newfallen snow, while Angel could not be considered innocent by any stretch of the imagination.

Shoving this disturbing thought from his mind, as the

music ended he returned Angel to Hilary's side, sought out his future fiancée, and secured two dances with her.

His mood was not improved when, as he and Lady Sarah danced, his previous impression was proven correct. Holding her felt rather like holding a clump of thorny honey locust rather than a dream in woman's form. And she was not smiling.

A suspicion flickered to life in his mind. Could Lady Sarah be in love with Simon? Surely not! The thought was ridiculous!

He looked down at his beautiful future wife as they passed by Evanstone, and was shocked and not a little dismayed to see her fine blue eyes follow Simon almost wistfully. Raising his gaze a bit wildly, Sebastian found himself looking directly into Angel's face. She, too, was watching Lady Sarah and Simon. She looked lost, remote. Almost as if she'd lost her best friend.

But that was to be expected, under the circumstances. It was only too obvious that Angel was also in love with Evanstone. If she knew Lady Sarah felt likewise, it would naturally make his poor ward miserable.

He sighed.

What could he do to find out if his suspicions were correct? It would never do if he were to wed Lady Sarah—despite losing her father's prime bloods if he did not—if the girl were in love with another man. Although other men of his acquaintance married for convenience all the time, the very thought turned Sebastian's stomach. There had to be at least some affection between a man and his wife.

The question was, Did Evanstone truly return Lady Sarah's affection? He had been squiring Angel about for nearly three weeks, now, and seemed quite taken with *her*.

Was his attention to Angel a front, to keep Sebastian

from noticing how Evanstone felt? Recalling Simon's reaction to Sebastian's betrothal announcement at the race in which Sebastian had lost Windywood Abbey to Sir Corbin Pugsley, the earl was forced to admit the tall, thin lord had hardly seemed pleased by the news.

Not that it really mattered if Evanstone was in love with Lady Sarah, Sebastian thought darkly, because unless Lady Sarah actually broke her agreement with *him* there was little he could do to remedy the situation. As a gentleman he could not back out of their understanding.

It would be totally dishonorable.

Nevertheless, he would prefer to go into the marriage with his eyes open on all counts. Though there appeared to be no way out of the betrothal, he still wished he knew Lady Sarah's mind.

If Lady Sarah did love Simon, and if Sebastian were free, would Angel want him? Had she really felt anything for him during their kisses, or had her heated response to his kisses merely been part of her passionate nature, that nature she seemed willing to share with any Tom, Dick or . . . or Pugsley who possessed coin of the realm?

Or was she so bent on having Evanstone that, if Simon decided he wanted Lady Sarah, Angel's heart would be broken? Sebastian knew he could not risk breaking Angel's heart, not at any cost. The only thing he could do was nothing at all.

Except what he'd planned while lying awake for so many hours the previous night.

As soon as the evening drew to a close, as all the dancers filed onto the floor for the last waltz, Sebastian sought out his ward. They came together as easily as they had the first time, and once again he was astonished at how easily she fit into his arms. No other woman— regardless how pure—had ever felt so right, so perfect, so wholly meant for him. It was as if she had been created especially for him, and no other woman would ever feel the same way.

Realizing that, if Angel agreed to the offer he intended to put forth after all the guests went home, this would be their last dance together, he pulled her close and was pleased when she pressed against him like a lost lamb. Although it was not proper and resulted in a few shocked glances as well as one furious glare from Hilary, he drew her closer still, until Angel's nipples brushed his chest.

He gazed into her eyes and tried to memorize her loveliness. "I would speak with you after everyone leaves," he whispered. "Try to get away from Hilary and meet me in the library. It is the third room on the left on the second floor. I have a proposition to make to you."

Angel stood on the step and watched as the last guests climbed into their carriage and drove away. Then, turning to Lady Cartwright, she said casually, "I think I left something inside. I will fetch it and be back, directly."

Hilary nodded. "Do not take long, dear. I have developed quite a headache. Too much champagne, I assume. Alcohol does not sit well with me; it never has."

"I shall return immediately."

Angel climbed the second staircase and moved down the dim third floor hall. As she came to the library door, she pushed it ajar. It squeaked faintly and she became aware how completely silent everything was now that the ball was over and the house was nearly deserted.

A nervous shiver rippled down her spine. "Sebastian?" she called softly. "Are you here?"

"Yes."

A match flared in the darkness and she watched as Sebastian lit a lamp on his desk. A golden glow flooded the room.

Angel moved toward the light. Her guardian was seated behind a desk, a low fire flickering in the grate behind him. Scattered about the desk were numerous sheets of paper. When he did not speak, but only gazed at her as if his tongue would shatter if he uttered a syllable, she said tentatively, "You . . . you wanted to see me, my lord?"

He cleared his throat. When he spoke, his voice was gravelly with emotion. "I did." He waved her to a chair opposite him. "Sit down, Angel."

Angel sank onto the plush brocade seat and, clasping her trembling fingers together, rested her forearms on the desk. Her attention briefly fell upon her new amethyst bracelet, as it sparkled in the firelight. Then she looked up as Sebastian pushed a sheaf of papers toward her.

"Read them."

She complied. By the second paragraph a burning fury had seared its way up from her stomach to her face. She drew a deep breath. "I do not understand, my lord."

The earl sighed impatiently. Angel smelled the sour tang of spirits.

"It is quite clear," he growled. "I had my solicitor draw up the papers this afternoon."

Sick with pain and fury, Angel made as if to rise. "You have obviously had too much to drink, my lord. You do not know what you are suggesting. I will leave you and attend you on the morrow when your mind is more clear."

Sebastian surged to his feet and loomed over the desk, his eyes glittering like faceted onyx. "Sit down!"

Heart pounding, Angel sank back onto the edge of her chair.

"Now then," he said unsteadily as he, too, retook his seat, "in case you do not understand completely, I shall explain what those papers entail.

"Conscious of your desire to live in the country so that you might follow your . . . whims," he said with a twist to his lips, "I have deeded a small but beautiful estate in Yorkshire to you. It is not far from Windywood, and should suit you admirably."

Angel looked down at her hands. They were trembling, and she clenched them together so Sebastian would not notice. "Why?" she demanded quietly. "I thought you wanted me to find a husband. Is that not why you insisted I come to London?"

He shifted uncomfortably. "Yes, but I have changed my mind. Upon further consideration, I do not think married life would suit you. Anyway, it was unfair of me to uproot you like I did. You are easily of an age to choose your own lifestyle, even if it is not one of which I approve."

"I do not know what you mean."

His eyes bored into hers. Longing etched deep lines in his face. "I believe you do. I also believe you know precisely what will happen if you remain in London for much longer. Are you willing to tempt me to betray my intended, Lady Sarah? For that is what will happen, you know. I cannot resist you, Angel. I would give you anything, any amount of money, you desired. But I cannot hold off my yearning forever. I am simply not that strong."

Angel rubbed her eyes and tried to determine the best reply. It appeared that Sebastian was offering her a carte blanche, yet that was impossible. He was still fixated on the idea that she had sold her body to earn the money to buy Windywood.

The entire situation had gotten out of hand. She had to explain herself, but could not. How could she make Sebastian understand she had not sold her body to Pugsley, or anyone else, without telling the earl the whole about Jonas and Vortex? And then she would, surely, lose the Abbey completely. Even if Sebastian gave her the remaining sum to win her wager, she knew beyond a doubt that if the baronet discovered her perfidy he would be furious enough to rip the Abbey apart with his bare hands. She simply could not risk that.

"My lord," she said helplessly, "I know you may not believe this, but I assure you I have done no wrong. I am still pure."

Sebastian gave a bark of laughter. The aroma of spirits grew stronger. "Pure? My dear girl, I was not born yesterday. Do you expect me to believe you know nothing of the ways of the flesh and still responded to my kisses the way you did?"

Angel's cheeks burned. "I do. My response to you was—it was—"

"It was what?" he asked, quirking a mocking brow.

"It was because I imagined myself infatuated with you," Angel cried. She jumped up from her chair. "I am sorry if you found my behavior forward, my lord, but I promise you I am not ruined. And I will not be banished from London like a naughty child simply because you cannot control your lust."

The earl's eyes blazed yet again.

"Why do you believe this of me?" Angel demanded. "What have I done that makes you so certain I am a whore?"

Although he winced visibly at her choice of words, Sebastian met her gaze squarely. "I saw you sneaking back into the house twice after assignations," he replied. "And you yourself told me you had earned the money to buy Windywood Abbey that way. Either you lied then, or you are lying now."

"I never told you that. *You* implied that I obtained the money that way. I simply did not disagree."

"Precisely. And what woman would have hesitated to defend her virtue if it were, in truth, unsullied?"

Angel stared at him. He was right.

God help her, he was right. Given the circumstances, what else could he believe? She could not blame him.

She shook her head slowly. "Again, I give you my word I am untouched. Except by *your* hands." She laughed bitterly. "But I will not leave London. I do not want your estate. The only estate I want is Windywood, and you have already taken that away from me."

He studied her soberly. "I have already apologized for losing the Abbey. If I could, I would get it back at any cost." He was silent for a time. At last he sighed and waved a hand wearily. "You must agree that, if I allow you to stay in London, we will not meet again until we are both safely wed."

Angel bowed her head. "I agree."

Sebastian's next words sounded as pained as if a saber had pierced his heart. "If I have wronged you, I am doubly sorry, Angel. If there is something you feel you cannot tell me, perhaps you will come to trust me, someday."

"It is not a case of trust, my lord," Angel assured him brokenly.

He shook his head, wearily. "It matters not. At any rate, I feel it necessary to avoid you in future until you choose your mate. Not only do I have Lady Sarah to think about, but I believe it would rip me into tiny pieces if I had to watch you and your future husband together. Do you understand?"

Their eyes met and held, and it seemed to Angel as if her heart left her breast and traded places with his.

He loved her. Of that there could be no doubt, although he would never tell her so. The emotion scintillated like moonbeams from his dark eyes, and the agony and remorse in his face was too much for her to bear.

She caught her breath. "I understand, my lord."

Sebastian bowed his head. His despair was almost palpable in the shadowy room. "Then I will bid you good night," he said softly. "I shall not see you again until you are betrothed. But if you do not find someone who suits you, please rest assured the estate I have deeded to you will remain in your name. I want you to have a place to go, Angel, no matter what you decide to do."

She moved to the door, but paused as he whispered brokenly, "God go with you, my sweet Angel. You will forever be in my heart."

Chapter Twenty

One morning some weeks later Angel sat at her writing table still garbed in her nightrail and wrap, gazing down at Jonas Spindle's most recent note. Her chest ached with worry, and her throat constricted. The news the short letter contained was the same as that in the last several notes she'd received.

Beginning over a month ago, Vortex had begun losing races to Sebastian's black stallion, Hughes Pride. Enclosed in the letter was the most recent *Times* article. The big gray, the newspaper read, had not won a single race in five weeks, although he'd come in only a stride behind the black stallion. The two horses were now even in wins, both having taken first prize in ten events. There had never been two such perfectly matched horses in England's history.

Furthermore, the Prince Regent was still pressing Vortex's anonymous owner to sell.

Folding the letter and article, Angel tucked them into her reticule. She tried hard to keep her panic at bay, but could not contain the pangs, like a pack of rabid, fighting wolves, that seemed to have taken up permanent lodging in the pit of her stomach.

With each successive loss it became less likely she would have enough money to win the wager with Sir Corbin Pugsley. Jonas had included in his last letter a tally of their finances. Although they'd managed to raise sixteen thousand pounds during their winning streak, they'd had to pay one thousand in entry fees. Thus, their entire worth was just barely fifteen thousand pounds.

Unless they raised another five thousand, Angel reminded herself yet again, she would lose the Abbey forever; she would not even allow herself to think about her vow to submit to Pugsley's desires.

Each time she tried to imagine what the baronet would do to her when he had her alone and at his mercy she fell victim to stabbing migraines. This morning was no different; already sparkling lights had begun flashing before her eyes and an aching heaviness settled over the right side of her head. Still, not one to give up without a fight, she rubbed her temples and tried to ignore the pain in order to concentrate on finding a solution.

The only race remaining in the Season was the Grand London Gold Cup, with its twenty-five hundred pound prize. Since there would be no other opportunity to raise the necessary funds, Vortex had to enter the race. And he had to win. Even then, however, the sum total of all the gray stallion's races would remain deficient to that same amount.

Her thoughts turned to her guardian, and the throbbing in her head grew more insistent.

Although she loathed the possibility she might steal the Gold Cup from under Sebastian's nose, she knew she had no choice but to try. And God alone knew what Sebastian would do, or how he would feel, if he discovered her perfidy. He was such an honorable man that Angel doubted seriously that he would be able to forgive her deception—much less her snatching his victory of his prized Gold Cup.

Her heart ached in rhythm with her head.

Although she was constantly surrounded by attentive, wealthy, titled males, the last nine weeks had flown by in a fog of loneliness. True to his word, Sebastian had made himself scarce from her presence. She'd seen him only a few times in the last two months, and on every occasion he had been with Lady Sarah. It appeared that the promised couple would publicly announce their betrothal any day.

To her shock and utter disbelief, despite her newfound confidence in her improved looks, Angel, herself, had received three offers of marriage. But though she knew she should accept one of the fine gentlemen's offers, every time she opened her mouth to say "yes," her lips somehow formed a negative response. And her gentlemen friends, as if realizing her heart was otherwise engaged, and they stood no chance, had begun deserting her for more receptive maidens.

Fortunately, this decamping of Angel's suitors did not trouble her overmuch. If she could not have Sebastian, she wanted no man. And since it would shatter her heart into a million fragments to watch him and Sarah wed, she knew she had to leave London before the "happy event." And that meant winning the Grand London Gold Cup so that she could return to Windywood Abbey.

At the thought of Windywood, her spirits sank even lower. She tried to think of returning home triumphantly as its new owner, but for some reason the thought of living there by herself no longer held any charm. For that matter, the thought of living at all held little appeal.

How could she ever be happy now, knowing what love

truly was, and loving a man who loved her in return but would forever belong to another? How could she be content knowing that, in marrying Sarah, who loved Simon, the best Sebastian could hope for was a comfortable marriage?

And what of poor Simon and Sarah?

Angel's hands left her temples and slid to massage the back of her neck. How could she love someone more than life, as she did Sebastian, and not want more for him than the kind of life he would have with a woman who loved another man?

If Sebastian had loved Sarah, while seeing them wed would have hurt every bit as badly as the prospect did now, it would still have been easier for Angel than seeing her beloved settle for a marriage of convenience. But she knew that, though she might not be able to stop herself from brooding about the matter, there was little she could do for Sebastian. Although her heart felt like it cracked every time she thought of him, he would have to take care of his own future. As would Sarah and Simon.

Since there was nothing she could do about her own beloved or her two friends' affection for each other, logic demanded that she concentrate solely on winning the wager with Sir Corbin.

It was her own life that should concern her. Since she did not delude herself into thinking that women ever truly died of broken hearts—no matter how much they might wish to, she must think of what would become of her in the future.

The Grand London Gold Cup was to be run in five days time, on the thirty-first of July. Again she reiterated these facts in her mind: if Vortex won the Gold Cup, he would have won 17,500 pounds. That left a glaring 2500 pounds remaining in order to win the wager.

Where, in God's name, was she to find another 2500 pounds?

As the little crystal clock on the mantel chimed noon, she pushed the troubling thought away. Rising, she donned a blue muslin day dress, smoothed a faint dusting of powder over her freckles, settled a chip-straw bonnet edged with cornflowers on her hair, picked up kidskin gloves, and left her room to find Lady Cartwright, who wished to visit a new milliner in Covent Garden.

Sebastian's sister was already standing near the front door of the town house, leaning close to a looking glass as she settled a pert primrose yellow hat more securely on her dusky curls. Seeing Angel, she smiled, looking much younger than her years. "Hello, dear. Ready?"

"Yes. You look charming, Hilary. Is that a new bonnet?"

"It is. I adore yellow. I know the shade doesn't exactly match my gown, but I intend to find a bit of fabric it will match, today, to have a new gown made up. Perhaps we should buy you a new gown, as well. You have seemed a bit glum of late. Maybe a new dress is just what you need to perk you up. You have surely heard the saying, 'Where's the man can soothe a heart like a satin gown'?"

"I believe I have. However, I hardly think such a measure is necessary to cheer me up," Angel demurred, certain that nothing short of marrying Sebastian would ever change her heart back from the cold hard stone it seemed to have become. "The Season is almost over and I still have several ensembles I haven't worn. Another would be a wretched excess."

Lady Cartwright studied her, solemnly. "What do you plan to do when the Season ends, Angel? Of course, I'd love to have you stay here with me, but I doubt you'd be willing. And it doesn't appear that you intend to choose any one of your suitors as a husband."

Angel turned away as tears pricked her eyelids. "I truly do not know."

But Hilary had apparently seen the sadness on Angel's face. "Oh, my dear," she said sympathetically, "are you quite up to our excursion today? If you would prefer to stay home, I will understand completely."

"Oh, no. I want to go. Please forgive my megrims. It is just that I have a headache," Angel lied. She saw no reason to subject Hilary to the same heartbreak *she* felt, and was certain the older woman would also feel, given her genuine fondness for Angel and her love for her brother.

Nevertheless, Lady Cartwright frowned and gazed deeply into Angel's eyes, a worried frown creasing her brow. "Are you quite sure you feel well enough to go out? Perhaps we should stay in and order Cook to make raspberry tarts. We could eat an entire tray of them with our tea."

"Oh, no." Angel forced a smile. "I am positive I will feel better if we do go out. I could not bear to return to my room. I fear that if I did I would do nothing but weep for the rest of the day."

Though still obviously concerned, Lady Cartwright nodded. Then she turned as the door chime rang and the butler moved past them to answer it. In a moment he closed the door and handed his mistress a rich envelope of creamy parchment. On its flap was a bit of red wax imprinted with three feathers—the mark of the Prince of Wales.

"Good heavens! It's from the Regent." Lady Cartwright's eyebrows flew skyward. "Angel! It is for you."

Angel took the envelope, snapped the wafer, and removed a single sheet of paper. She scanned the rather messy scrawl rapidly, then smiled a trifle wanly.

"It is indeed from the prince," she informed the earl's

sister. "He wishes my presence at his stables tomorrow afternoon, and naturally invites you as well to act as my chaperone. He also invites us to attend the Grand London Gold Cup with him, in his box."

"In his box!" Lady Cartwright clapped her hands, delightedly. "What an honor. You certainly charmed him, darling."

Angel shrugged. "Oh, I think it is more that he is just a charming man." She glanced back down at the Regent's missive. "He writes, further, that he has also invited several other people to join his box. There will be lunch and champagne." Then she frowned.

"What is wrong?" Lady Cartwright asked.

Angel glanced up but was scarcely aware of her friend's curious gaze. "He has also invited Sebastian and Sarah to the race. He is certain we . . ." She swallowed. "That we will enjoy their company and be glad of their presence."

Lady Cartwright's expression did not reveal her thoughts. "Would you prefer to send our regrets?"

Although Angel would have liked nothing better than to avoid seeing Sebastian with Sarah, she knew it was impossible. She had to be at the race, and the prince would be deeply offended if she attended but did not accept his invitation. "No. We must go. It is, truly, a great honor."

"Yes, but—"

Angel smiled bravely. "Really, Hilary," she interrupted. "I do not know what all the fuss is about. So your brother kissed me. So we shared a moment of passion. We did nothing that thousands of other people do in London every day. And I am sure his lordship has gotten over it quite as rapidly as I."

Angel did not give Hilary a chance to respond.

"I promise you, I am quite recovered," she finished with a brightness she did not feel. "Now, shall we go?"

Moving forward, she hurried out the door and down the steps to the Cartwright carriage.

The next day dawned clear and bright. Although a fierce storm had shaken the windows at Cartwright House the night before, fresh breezes had chased away the clouds, and the rain had merely left the air fresh and clean as Eden the day after its creation. The sun, a glorious golden orb, beamed down on England, making it look to Angel every bit of Shakespeare's "precious stone set in a silver sea."

It was impossible to dwell on her difficulties on such a magnificent day, and she was relieved to find that, along with the clouds, the wind seemed to have blown away some of her distress as well. When the Regent's carriage arrived, she and Lady Cartwright hurried down the steps of the town house, not wanting to keep their royal host waiting.

Angel was somewhat surprised by the prince's carriage. Instead of gleaming with pomp and circumstance, it was a rather drab looking vehicle, black with purple velvet draperies, and no royal crest. Nevertheless, a chilled, open bottle of champagne and two exquisite crystal flutes awaited her and Hilary inside.

As they laughed over glasses of the ambrosial beverage, they pointed out various sights about the city as they drew close to the palace. Soldiers in scarlet came to attention as the carriage swept through the palace gates. Then, instead of taking them to the front entrance, the driver directed the carriage around to one side of the building.

The moment they drew to a stop, the carriage door flew open. Angel gasped as the Regent himself appeared and offered his plump, beringed hand. His overweight, florid face beamed up at her, delight apparent in every royal crease.

"Lady Angelique! And Lady Cartwright! How splendid to have you here today. I do hope you do not mind my instructing the driver to bring you directly to the stables, but I was simply unable to stomach the idea of spending three or four hours over small talk before politely suggesting we look at my horses."

"Indeed, Highness," Angel replied with a confiding smile. "I, too, would have been sitting on pins and needles at having to wait."

Lady Cartwright curtsied and smiled. "Your Highness, this is such a great honor. Thank you so much for your invitation."

The prince bowed. "Good day, Lady Cartwright. You are looking most beautiful this morning." He straightened. "Now, ladies, if you will be good enough to come with me, I shall take you on a personal tour of my stables."

Proffering both his arms, the prince waited until the two women tucked their hands into the crooks of his elbows, and then the trio walked down the courtyard toward a group of magnificent red brick buildings. Now and then a stableboy led a horse in or out through the wide white doors. Each successive steed seemed, to Angel, more magnificent than the last.

As they reached the last building, she gasped as a young lad led a beautiful silver mare through its doors. Angel stopped dead in her tracks, inadvertently removing her hand from the prince's arm. "Oh, Your Highness! What a lovely creature. She is absolutely breathtaking!"

The Regent beamed. "You should think so. She is descended from your grandfather's stock. Her name is Luna—the moon—and, though she is getting older now, she has given me many lovely foals. There is one filly in particular I would have you see." He proffered his arm again. "Come along, my dear."

Throwing a last longing glance after the silver mare, Angel went into the stable with the prince and Lady Cartwright.

Row after row of roomy, fresh straw-filled stalls lined the interior of the building. Out of each a velvety nose was thrust, inquiringly. The Regent absently stroked every one, pointing out numerous animals that had belonged to Angel's grandfather, and which she usually recognized, while heading as unerringly as one of Robin Hood's arrows toward the rear of the stable.

When he neared one of the back stalls, the prince hesitated. Angel raised a brow inquiringly.

"You are about to see my pride and joy," he murmured almost reverently. "Her name is Moonbeam. She is Luna's last foal. I have several other young fillies that are equally promising, but Moonbeam has that certain something, that special spark, that sets her apart from all the rest. You will see what I mean in a moment."

As if called by his voice, the filly trotted forward and thrust her head over the door of the stall. Her head was a delicate, almost luminous white. Her nostrils were flared curiously, and her uncommonly lovely brown eyes gazed interestedly over the gate at the intruders.

Angel caught her breath. For several moments all she could do was stare. Then she said breathlessly, "Can we get a closer look at her?"

The prince grinned. "Of course. I can see that you also recognize the special aura about my lovely Moonbeam."

The prince waved a finger and a lad scurried forward to release the stall door. Throwing a halter over the filly's head, the youth then led her out into the hall.

Even in the dim stable light it was obvious to Angel that, next to Vortex, the filly was, indeed, the most magnificent horse she had ever seen. For a long time she said nothing, content with gazing in open-eyed awe at the well-muscled flanks, superbly sculpted head, and exquisite contours.

When the Regent asked the stableboy to lead Moonbeam outside into the sunlight, Angel followed closely. They moved to stand next to the horse.

The sun glinted off the filly's silky, pure white coat. No hint of yellowing marred the flowing mane and tail, and her nose and hooves were a gleaming coal black. Her hindquarters, while feminine, were strong and high, while her forelegs stood straight and solid.

At that moment a passing butterfly swooped too close to the long, fine-boned nose. Moonbeam reared sharply, showing her superb rib structure and the muscles that moved so smoothly beneath the luxuriant, satiny skin.

But, even though the filly was undeniably lovely, the thing that caught Angel's attention the most was the flicker of intelligence in the soft brown eyes, eyes that seemed to be investigating Angel as much as Angel was investigating Moonbeam.

Vortex was the only horse in which Angel had ever before seen such easily apparent intelligence. Absently she wondered how closely the filly and the stallion were related. And, if only she could obtain the little horse, what their offspring would be like.

Then the Regent gave a laugh. "You know, Lady Angelique," he said confidingly, "if I thought there was a prayer the owner of that big gray stallion—you know the one, named Vortex, who has taken everyone by storm—would sell, I'd pay anything he asked."

Angel did not know how to respond.

The Regent stroked his filly's nose. "He is the stallion I would have for my darling Moonbeam. Can you imagine the foals they would have?" he demanded, echoing

Angel's previous thought. "Nothing in Britain, possibly in all the world, would be able to match their offspring."

Angel nodded politely.

Of course she could not sell Vortex. For any price. But it *would* be magnificent to see him and his little white cousin together.

Moonbeam was everything she had ever wished for in a mate for Vortex. And somehow she knew that Vortex would second this opinion eagerly.

The prince's voice interrupted this pleasant daydream. "You must know," he said a trifle testily, "I have placed any number of offers in the *Times,* since no one seems to know the identity of the Vortex's owner. I keep hoping the gentleman will see one of my notices and decide to sell."

He ran a hand possessively over Moonbeam's silken flank. "Thus far, I have been unable to give my little darling here to any of my own prime stallions. I cannot seem to shake the feeling that she belongs, heart and soul, only to Vortex." He laughed self-consciously. "Does that sound ridiculously sentimental to you, my lady?"

"Not at all, sir. I can see why you would feel that way. Two such magnificent specimens should be together." She pursed her lips, thoughtfully. "If you could not own Vortex, would you perhaps consider a loan of the stallion, Highness?" she asked hesitantly. "Perhaps the owner would offer her—*his*—horse as a stud."

The Regent shook his head. "No. I will only settle for ownership. I want that stallion enough to give almost anything I own to possess him. I could not stand merely possessing him for a few weeks. It would never be enough."

Angel sighed and stroked Moonbeam's velvety nose. Somehow, she thought determinedly, she had to have this filly. After seeing this exquisite creature, she knew no other filly in England would satisfy her when she set about seeking a companion for Vortex.

At their side, Lady Cartwright, obviously not as enthralled with the stable or the horses as Angel and the prince were, spoke up suddenly. She pointed to a low bench beneath a willow not far away. "I think I shall go sit down, if you do not mind, Highness, Angel."

Angel and the Regent both shook their heads. After escorting the older woman to the bench, the prince returned to Angel's side.

Angel eyed him covertly. "Highness?" she said boldly. "Do you think you might be willing to place a wager on the outcome of the Grand London Gold Cup?"

The Regent looked scandalized at her even suggesting such a thing. It was obvious that, despite his invitation to examine his prime bloods, he nonetheless did not feel the turf a fitting subject for discussion between himself and an innocent debutante. "Well-er- that is to say—" he stammered incoherently.

Angel flushed. "I meant, of course, between you and Vortex's owner. Perhaps, since you say you believe Moonbeam belongs with Vortex, you might offer her as bait. Make her an additional prize, along with a sizable sum of money. While I would not presume to know if you would win or not, surely it would be worth the risk. And even if you lost, your lovely Moonbeam would still be able to produce the foals you imagine."

The prince brightened. "Oh, yes! You might have something there, Lady Angelique. Surely if the man enjoys entering his horse in races he is a betting man, and would enjoy a friendly wager. And, although I should hate to lose Moonbeam, I know anyone who owns a horse like Vortex would appreciate her true value. And I would not lose contact with her, completely. I am certain a man with an appreciation for horseflesh like Vortex's owner would be very interesting to know, and might even wish to exchange studs in the future."

Angel nodded enthusiastically. "I am sure you are right, Highness. Maybe if you were to place a notice in the *Times* to that effect, you would get a more satisfactory response than you have to your previous inquiries."

The Regent beamed. "I shall do that very thing, as soon as we have taken tea. Come along, dear girl. Let us retrieve your chaperone and go inside. And I find I am suddenly devilish overset. Good news always makes me hungry." He frowned suddenly. "For that matter, so does bad news."

Angel grinned fondly as she took his pudgy arm and they went to collect Lady Cartwright.

Later that afternoon, while reading the afternoon paper at her writing desk, Angel perused the Regent's suggested wager with Vortex's owner. He was offering ten thousand pounds and his prize filly, Moonbeam, if the big gray should win the Grand London Gold Cup.

Angel's heart gave a lurch. Even though she had realized that her last chance at obtaining the Abbey stood with winning this wager with the Regent, if she accepted the prince's terms, there was a genuine possibility she might actually lose Vortex forever.

If Vortex lost the race, the prince, according to his offer, would take possession of the big gray stallion immediately—although he was offering a tidy sum along with the filly, the prince was asking the stallion's owner to wager nothing but Vortex.

Despite the shaft of pain that shot through her at the thought of potentially losing her beloved horse, Angel knew that if Vortex did lose, at least he would go to the one person in all England that would undoubtedly value him as much as she did. The prince would prize the gray stallion above all his other stock save the little white filly. And Vortex would have Moonbeam as his mate, regardless of the outcome of the race.

With trembling hands, Angel plucked a bit of parchment from her desk drawer and scrawled an acceptance notice in her most masculine hand. Then she also wrote a letter, informing Jonas of her intentions.

She would go to the race, sit in the Regent's box, and either win enough money to pay Pugsley for Windywood Abbey or lose both her horse and herself.

Chapter Twenty-one

The day of the big race dawned dark and cloudy. Angel stood at her window, looking out at the dreary landscape, watching the rain pelt everything and everyone that was unlucky enough to be out in the foul weather.

She had a sudden premonition that the gloom outside was a direct indication of the way her day would end. She tried not to dwell on the overpowering sense of doom that seemed to hang over her head like the thunderclouds hanging over the London streets.

While she waited until it was time to leave for the race, she sat down at her writing desk and scrawled a quick note. Then, without giving herself time to tear it up, she rang for a footman and instructed him to deliver it, posthaste. Afterward, moving to her window once again, she watched the servant plunge into the rain and disappear down the street.

Forcing herself to lie down, she tried to calm her nerves and quell the headache that threatened to rip her head and neck from her shoulders. Surprisingly, despite her agitation she fell asleep until the clock on her mantel chimed noon. At that hour a maid entered the bedchamber to help Angel dress for the race, which was to begin at two o'clock.

Her short nap had relieved neither her headache nor dissipated her forbodings.

When she was ready to go downstairs, she glanced into the cheval glass resting against one wall to give her gown a final check. She could not help observing that she looked unpleasantly wraith-like in the dove gray walking dress, matching kidskin gloves, and her charcoal-colored spenser. Her bonnet, a silver confection made of lace and satin, covered all but a few curling strands of her coppery hair, which had been trapped in a gauzy silver net on the back of her neck and lent the only color to her entire ensemble.

She descended the staircase and found Lady Cartwright awaiting her in the foyer.

"Ah, there you are," the older woman said brightly. "A rather dismal day, isn't it? I do hope the horses don't slip on all this mud. I always worry that someone will be dreadfully hurt when the weather is not optimum for one of these big races." Then she glanced at Angel's hem, speculatively. "I do hope you have worn your black leather half boots. You shall have very wet feet, otherwise."

"I have," Angel affirmed. "You look lovely, Hilary. That shade of lavender complements your beautiful complexion perfectly."

Lady Cartwright smiled. "Thank you. It is my husband's favorite color for me to wear, as well. I was missing him today, which is why I wore this gown. I do hope he returns from the country, soon." She cocked her head toward the front door. "I believe I hear the carriage His Highness planned to send for us. Are you quite ready?"

Angel nodded and, following her sponsor's example,

opened one of the black umbrellas that filled the stuffed rhinoceros leg standing in the hall.

The knocker sounded on the door, and Fipps moved to admit the visitor. It was an elaborately dressed footman. The lad informed them, as Lady Cartwright had suspected, that the Regent's carriage awaited their pleasure to take them to the prince's box at the Grand London Gold Cup.

Angel followed Hilary down the town house steps and allowed the footman to aid her ascent into the carriage. There she glanced curiously about the vehicle's interior. This time, rather than cold champagne, a small brazier rested on the carriage floor. It heated the vehicle nicely, and warmed a small cauldron filled with spiced cider.

By the time the carriage reached the racing track on the outskirts of London, the rain had slowed to a mere drizzle. The sun peeped through the clouds, lending them the proverbial silver lining. Angel hoped this was a good omen, although her intuition still declared otherwise.

The carriage pulled to a stop and the same footman opened its door. Angel caught her breath as she saw Sebastian, who had apparently been awaiting them, standing on the curb. Lady Sarah Moreton, gloriously beautiful in indigo velvet that brought the color out in her eyes, stood beside the earl. Atop her head the exquisite girl wore a matching velvet hat. Tiny silver stars dangled from the bonnet's brim, dancing with each movement Lady Sarah made.

Lord Evanstone hovered several feet away from Lady Sarah and Sebastian. A mask of indifference, belied by the glimmer of agony in his blue eyes, rested upon the tall lord's face. His mouth was a tense, white slash. He did not once remove his gaze from Sebastian's future betrothed.

Lady Sarah smiled brightly. "Hello, Angel! You have been rather reclusive, lately. I have hardly seen you.

You've not been present at any of the functions Lord Darcy and I have attended."

Angel tried to return Sarah's smile, but her lips seemed numb. "Oh," she replied stiffly, "I suppose it is just that Hilary and I have gone to different entertainments. There are so many, you know."

"Yes." Lady Sarah laughed. "Well, I never thought I would see the day that I'd actually be attending a function in the company of the Regent. I know I have you to thank for that, Angel—though I am not certain gratitude is what I am feeling. Just between us, I am absolutely terrified I will do something gauche and disgust him forever."

Angel gave a forced laugh. "I do not understand why everyone thinks the prince is such an ogre. While I will agree his spending habits frequently trouble those in and out of his sphere, I assure you he is a charming man, and has always been kindness itself, to me. I am sure he will love you when he gets to know you, Sarah, as you will him."

Sebastian made a slight movement. "Ahem. If you ladies will allow Simon and me, we will escort you to the Regent's box."

Lady Cartwright nodded. Linking one hand through Lord Evanstone's arm, she reached out for her brother's arm as well. "Leave the girls to walk together, gentlemen. I am sure they have a lot to talk about. Tell me, Sebastian, are you nervous about the big race and how Hughes Pride will run today?"

"Without a doubt. You must remember that I have spent the last twenty years trying to win this race. And our father before me."

From behind, Angel gazed at him with her heart in her eyes. She felt a rush of guilt at the thought that she might take the Gold Cup away from him. Then she flushed hotly and wondered if anyone had observed her loving attention to the earl.

A sideways glance relieved her somewhat, although she noticed that Sarah was watching Evanstone, her eyes mirroring the love Angel knew had been in her own glance toward Sebastian moments before. The girls did not, as Lady Cartwright had implied they would wish to do, exchange a word.

"Of course," Sebastian continued, "the Regent is also hopeful. He has a horse of his own in this race—although that it not why he is so excited. I understand that the owner of the big gray stallion, Vortex, has finally agreed to a wager."

"Never say so!" Hilary exclaimed. Then she blushed. "Oh, I know I am not supposed to be all that interested in the racing circuit, being a lady, but who could help but see all His Highness's pleas in the *Times?*" Then she asked, curiously, "What are the stakes?"

"If the gray wins, the Regent must pay ten thousand pounds as well as hand over his prize filly, a lovely white horse named Moonbeam. If Vortex loses," Sebastian informed his sister, "he immediately becomes the prince's property. The prince has asked for no money, just the stallion. It appears it was an offer Vortex's owner could not refuse."

Hearing this, Angel's chest contracted painfully. She sent up a silent prayer to God that, if it was His will, her beloved horse please not lose the race.

They drew nigh the Regent's box, which was placed close to the finish line so that he and his guests would be the first to know the race's outcome. A purple canopy had been set up over the box, and flags bearing the royal crest snapped in the crisp breeze.

When the prince saw Angel's party, he rose from a plush velvet chair and beckoned them to his side. "Welcome, my friends!" he cried merrily, waving a full champagne flute in their direction. "Come, have some champagne and enjoy the fine luncheon my chef has prepared. There is every kind of food you might desire."

Gazing at the prince's rotund figure and wiggling chins, Angel swallowed an affectionate smile. Yet again it became vividly apparent that the Regent held the pleasing of his palate in very high esteem.

Then the prince set his glass down and came to claim her hand for a royal salute. "You will sit on my right side, Lady Angelique," he said then, firmly tucking her fingers against his arm, "and Lady Sarah will sit on my left. Or vice versa. Would either of you mind very much if we walked down to the paddock where the horses are awaiting the start of the race, before we take our luncheon?"

Sarah, standing near Sebastian, blanched but shook her head weakly. "No, Highness."

"I would love to." Angel's heart fluttered at the thought of seeing Jonas and Vortex again after so many months. Both should be at the paddock, preparing for the event.

"Excellent. Darcy," the prince commanded Sebastian, "you will attend us as well. Lady Cartwright, I am sure you know the other ladies present. While you may accompany us, you needn't feel obligated."

Hilary curtsied. "Thank you, Your Highness. I will remain here."

"We shall return momentarily."

From the corner of her eye Angel saw Evanstone frown and clench his fists as Sebastian extended his arm to Lady Sarah, and the dark beauty accepted her promised fiancé's escort. With difficulty Angel kept a similar anguish from appearing on her face, and smiled weakly at the Regent as he patted her fingers and turned toward the walkway edging the race track.

As they walked, she tried to concentrate on the sights and sounds around her.

There must have been upward of two thousand people present, as high up on the social scale as the Regent and as low down as the humblest stableboy. Here and there hawkers called their wares: meat pasties, gingerbread, cloved oranges, spiced wine. Curious onlookers, who had gathered to gawk at the royal party, were kept at bay by members of the Regent's finely dressed regiment, the 10th Hussars.

The race track curved away to the right, while the packed grandstands sat on their left. It dismayed Angel to hear some of the English citizens shout obscenities and hiss in the prince's direction. While she knew His Highness was not perfect, as made evident by his treatment of his wife as well as, as Angel had already quietly mentioned to her friends, his spendthrift manners, she had grown to like him very much.

Then Sebastian spoke. "I shall do my best to see that you win your wager, Your Highness. As you know, my stallion Hughes Pride is running against Vortex. He and the gray are the favorites in today's event, as you must also know." Then he grinned. "I confess to being exceedingly nervous about the outcome."

"I'll wager so," the Regent replied easily. "But I trust you shall not disappoint me." He smiled, to take the edge off his words. "However," the prince continued as they left the walkway and reached the group of paddocks wherein the horses awaited the race, "even if Vortex wins today I shall have the pleasure of seeing him sire my Moonbeam's foals. And though I'd hate to lose her, I could not help but be delighted with the prospect of seeing their future progeny."

Angel searched the area for her horse and the diminutive form of Jonas Spindle. When she finally saw them, she smiled and barely caught her hand as it rose in a salute. Naturally she could not disclose her familiarity with them. Where would she have met members of the circuit, after all?

From where he stood, bent against Vortex's broad back and inspecting one of the huge stallion's hooves, Jonas's head jerked up abruptly as if he had felt Angel's presence. When his eyes met hers, he smiled broadly, then carefully straightened his lips and bowed respectfully to the prince.

"Ah, my good man," the Regent said amiably, "how is the big fellow today? I trust he is well, but also that he will lose this race so I might add him to my stables. Naturally you are welcome to come with him, in that event."

Jonas's eyes sought Angel's once again. They seemed to say that he understood her accepting the Regent's wager, since he was well aware of exactly how much money they possessed and how much they still needed in order to win the wager with Sir Corbin Pugsley.

"Vortex is doing very well, Highness," Jonas answered deferentially, tugging his cap. Then he added, a glint of mischief in his eye, "But naturally I cannot second your hope that he comes in less than first."

The prince frowned.

As if in agreement with the groom's comment, Vortex reared suddenly, then eased gracefully back to earth. "Excepting an act of God," Jonas continued, "I am quite certain he will take the Cup today. Perhaps you would be better served to cancel your wager with his owner before the race starts—begging your pardon, sir, of course."

The prince roared with laughter, doubling over so that he tugged on Angel's arm. "By all that's holy," he cried jovially, "you have my pardon, my good man. However, my wager stands. I cannot cancel it, now. You see?" He nodded at a spot just opposite Vortex's paddock. "My lovely Moonbeam is present and seems quite taken with Vortex. I could not think of disappointing her at this late hour."

Truly, Angel saw, the lovely white filly was gazing adoringly over the fence at the big gray stallion. Her ears were pricked forward, intently, while her intelligent, soft brown eyes never left Vortex's prancing body.

Angel smiled at the eagerness in the mare's face. Then, as Sebastian accidentally brushed against her arm, causing delicious goosebumps to rise on her flesh, she swallowed heavily. How well she could understand Moonbeam's eagerness to be possessed by the virile stallion. Her cheeks flamed as she remembered Sebastian's caresses and experienced a similar eagerness for him.

Sebastian cleared his throat as if he, too, had felt the longing. "So that is the famous Moonbeam," he said almost too quickly. "She is truly beautiful. I can see why you are so partial to her, Your Highness. I certainly would not be averse to adding her to my own stable."

"Unless you secretly own Vortex and plan to throw the race by seeing to it that Hughes Pride loses, you can put that thought right out of your mind, Darcy," the prince replied repressively. "Moonbeam is destined for Vortex and none other."

At that moment a disturbance in Vortex's paddock made them all glance over at the stallion. Angel caught her breath as her eyes met Jonas's. Obviously the big gray horse had just recognized her and was trying to get her attention.

Curious, the prince drew Angel back over to the gray. "Why, I do believe he likes you, Lady Angelique," he said affably. "Isn't that something? Just look at the way he's stretching his head over the bars as if he wants you to stroke his nose!"

The instant they stood beside the paddock Vortex's huge head nuzzled Angel's breast, searching, she knew, for the bit of sugar she had always kept in her pocket in the stables at Violet Cottage. Raising a gloved hand, she pushed Vortex's nose away gently.

"Hello, beautiful," she said brightly, hoping she merely looked like an admirer of fine equines.

To her relief Vortex ceased his seeking and settled for a good scratch between his ears. Angel raised her eyes to find Sebastian's gaze upon her, searching her face with a strange expression, as if he were trying to remember something long forgotten.

Lady Sarah had said little during the walk, but when Angel glanced over at her friend's beautiful face the girl's terror at being so close to the big gray stallion was obvious. Sympathetic, Angel said quickly, "I am feeling a bit tired. Do you think we might return to your box, Highness?"

"Certainly, my lady," the Regent replied gallantly. "I cannot have one of my guests collapsing from exhaustion. Besides, I believe that since the race is due to start in under an hour, we should make use of the luncheon provided us by my chef."

When they arrived back at the box, they found that the royal servants had spread fine linen sheeting over a long table and were busily laying out dinnerware. When the baskets of cold chicken, hot beef, stuffed mushrooms, deviled eggs, sharp and mild cheeses, and innumerable bottles of wine had been set in the center of the table, the servants quietly disappeared.

There were many other couples in the Regent's party besides those few who had walked down to the paddocks, and the men seated their ladies before taking their own chairs. True to his word, the Regent himself seated Angel and Sarah on both his sides. Lady Cartwright sat only a few places away, between Sebastian and Evanstone.

With all the other ladies casting envious glances in Angel's direction, where she sat in the place of honor, Angel had to smile. It still never failed to astonish her that she was here, after worrying so badly in the beginning that the ton would laugh in her face. However, when she looked up to find herself seated directly across from Sebastian, she found her delight in the day dimmed substantially, and it was all she could do to keep from bursting into tears.

To counteract the pinpricks behind her eyelids, she directed all her attention to the superb food. She could not help noticing that Evanstone did not eat a bite, and that his pained expression seemed no less agonized than when she'd first seen him, earlier that day. Angel also noticed that the lanky peer still gazed at Lady Sarah as frequently as he could without being obviously observed.

"Gracious," the Regent remarked with astonishment as Angel reached for a third helping of salmon aspic, "you must have been ravenous, my lady. Did you not take your breakfast?"

Angel choked, and blushed furiously. Sputtering, she managed, "I did, Highness. It is just that . . . it is just that your chef has such a way with food," she said lamely. "He lives up to the fantastic salary you pay him."

The prince beamed. "I also think he does. And I am quite certain Monsieur Careme would be pleased to see his efforts enjoyed in such a wholehearted manner."

Sebastian glanced at Evanstone. "What about you, Simon? Is the food not to your liking? Every other time I have seen you eat, you've dined as if you were possessed of a hollow leg. And yet you have eaten hardly a bite. You also look quite pale. Are you unwell?"

"Not really," Evanstone replied glumly. "I just have no appetite today. Feel a bit queasy, if you must know." He glanced back over at Lady Sarah before looking quickly down at his loaded plate.

The Regent looked concerned. "I do hope it is not something contagious."

"Oh, no," Simon averred. "I am merely not feeling quite the thing, today."

Sebastian nodded. "Got a lot riding on this race, have you?" Without awaiting a reply, he went on quickly as if, Angel thought lovingly, to remove attention from his uncomfortable friend. "I do, as well. Too much, in fact. Can't blame you for not feeling up to par. Perhaps you should have a glass of His Highness's excellent wine. Where did you come by this superb Bordeaux, Highness?"

To all four of the discomfitted friends' relief, the prince launched into a lengthy lecture of fine wines.

As the meal drew to a close, Angel became aware that she had drunk quite a bit too much wine. Her cheeks felt warm and her head seemed a bit too large for her body. How many glasses had she had? Five? Six? It had been easy to lose track, since there were at least a dozen different kinds, and the prince had demanded her opinion of each and every bottle.

Just then a bell rang somewhere in the vicinity of the starting gate, signaling the imminent beginning of the race. As the Regent stood, Angel followed suit only to find that the table and other guests seemed to sway wildly. She was vaguely conscious that Sebastian had come around the table to collect Lady Sarah.

As if aware of Angel's distress, the prince tucked her hand under his arm and smiled. "Please," he said gently, "I would like you to stand with me at the rail, Lady Angelique. I find I am, much like poor Darcy, too nervous not to be holding on to something, and a lovely lady's arm is one of the nicest things I can imagine grasping."

Angel smiled gratefully. "Thank you, sir," she whispered. "You are most kind."

"Not at all," he said softly as the other guests joined them at the rail. "It should be obvious to everyone that I am not an infrequent victim to overindulging in good food and drink, myself."

In the distance Angel could see the stallions lining up at the starting gate. She tried to single out Vortex and Jonas, but could not see them for the bustling crowd of equine bodies. She looked down at the track, gauging its slipperiness. At least the rain had stopped and the ground was not too wet. To the best of her knowledge, Vortex had never run on a muddy course.

When the starter fired a shot into the air and the horses all burst from the gates, she leaned over the rail and watched, her heart in her throat.

Chapter Twenty-Two

Angel tried to keep from thinking about what would happen if Vortex did not win the race. She also tried to keep from thinking about Sebastian's disappointment if the big stallion *did*.

The horses, their huge bodies straining for their fastest paces, surged past where she and the prince stood near the railing. The jockeys, dressed in colorful silks, waved their crops and shouted encouragement to their mounts. On the sidelines, people jumped up and down with excitement.

The only people present who did not look thrilled with the event were Sarah, who had pulled away to the back of the box and had pressed her gloved hands to her ears, and Evanstone, whose worried eyes had obviously seen his beloved's distress.

It seemed to Angel as if she was watching the commotion from a distance, and could not quite hear anything. She watched, fascinated, as Sebastian raised an arm and yelled something she could not discern as the horses made another pass. Then she caught a glimpse of Jonas atop Vortex's broad back. His wrinkled face was clenched with concentration.

The next time the stallions drew near, Angel observed that Vortex and Hughes Pride had broken away from the pack. Neck and neck, they hurtled past the fence. The Regent had pulled away from Angel's arm and was clinging to the rail, leaping up and down for all his pudgy body was worth.

Then there was only one lap to go.

Swallowing, Angel forced herself to attend to the horses, and clamped her mouth shut on her cries of encouragement for Vortex. None in the royal box would understand if she were to favor the wrong stallion.

As the two leading horses rounded the bend for the final time, she found that she could not bring herself to watch the end of the race. Her entire future hung in the balance, and she knew that if she kept her eyes on the stallions, she would faint. Instead, she moved away from the rail to stand beside Sarah, and tried to act as if she were there to lend her support to Sebastian's terrified betrothed.

When the cries of triumph erupted in the royal box, Angel felt her heart freeze in her chest. She knew she had lost everything in the world that mattered to her.

She collapsed into a nearby chair, still clenching Sarah's hands. Unable to speak, she turned to watch blindly as Hughes Pride was led into the winner's circle and draped with a circlet of roses. Part of her was aware that Sebastian had left the box and was stretching out his hands to accept the Grand London Gold Cup he had coveted for two decades.

Unable to watch any more, Angel rose very unsteadily to her feet. There was no putting off the inevitable. Pugsley was probably at the Gilded Calf by now, waiting for her, as the note she had sent earlier that morning had requested.

As Jonas, still astride Vortex, turned and gazed sorrowfully at Angel, she whispered shakily, "Sarah, I believe I am going to be ill. Would you excuse me? I am sure, under the circumstances, the Regent will not mind if I ask his driver to take me home."

Sarah nodded. "I shall accompany you. I, too, feel quite faint from all this shouting and from all those smelly horses."

"Oh, but . . ." Unable to think of any way she could convince Sarah to stay behind, Angel agreed. She would simply ask the driver to drop Sarah off, before taking *her* to the Gilded Calf.

The two of them slipped away quietly, unobserved by the other box occupants. In moments they were on their way to Sarah's parents' town house. Angel's last view of the race track, as the royal carriage lurched into motion, was to see the Regent smilingly accept Vortex's reins from Jonas's hand. Unable to contain her grief, she turned her head into the plush velvet carriage squabs and began to sob.

"Angel!" Sarah cried. "You must be very ill, indeed!"

"It is nothing. I shall be all right," Angel insisted. But she cried all the harder.

Sarah clamped a hand around Angel's forearm and pulled until Angel turned around to look at her. "Nothing, my eye! What is it? What is wrong? Tell me at once, Angel."

"I cannot."

"I thought we were friends," Sarah retorted heatedly. "If that is true, you will let me help you. I do not know what is wrong, but it is obvious that something is troubling you desperately. And do not lie, for I know you are not simply ill. I am a very sensitive person, myself, and recognize heartbreak when I see it." Her beautiful blue eyes shone suspiciously for a moment, but she cleared her throat and managed to restrain her own grief.

Angel gave a broken sigh and nodded. "You are correct; I am not ill," she admitted. "But I cannot tell you what is wrong, Sarah. I can only say that I have made a very unwise wager with a very bad man. And, since Vortex lost this race today, I must now pay my price, or watch my family home be ripped to the ground, piece by piece. And if that happened, I might as well tear out my own heart."

"A wager!" Sarah sounded mortified. "You could not have done such a shocking thing, Angel! Ladies do not make wagers!"

Angel wiped her streaming eyes with one kid glove. "Nevertheless, I did. And now I must pay the forfeit."

"Does Darcy know?"

"Of course not. He would never have allowed it, and, as I had no choice but to commit to this wager, I did not see fit to inform him just to have him stop me."

"What kind of gentleman would lure a lady into doing such a thing?"

"No gentleman. His name is Sir Corbin Pugsley—an old neighbor when I lived at Windywood Abbey."

Sarah looked blank. "Who?"

"Sir Corbin Pugsley. He's a baronet, and recently won my family estate from Lord Darcy. He offered me the chance to win it back. He said if I did not agree to his terms, those being the deliverance of twenty thousand pounds by the first of next month, he would demolish the Abbey."

Sarah thought for a moment. "I see. But why did you not simply ask Darcy for the money?"

Angel sniffed. "Because, as I told you, he would never have allowed it."

"Surely that would be better than losing the wager altogether."

"Not necessarily. Pugsley told me that if he found out I'd informed Sebastian of the wager, he'd tear Windywood down immediately. And since I knew it would be just like him to put a spy in either Sebastian or Lady Cartwright's household, I dared not risk telling Sebastian anything."

"I think I understand," Sarah said slowly. "And rest assured, had I any funds of my own beyond pin money, I would gladly give you every shilling. Unfortunately I do not. So what now? I know the baronet wagered the Abbey, but what did you have to offer him?"

Angel averted her gaze. Her cheeks heated. "I promised to spend twenty-four hours in his company, doing whatever he commanded."

Sarah looked as if she could not breathe.

Angel rushed on, hoping to avoid a scolding. "Since, win or lose, I knew the outcome of this race would decide our wager, this morning I sent Pugsley a note telling him to meet me at the Gilded Calf Inn just outside London this afternoon," Angel said. She still felt markedly tipsy, and, thus, foolishly brave. "I hoped it would be to have him deliver the title to Windywood Abbey into my hands. Now I mean to deliver myself into his."

"You cannot!" Sarah cried. "I will not allow it. Angel, I absolutely forbid you to do such a mad thing."

"You cannot stop me. I repeat, I will do anything in this world to protect my home. And if that means placing myself at Sir Corbin Pugsley's disposal, then that is precisely what I will do." Angel straightened on the carriage seat. "Now, I already asked the coachman to go to your father's town house, where I intend to leave you. If we are friends, Sarah, tell no one where I have gone."

Sarah paled. "You cannot ask that of me. And you must not go to the inn. You know 'twould be utter madness!"

"I can!" Angel again wiped her eyes with the back of one glove. "I must."

"But why?" Sarah wailed. "What if you go along with the baronet's wishes and he tears down the Abbey, anyway?"

Angel sighed and shook her head. "I have no choice," she repeated dismally. "There is nothing else I can do."

Both women were silent for several moments. Then Sarah narrowed her blue eyes, speculatively. "I have an idea. I will go with you. Surely Sir Corbin will not dare do anything unspeakable to you if I am present."

Angel ruthlessly squelched the glimmer of hope that rose in her breast. "Absolutely not. You do not know him. He would probably be delighted to have two women at his disposal instead of only one."

Although Sarah trembled, she held firm. "Well, I shall not leave your side. You have no choice but to take me. If you do not, I shall go straight to Lord Darcy and tell him where you have gone. So you see, the only way to ensure my silence is to keep me with you."

Despite her perturbation, Angel grinned. "You are impossible, Sarah, but you are a true friend. Thank you."

"Then you will take me?"

"I suppose there is little else I can do."

"Good." Reaching up, Sarah pounded on the carriage roof. When the vehicle slowed and the driver peered down, she commanded rapidly, "We have changed our mind. Instead of going to the Appleby town house, take us both instead to the Gilded Calf Inn on the outskirts of Town. You know where it is?"

"Aye," the driver replied hesitantly, rain dripping from his low-brimmed hat. "But I don't think His Highness will like it much. 'Tis a disreputable place. None but cut-throat and thieves would be caught dead there—literally.

Besides that, it's begun rainin' again, and the road leading to the Gilded Calf can get terrible muddy."

Thunder growled its agreement.

"Isn't there somewhere else I could take ye?" the coachman inquired hopefully. He pulled his coat closer around his neck. "Like to your homes? It's gettin' cold, ladies. Young gentlewomen ain't got no business out in weather like this, and as God's my witness they certainly do not have any business going to a place like the Gilded Calf."

When neither Sarah nor Angel replied, he shrugged, muttered, spat off the edge of the carriage seat, and slapped the reins sharply over the horses' flanks.

In the darkness of the carriage, Angel's hand crept out to grip Sarah's. Neither girl spoke as the horses slowed before the Gilded Calf Inn and they climbed out to stand in the muddy courtyard.

Over the inn door, which hung open a few inches, a sign with a painted, peeling golden calf creaked back and forth in the chilly, damp breeze. There was no sign of any other guests. The inn windows, layered in thick, dirty grime, looked as if they hadn't been washed in decades.

Turning, Angel addressed the coachman as imperiously as she could manage, hoping the man would obey. "Thank you; you may go."

When the coachman did not reply, she said in a gay voice, "Please do not worry, my good man. We are meeting several good friends here today. I vow we shall not get into any trouble. Be at peace on that matter."

Though the coachman frowned he nodded stiffly and tugged his cap. "Aye, milady." He jumped back onto the carriage box and drove away.

With the carriage's departure the inn door immediately swung open wide. The tall figure of a man seven sheets to the wind lurched out into the storm. His greatcoat swirled about his legs, and rain dripped from his greasy golden hair. He executed a low bow and nearly fell to the muddy earth, but recovered his balance just in time.

Angel swallowed. It was Pugsley. Suddenly she felt off balance herself. The wine still in her veins made her feel queasy.

The baronet smiled blearily. His white, left eye weaved to and fro like the broken-down inn sign. "Well . . . well . . . well. Two cherub-ettes for the price of one," he said softly. "And unless I mistake matters, it is unlikely either of you has told anyone where you are. How utterly lovely. And how utterly stupid."

As Angel opened her mouth to object he raised a hand. "Please, my dear, do not try to convince me that you told your illustrious guardian your destination before you came here. While you might not give any thought to your own reputation, it is doubtful you would have risked that of your beautiful little friend, here. Why, I shudder to think what the good Society dames would make of such a shameless thing as two unattended young women meeting a man at a disreputable inn. I fear I have no choice but to think you completely at my mercy." Throwing back his head, he roared with glee.

Sebastian was elatedly flaunting the Grand London gold cup to the rest of the Regent's guests when he saw the prince's coachman running toward the Regent, waving his hands wildly. Despite the earl's happiness, a cold lump settled in the pit of Sebastian's stomach. He glanced over toward the track, where the prince was speaking with Vortex's jockey.

When the coachman reached his master's side, the earl thrust the gold cup into his sister's hands. "Take care of this," he said hastily. "I'll be back."

Hilary gaped after his departing form. "Sebastian!" she called. "Where are you going?"

Without responding, Sebastian hurried to the prince. The drizzle had become a downpour, now, and he had to lean toward the prince's mouth to hear his words over a sudden murmur of thunder.

The Regent's face had gone a sickly shade of gray. "Have you any idea why Lady Angel and Lady Sarah would have wanted to go to the Gilded Calf Inn, Darcy?" he asked worriedly. "Devilish bad place, that. My coachman tells me they bade him leave them there—gave him some story about meeting a group of friends. He wisely did not believe them and came straight to me with the information."

"The Gilded Calf?" Sebastian frowned, the sick feeling in his stomach, oozing like sewage, upward through his entire body. "No, I do not believe I am acquainted with it." He turned as Vortex's jockey suddenly threw himself back into the gray stallion's saddle.

"No time to lose, my lords!" the little man shouted over the storm. "Get your mounts and come with me! If you do not, both girls'll be dead before you can whistle up Old Snatch! I'll explain as we go."

Sebastian's heart pounded. He raced to Hughes Pride's stall. Though a groom was beginning to remove the stallion's tack, the black horse was still saddled. Leaping onto the stallion's back, Sebastian urged Hughes Pride into a run. As he reached Vortex's side the jockey also kicked the gray into motion. Several seconds later Sebastian realized Simon had borrowed a third race horse and was speeding along at their sides.

"I don't know where you're going," Simon cried, "but if it involves Lady Sarah's safety, I'm going with you."

Sebastian stared at his tall friend, then nodded swiftly. "I do not know precisely what is going on," he shouted back, "but I fear for both Lady Sarah and Angel's well-being."

Vortex's little jockey urged the big gray between Sebastian and Simon's mounts. "I'm Jonas Spindle," he shouted over the thundering hooves. "And I've some things to tell you that you may be interested in hearing, Lord Darcy."

The jockey continued shouting and, with each step they grew nearer to the Gilded Calf, the tighter Sebastian's jaw clenched, until he was grinding his teeth so tightly he thought they would be turned to powder. With renewed effort, he bent lower over the saddle and urged even greater speed from Hughes Pride.

Chapter Twenty-Three

Before Angel knew what was happening, she and Sarah had been bundled into Pugsley's carriage. The vehicle sped northward. Sir Corbin sat across from the girls, never taking his good eye off of them, and never losing the delighted smirk that twisted his deformed lips.

Glancing over at Sarah, Angel saw that her friend's face was milky-white with terror and her lips were trembling. Angel cursed herself silently. She should have insisted Sarah go home where she belonged, instead of along on this fool's errand. She saw now that her argument for sending Sarah home had had genuine merit. Sir Corbin looked unmistakably delighted by the prospect of having two women at his mercy instead of just one.

Then the baronet spoke. "You'd best try to relax and become accustomed to my company, my darlings. Perhaps you might take a nap. It is a long way to Green Willows." He turned and said in an aside to Sarah, "That is my home. I am sure you will find it very beautiful." Then he continued addressing both girls, "If we are to get halfway today we will be unable to stop at an inn until well after midnight."

"You are taking us all the way to Yorkshire, then?" Angel asked.

"Correct. We should be there by two or three A.M. tomorrow night. I have already sent word on ahead for my friends to be get everything ready for our arrival." He gestured toward his contorted features. "And then I shall repay you for this."

Sarah gasped faintly. It was obvious she had been trying, unsuccessfully, to keep from staring at Pugsley's wildly gyrating left eye as it rolled freely in its socket. "You . . . you did that to his face, Angel?"

"She did, indeed. A bit quicker with her 'blade' than I was with mine," Pugsley said with bitter amusement. "My two friends, those who will be meeting us at Green Willows, and I were merely trying to be friendly to Angel many years ago. She repaid our flattering attentions with brutality. I intend to return the favor."

Sarah fell silent. Her eyes, below her lovely blue velvet hat with its spangled stars, were wide with fear, but also flickered with a determination Angel had never before seen in the beautiful girl's face. She had always seemed so obedient and biddable, before. She looked nothing like that now. Angel wondered what it could be that Sarah was planning.

After a time it was Pugsley, rather than either girl, who drifted off to sleep. Soon the baronet's gusty, drunken snores filled the small compartment, gently vibrating the velvet carriage squabs.

When they had been traveling for several hours and darkness had fallen, they turned onto the Great North Road. Sarah quietly removed her spangled hat. Glancing at Pugsley, she pushed the hinged carriage window open slightly and tossed the bonnet out into the rapidly gathering darkness.

After waiting for a moment, tensed expectantly as if she expected the baronet's outrider to notice the hat, Sarah finally turned back toward Angel with a tremulous smile. Her eyes seemed twice their normal size.

Angel smiled, encouragingly.

She could not help a pang when she realized, however, that if it weren't for Sarah's presence, she would have risked throwing herself out the carriage door and making a run for it. But, while she knew *she* would have stood a chance at escaping, she did not know how fast or how far Sarah could run.

And, no matter what became of the both of them, Angel could not desert her faithful friend.

They would simply have to wait until a more promising time to make their escape, and hope that, should anyone find out they had been abducted (which was doubtful, at best) and come after them, they would see Sarah's hat lying on the road and know which direction Pugsley had taken.

She was very impressed by her friend's ingenuity, and a trifle ashamed of herself for believing Sarah to be less intelligent than *she*.

Angel was relieved when Pugsley's carriage rolled into the yard at an inn called The Stuck Pig, as she hoped for a chance to escape their captors. She'd known she and Sarah would have no opportunity until the vehicle stopped. She soon realized, however, that there would be no chance for escape—or a good night's sleep after their long, grueling journey.

Blithely wishing the girls a good night, and telling them that if they made any noise that might cue passersby to their presence his coachman would gag and bind them both, the baronet entered the inn for a hot supper and a warm bed. Angel and Sarah, on the other hand, were left behind, locked inside the chilly carriage with nothing to chew on but their thoughts.

After driving the coach around to the back of the inn, where it would be hidden from curious eyes, the burly coachman settled himself on a pallet on the ground beside the carriage door. Sarah, giving a sigh, resignedly settled herself on the opposite seat and, as made evident by her steadily deepening breaths, gradually drifted off to sleep.

Angel swallowed a lump in her throat, and wondered where Sebastian was, and what he was doing.

Was he at White's, perhaps? Celebrating Hughes Pride's win over bottles of the club's best cognac? Or was he lying in his bed, his black hair tousled and his beautiful dark eyes dreamy with drowsiness?

Finally, following Sarah's example, Angel decided to try to sleep.

The night air was very cold. Finding two lap rugs beneath the cushion, Angel lay one over Sarah and pulled the second over her shivering body, glad the baronet had not thought to take the blankets with him. Had he realized they were within the carriage, Angel had no doubt, he would most certainly have removed them if only to cause her and Sarah more discomfort.

Closing her eyes, she put the baronet out of her mind and tried to think only of the feel of Sebastian's lips on hers. It didn't work. All her thoughts could conjure up were imaginings of what Pugsley and his friends would do to her and Sarah once their entourage reached Green Willows.

Sebastian was not surprised to find the girls gone from the Gilded Calf once he and the other men reached the inn. However, a discreetly proffered sovereign brought instant news of the disreputable-looking man who had met Sarah and Angel, and with whom they had ridden off toward the north.

Sebastian felt a chill threaten to freeze the marrow of his bones. The man fitting the description could only be Pugsley.

Now that Jonas had told him the truth of Angel's relationship with the baronet, that of the secret wager, Sebastian could have kicked himself for thinking his darling girl would ever have sold herself to Pugsley. How could he ever have thought her experienced? It was clear, now, that her passion for his kisses had been just that—the delightful passion of an innocent maid in love.

Even now he could not contain the agony he felt at the realization that, if he had not made the wager with Pugsley in the first place, Angel would not be in danger now. If he had not lost Windywood Abbey, she would have been able to purchase the property from him without having to go to such gyrations to achieve her goal.

And Jonas Spindle had had other information to share about Angel and Pugsley.

It had shocked Sebastian to the core to learn why the baronet hated Angel so passionately. He recalled how famous Pugsley had been in tonnish circles because of his handsome face. And, because the baronet—although as a result of his own perversion—owed his present hideousness to Angel, he surely must have been planning his revenge for years.

The three men were forced to leave their exhausted mounts behind at the Gilded Calf and send a dispatch for a servant to pick them up. Fortunately the innkeeper had a battered carriage available, and four weary-looking hacks to pull it. There was no driver, but Jonas, ignoring the rain, instantly leapt up into the box.

Climbing inside the vehicle Sebastian sat rigidly and

tried to keep his hands from clenching into fists. The road was becoming treacherously muddy. If they had an accident now, they could forget all about rescuing the two girls.

At this rate, he thought desperately, they would never catch Pugsley before whatever ugly deed the baronet had planned was done. How could they? They still had no definite idea as to where the baronet was headed, although all three men were determined to drive all night and check every inn along the road in their search.

Sebastian did not give much hope to the baronet's stopping for the night; with as much hatred as Pugsley harbored for Angel, he would *also* likely drive all night in order to reach whatever destination he had in mind.

However, luck had not entirely deserted them. Remembering the lurid rumors that had gone hand in hand with the baronet's name over the years, Sebastian had a fair notion of where the girls were being taken. He did not like it. Not at all.

But at least the notion gave him some hope.

So the old carriage pounded along through the mud and potholes. They stopped and rushed into each inn or posting house they passed, but found no word of the party they were pursuing. All three men began feeling an overwhelming sense of doom and hopelessness, though none spoke his innermost fears to his companions.

Then, against all odds given the pitch darkness of the night, Jonas saw an obscure object lying on the left side of the road. Slowing the horses, he called down to the others, "My lords! Look you there!"

The two men craned their heads out the window. Sebastian's mouth tightened, and Evanstone gasped. As the carriage slowed, Simon leapt from the vehicle and raced to snatch up the item. In his long fingers he held Lady Sarah's blue hat with the silver spangles.

The tall lord said nothing as he stepped back into the carriage, but his anxious expression seemed almost to dare Sebastian to inquire as to why he held the hat to his chest like a precious treasure. Sebastian gave Evanstone an understanding smile that made the lanky lord's face relax, and the earl resigned himself to losing the seven horses that were to be part of Lady Sarah's dowry.

While the lightning crashed about them, illuminating the countryside like a ghostly dreamscape, the steady rain became a torrent and mud began collecting on the carriage wheels. The carriage slid from right to left until it seemed to Sebastian as if they were riding in a sled, rather than a coach.

Then disaster struck.

About a hundred miles out of London, the carriage slid sideways in the mud and tilted headlong into the ditch at the side of the road. With a loud cracking sound, the back right wheel came loose and rolled lazily off into the brush.

Jonas managed to jump off the box and escape injury. When Sebastian and Evanstone crawled out of the wrecked carriage into the rainy night, they and Jonas glanced at each other and, without a word, released the broken-down horses from their traces, mounted, and began riding for the nearest posting house. By the time they entered the common room of an inn called The Stuck Pig, all three men were dripping wet.

The common room was empty, which was not surprising considering the hour was well into the next day. It did not help any of the men's dour dispositions to learn that the innkeeper had no extra carriage for their use, or any fresh horses. They would have to wait until morning for their carriage to be repaired and their own animals rested enough to continue.

And, as if that weren't enough bad news, the innkeeper regretfully informed them that his one remaining free

room had only a single tiny bed, which they would have
to share among themselves.

After promising to meet in the common room at first
light the following day, the three men drew straws for
the free chamber from the innkeeper's wife's broom.
Evanstone won and stretched his lanky body out on the
lumpy mattress, still clutching Lady Sarah's hat to his
chest. Jonas and Sebastian headed for the stables, deciding
it would be more comfortable to sleep in a pile of warm
straw than on a hard wooden floor.

The innkeeper, holding to his word, had the wrecked
carriage pulled out of the ditch and repaired before the
sun rose the following morning. By the time Sebastian,
Evanstone, and Jonas walked to the front of the inn, the
still weary-looking hacks were standing in their traces,
snorting clouds of white steam in the chilly air. Sebastian
and Evanstone piled into the carriage, while Jonas took
up his position on the box.

In no time at all the party was racing across the countryside.

Evanstone remained silent during most of the journey.
Had there been any doubt in Sebastian's mind about how
his friend felt about Lady Sarah, it would have been
demolished by Simon's current behavior.

When the tall lord was not gazing down at Sarah's
spangled hat as if it were a holy relic, he was fingering
the pistol he'd purchased from the innkeeper at the Stuck
Pig (unfortunately the only weapon the man had had to
sell) and gazing out the window into the darkness. His
face registered an expression of such enraged malevolence
that Sebastian shivered, entirely relieved that such antago-
nism was not directed at *him*.

Seeing Evanstone's heart-wrenching distress, Sebastian

did not voice the worry that had crept into his mind during the long, sleepless night. He could not bring himself to worry his friend, further. But his own heart pained him as severely as he was certain Simon's was hurting, for not only was Sebastian worried about Angel but he was also terribly concerned about something that had been chewing on the back of his thoughts since they'd left the Stuck Pig.

What if Pugsley had not taken the girls out of London, at all? Suppose they were still in Town, already suffering God knew what at the baronet's hands? Was it possible that, even now, both girls were dead?

Sebastian shook himself. No, they could not be dead. Surely he would know if anything had happened to Angel.

Yet it seemed devilishly peculiar that no one along their route had seen the girls, or Pugsley, who could not have been missed with his horrid disfigurements. They had not bothered asking back at the Stuck Pig, since, if Pugsley and the girls had been there, Sebastian and his party would have seen them.

Therefore, unless Pugsley and the girls had remained in the carriage when stopping at inns for food, and instructed the coachman or outriders to take care of their journey needs, the baronet and his captives had not passed this way at all.

Unwilling, however, to suggest such a ghastly idea to his companions, Sebastian merely tightened his jaw and stared resolutely out the grimy rental-carriage window. Since they had come this far, there was no point in turning back. Either they would find the girls at Sir Corbin Pugsley's hidden torture chamber at Green Willows, or they would not see the girls until they returned to London.

If they ever saw them again at all.

Chapter Twenty-four

Since the baronet slept late, and lingered over his breakfast the following morning (again without offering any food to the girls), it was well into the next night before Pugsley's carriage rattled up the drive at Green Willows.

As the vehicle rolled to a stop, the baronet woke abruptly.

Peering out the window, he watched his groom run to unlock a huge iron gate set between stone pillars. Then, as the boy returned to the carriage, the coachman slapped the reins and the vehicle lurched through the twin granite columns. The groom repeated his actions in backward fashion, locking the gates securely and then once again climbing back onto his seat. The carriage rolled up a long circular drive lined with pebbles, stopping before a magnificently beautiful manor house.

Stretching his arms, Pugsley yawned widely and then smiled. "Welcome to my home, ladies. I hope you will find it comfortable." Then he laughed. "For a time, at least. I would not want you to get too comfortable.

That wouldn't be at all entertaining for my friends and me."

Neither Angel nor Sarah replied.

When the footman opened the carriage door, the three passengers climbed out and stood at the manor's front stoop. The night was pitch black. Angel supposed it must be around three or three-thirty in the morning. Reaching out, she gripped Sarah's fingers tightly; they were icy cold.

Just then a large black shape hurtled through the darkness.

Angel and Sarah gasped and jumped backward as the biggest, blackest, most vicious-looking dog either of them had ever seen came to a stop mere feet away. The dog opened its cavernous mouth and snarled, exposing ivory teeth like icicles that dripped saliva instead of melting water. Lowering its head, the creature rocked from side to side as if it would like nothing better than to devour both girls for its midnight snack. It wore a collar studded with thick iron spikes.

"Easy, Cerberus," Pugsley said disinterestedly.

The big dog sank into a crouch without quite touching the ground, as if it might break free from its master's command at any second. Its teeth gleamed in the light from the carriage lanterns.

Moving swiftly, the baronet climbed his front steps and threw open the doors. "Come along, ladies," he instructed amiably. "Don't dawdle. I promise you a most diverting visit to my home."

He stood to one side as the girls moved past him and into the dark house. Rising, the big dog followed, its nose pressing the backs of the girls' legs. At any moment Angel expected to feel the huge teeth sink into her calf. Already she could feel the animal's moist breath wetting her gown and petticoats as it snuffled her flesh.

Pugsley followed. He paused by a barely visible table and lit a lantern, which he held high. "I gave my servants a few days off when I discovered that I would have the pleasure of your company. Although," he added with a leer in Sarah's direction, "I didn't expect to have twice as much."

Sarah glared, though Angel could see the dark-haired girl was also shaking with fear.

Pugsley waved the lantern. "Hurry, now. We have an appointment to keep. We don't want the other gentlemen to become annoyed. I assure you, they can both become very unpleasant when they are kept waiting."

He laughed again, and Angel shuddered. Squeezing Sarah's hand even harder, she whispered, "Can you ever forgive me for getting you into this mess?"

To Angel's surprise, Sarah smiled sardonically. "What is there to forgive? I forced myself into this situation. You had little to say about it."

Fighting an urge to run, since she was confident the dog would not let her escape with her life, or if not hers, Sarah's, Angel gritted her teeth and obeyed the baronet's command. Now and then Pugsley glanced back as if making certain the girls were following. He did not seem overly concerned with their losing themselves in the big house, however, since his dog never left their sides.

The baronet led the way into a large, musty-smelling library. He moved to stand in front of a portrait of himself as he had been, years before, prior to the incident in the meadow with Angel. Lifting a hand, he brushed his handsome image tenderly, then turned a glance of such intent malevolence upon Angel that she shuddered.

Seeing her discomfort, he laughed harshly.

Turning back to the painting, he touched a hidden mechanism and the painting swung back, revealing a dark corridor beyond. He moved ahead, set his lantern down on another table, struck a tinder box and lit a torch placed in an iron cup on one stone wall. Lifting this, he again beckoned them forward.

They descended for what seemed an eternity, then came to a vast chamber.

The entire room was decorated with coal black marble. The draperies lining the walls and windows were also black, like curtains in a hearse. A crimson rug, thick and plush, ran the length of the hall like a gash against the gleaming jet floor. The few pieces of furniture were of intricately carved, polished ebony.

Studying the furniture closer, Angel felt her stomach lurch sickly as she recognized images of twisted bodies, wrapped around each other in carnal embraces, with figures of demons and devils prodding the lovers with pronged pitchforks.

"Beautiful, isn't it?" Pugsley sighed with satisfaction as he stepped into the room. "This is my favorite chamber in the entire house. Please feel free to explore. I have been most eager to have *you* see this room, especially, Lady Angel. It was, as a matter of fact, designed with you in mind, many years ago. Most of the equipment is antique—though still quite useful, I assure you."

Moving ahead of Sarah, Angel stepped past Pugsley, pulling back in order to avoid touching him. He saw this and his mangled lips became even more obscenely hideous, twisted with pure hate.

The chamber was very large, at least five thousand square feet. The walls were lined with a collection of swords: sabres, rapiers, cutlasses, and oriental tools of destruction that Angel did not recognize. Their two-headed, curved blades looked capable of removing a man's head with one swipe.

Two huge fireplaces stood on either end of the chamber

like yawning mouths. Although lain with great chunks of coal and wood, they were not yet blazing. From the corner of her eye, Angel watched as Pugsley hurried to light them with his torch. Then, as the room brightened, she turned her attention to the "equipment" he had mentioned previously.

Even though she had read of the torture methods used in the great Spanish Inquisition, she had never before seen the actual instruments used in questioning hapless victims. She could almost hear the screams of the long-dead men who had suffered while in their iron clutches. She could not even imagine what some of the machines were used for, although she did recognize the infamous "rack," as well as one rather simply designed item that could only be thumbscrews.

Near the latter stood a low table complete with rawhide strips at each of its four corners. A bucket of water nearby was probably used to moisten the strips before restraining the victim's hands and feet. When the strips dried, Angel realized, they would tighten until the victim's bones were pulled from their sockets.

Another machine had two manacles hanging from a low bar suspended from the ceiling. At its base ran row after row of razor-sharp iron spikes, as if one would be tied into the manacles and, as long as he kept himself elevated over the spikes, would not feel their sharp teeth bite into his bare feet. As soon as he tired, however . . .

A large brazier, which Angel did not notice until Pugsley lit the coals in the oven's broad, cuplike center with a flaming timber, stood in one corner of the room. Several long iron objects protruded from the coals. They looked like brands of some kind, although some of them had sharp points.

A sudden burst of movement caught Angel's attention

and she turned to see two men enter the chamber through
the same door Pugsley had brought her and Sarah. The big
black dog, rising, vanished out the door as they entered.

Chapter Twenty-five

It was early morning, and still pitch dark, before Sebastian, Simon, and Jonas's hired carriage rolled to a stop before the pair of massive wrought iron gates in front of Green Willows.

Jonas leapt from the carriage box, ran to examine the huge lock securing the gates, and turned back to address his companions. "We can't get through here," the old man said gruffly. "We'll have to go over the fence."

Sebastian, noting vaguely that it was still raining, pulled his greatcoat around his shoulders more tightly. He climbed out of the carriage and joined Jonas at the gate. He placed a foot in the bottom of the fence and launched himself over the structure. Simon and Jonas followed on his heels.

The three men ran up the drive, pebbles crunching beneath their booted feet. As they neared the manor house they exchanged dismayed glances. The building was pitch black. Surely, if anyone were home, there would be a light somewhere in the enormous house.

Then Jonas whispered excitedly, "Look! Up there!"

Lifting his gaze toward the top of the house, Sebastian nodded. A thin wisp of gray-blue smoke hung wraith-like against the black thunderheads. Every few seconds streaks of lightning illuminated the sky, followed by deep growls, as if an invisible hellhound lurked amid the clouds.

"I see it." He squinted. "And I can just make out the chimney. Let's head around to the west. Maybe there will be a side door we can enter."

Grimly, the men resumed their resolute march.

Suddenly Sebastian hesitated. "What was that?"

Evanstone also paused, and tilted his head. "I didn't hear anything."

"Listen. Maybe it will happen again. It sounded like snarling."

"Don't you think it was just thunder?" Simon whispered.

Sebastian didn't have to reply.

All three men saw the massive black dog, with great white teeth gleaming like tombstones in the flashing lightning, at the same moment. It stood in the shadows, its shoulders impossibly huge and muscular, its short black hair standing up from the nape of its neck to the base of its tail. The spiked collar encircling its neck glittered.

"Back up slowly," Jonas instructed quietly. "Do you still have that pistol you purchased from the innkeeper at the Stuck Pig, Lord Evanstone?"

"I do," the tall lord replied softly. "It is right here in my pocket." He withdrew the weapon.

"Good," Sebastian said. "Now, it would be a damned nuisance if we were forced to use the one bullet we have on that miserable cur, so let's do as Jonas suggested and back up slowly. Maybe we will be fortunate and the animal will not attack."

However, the moment they moved, the dog hurled itself

off the steps, its teeth shining like lanterns in the flash of lightning that accompanied its leap. Instantly Evanstone's pistol shattered the silent night.

The dog dropped like a stone and did not move again. However, a solitary human figure appeared without warning. "Who are ye? What the devil are ye doin', and what was that blasted noise? Sounded like a gunshot!"

As Simon furtively dropped the empty pistol behind him, Sebastian moved forward with a wide smile, hoping the man wouldn't notice the dead dog, which lay twenty feet away. "I do not know what the noise was, my good man," he replied amiably. " 'Twas most likely just thunder. Devil of a night, isn't it? We are friends of Sir Corbin. Is he at home?"

"Aye. But he didn't tell me he was expectin' company." He grinned suddenly, exposing rotten teeth. "An' under the circumstances, he would have."

Sebastian's shoulder's tightened. "What circumstances are those?"

The man's humor vanished. "That be none of yer concern, mate."

"Do they perchance involve the abduction of two young ladies?" Sebastian's heart pounded.

"Aye."

"Well, take us to them, man!" Sebastian said with false joviality. "The night is wasting, and the girls aren't getting any younger. Has Sir Corbin instructed his servants to prepare chambers for us?"

The coachman went very still. "The servants?" He withdrew his own pistol from his pocket. "Sorry, mate, but ye just done yerself in. Any friend of Sir Corbin's woulda known the baronet always gives 'is servants the night off when 'e's playin'. T'only people here are meself and one groom, who has imbibed so much cheap brandy t'nigh 'e won't be walkin' 'til at least tomorrow afternoon."

Seeing that the man was not fooled by his pretending to be as debauched as Pugsley, Sebastian said coldly, "Does your master make a habit of abducting virgins, then?"

The coachman chuckled crudely. "Virgins?" he hooted. "Oh, no. The women allus act innocent enough, but unless I miss my guess they—and these here today—were just pretendin', to make things more interestin'. The girls he brought this morning acted the same, as far as I could tell, but they were better at their parts. 'Twouldn't be the first time his lordship has brought ladybirds here to act out a scene in one of his little fantasies."

He waved the pistol. "Go on. Up the stairs. We'll see what his lordship has to say about your unexpected visit."

Throwing a cautionary glance at his companions, Sebastian, preceding the others, did as instructed. As he passed a low table filled with statuary depicting numerous demonic figures, the earl furtively plucked one statue from its nest of black velvet and tucked it against his side.

The coachman paused in front of a full-length portrait of Sir Corbin—looking as he had before his perfect features had been rearranged into a less-pleasing facade—and pressed a hidden button. The painting rotated, exposing a flight of stairs leading downward at a very steep angle. Stepping aside, the coachman gestured for the three companions to precede him.

"My, what an interesting house this is. Did Sir Corbin design its decor, himself?" Simon asked conversationally. "Good God, look at that!" He pointed to a particularly hideous sconce some ten feet down the stairway.

The coachman leaned forward to see what the tall lord was indicating. "Aye, that he—OOF!"

The man crumpled to a heap on the floor.

Dropping the blood-stained carved figurine, Sebastian knelt to feel the man's pulse. He shook his head. "He's dead. I can't say I'm sorry." He picked up the coachman's revolver and he and his companions continued on down the steps.

"Where do you suppose this passage leads?" Jonas asked, his voice just above a whisper.

Sebastian replied in an equally soft voice. "I'd have to guess it leads to Pugsley's 'amusement room.' "

"Amusement?" Jonas shot the earl a dour glance. "Why don't I like the sound of that, my lord?"

"Actually," Sebastian said, as his eyes searched the blackness ahead for a light that would indicate the presence of Pugsley and his friends, "the chamber is reputed to be a replicated dungeon. Complete with instruments of torture the baronet has collected over the last twenty years. I have heard numerous tales of the chamber, but never actually thought I'd see it." He halted abruptly. "Look there! Firelight coming from that doorway a hundred paces further."

They moved silently forward until they stood at the entrance of the illuminated, hell-black room.

Before giving his eyes permission to see whatever ghastly spectacle awaited them, Sebastian checked the coachman's gun to make sure it was ready to fire. As Angel's terrified cry pierced the air, he leapt into the chamber.

Seeing the sudden movement, Angel craned her neck to see who had interrupted her torture. Her heart leapt.

Sebastian! He had found her!

Their eyes met for a split second; then Angel's attention was jerked away from her beloved as one of Pugsley's cronies withdrew a tiny pistol from one pocket and aimed it directly at the earl's heart.

"Sebastian! Look out!" she screamed, tugging futilely at the ropes that bound her hands.

The earl whirled about and, just before Pugsley's friend pulled the trigger, raised his own pistol and sent its charge straight through the other man's chest. Wasting no time, he tossed the empty gun away and, as the second man charged toward him, grabbed one of the double-edged oriental swords that hung on the wall.

Evanstone caught the second man by one arm as the blackguard raced toward Sebastian. Holding the man in a hammerlock, the tall lord pounded relentlessly at the man's face.

Jonas and Sebastian raced for the girls. Jonas, being closest to Lady Sarah, reached for her, while the earl turned toward Angel.

Sir Corbin stood, staring in blank miscomprehension, at Angel's side. His face had gone quite purple with shock and rage.

Abruptly he seemed to come back to his senses. Lifting the glowing poker, he turned away from Angel as Sebastian approached.

Seeing her opportunity, Angel gave a mighty kick, planting her toes directly between Pugsley's legs. The baronet screeched and doubled over, dropping the glowing poker and clutching himself tightly.

Pugsley's bad eye whirled from side to side, but his good eye was pinned on Angel's face with all the hate in hell. His twisted mouth was contorted with fury.

As he stumbled back to his feet, his attention completely on her, Angel knew she was about to die.

It seemed as if everything in the room began moving in slow motion. Angel's mind registered Jonas standing guard over the battered body of Pugsley's second friend, while Sarah and Simon stood locked in each other's arms, oblivious to everything but each other. Sebastian stood as still as a statue, holding the double-edged oriental sword high in one hand.

Pugsley's hand shot out to grip Angel's throat. Slowly, steadily, he pushed her backward toward the flaming brazier. She could feel its heat scorching her shoulders. Unable to help herself, she whimpered with fear.

Before the baronet could do more, Sebastian hurled himself the rest of the way across the room. Raising the double-edged sword over his head, he cried, "Angel, get down!"

Angel dropped to one side as Sebastian's sword sliced through the air, whistling like a willow branch in a high wind. As Pugsley's body dropped to the ground like a discarded mackintosh, Sebastian hurried forth and cut the bonds on Angel's wrists. Then he pulled her into his arms in an embrace so tight she could scarcely breathe. She was vaguely aware that Sarah and Simon were also wrapped securely in each other's arms.

"Are you all right?" Sebastian demanded. "You are not badly burned?"

Angel pressed herself closer to her beloved guardian. "No. I am fine."

After a moment the two couples separated, complete understanding of their new relationships mirrored in every face.

Simon raised his head and divided his gaze between Angel and Sebastian. "Does the fact that you are obviously enamored of your ward mean you will not be sending your seconds to call upon me, my lord?" he asked solemnly. "Because I fully intend to marry Lady Sarah."

Sebastian smiled, wearily. "Only if you do not take extra-special care of that young woman, sir."

Simon returned his grin. "I shall. You have my word."

"Excellent. Now, let's get out of this God-forsaken place."

Jonas spoke up. "My lord?"

"Yes?" Sebastian answered.

"What do you wish done with the wounded man?"

Sir Corbin's live friend rolled over and groaned with pain.

"Leave him. His two friends are dead; I doubt that he will be inclined to cause much trouble in the future. If he does, I shall make certain he never sees another sunrise."

"Aye, sir."

The group moved back up the dark stairs the way they had come. Once outside, they stood, grinning self-consciously at each other, not quite certain what to do with themselves now that the danger appeared, to all intents and purposes, to have ended.

It was Jonas who reached the perfect solution. "Forgive me for being presumptuous," he said, "but it seems to me that, being as close to the Scottish border as we are, you four lovebirds might be wanting to speak your vows over the anvil rather than return to London and wait another three or four weeks before you become men and wives. I'd be happy to drive you there."

Both Sarah and Simon blushed furiously, but Sebastian said sincerely, "Thank you, my good man. That would be most appreciated."

Stretching out his hand, the earl helped Angel into the dilapidated carriage, then held the door as Simon and Sarah also climbed inside. It was a tight squeeze, but no one seemed to mind, overmuch.

Epilogue

Twilight painted the sky with colors only Heaven could have imagined. Angel and Sebastian sat quietly, side by side on the balcony at Windywood Abbey. Off in the distance they could just see the road that ran south toward London. The view was serenely pastoral, and both Lord and Lady Darcy felt supremely contented.

Sebastian's arm curled possessively about his bride's shoulders, while Angel's head leaned adoringly against her bridegroom's muscular chest.

Sebastian was thinking of how surprised he'd been to learn, following his and Angel's wedding, that his friend Lord Barstow, that confirmed bachelor, had gotten himself betrothed not three days previous. Smiling, Sebastian gently squeezed his new wife, and silently wished Barstow as much happiness as *he* had found.

Angel was thinking of the delightful letter she had received from Hilary only that morning, informing her that Lord and Lady Cartwright were finally to be blessed with a child. Angel hoped it would not be long before she and Sebastian would share in the Cartwrights' joy. 'Twould be wonderful if their children could grow up together.

They had been relaxing thus, nestled in each other's arms, for nearly two hours, and were finally beginning to consider making their way to their warm, inviting bed, when they noticed, some ways away, a cloud of dust rising from the road as if someone were riding toward the Abbey at a steady, unhurried pace.

Glancing at each other, both rose and shaded the right sides of their faces from the rapidly falling sun.

"Who can it be?" Angel asked. A secretive smile played about the corners of her mouth.

"I cannot imagine." Sebastian grinned in a similarly furtive manner.

"They seem to have quite a number of horses with them," Angel noted with satisfaction.

"A number?" Sebastian's smile faltered. "Perhaps two, but surely no more."

Angel turned to look at him. Her eyes sparkled. "Oh, I assure you, they will have at least seven, plus those they are riding. Although their own mounts are of no interest to us."

"I am sure you are mistaken. Surely there will only be two horses besides their own mounts. You shall see." Giving his bride an indulgent glance, Sebastian turned back and watched the party near the manor house. Then, just as his smile faded to a perplexed frown, he noticed a second party of riders coming from several hundred paces behind the first. He grinned, again.

"There, you see?" Angel crowed. "I told you they had at least seven horses with them. Do you recognize them?"

Sebastian turned his attention back to the first party. His eyes narrowed, then widened with delight. "Angel!

Those are Lord Appleby's horses! The ones that were to be a part of Lady Sarah's dowry."

"I know." Angel leaned over and kissed his cheek. "When you were kind enough to purchase Windywood Abbey back from Pugsley's heir as a wedding gift for me, I found myself quite at loose ends as to what to do with all the money Vortex had won. Half of it I gave to Jonas, but the other half still posed somewhat of a dilemma. Then I hit upon the perfect solution. What better use, I asked myself, could I make of those funds than to buy my bridegroom a wedding gift I knew he would love?"

Sebastian drew Angel close and kissed her deeply and long. "*You* are what I love, sweet girl. But thank you very much. Having you has made me the happiest of men, but having those horses is the icing on the wedding cake."

Angel snuggled her head under his chin. Then she pulled back as he spoke again.

"However, you were not wholly correct about the sum of the horses."

She frowned and looked up into his face. "Whatever do you mean?"

Nudging her with his chin, he gestured back toward the road. "You miscounted by two." Grinning, Sebastian reached around and kissed her nose. "I had a note from the Regent the other morning, stating that he was sending us a very special wedding gift."

Angel's heart gave a lurch and she whirled about just in time to recognize Jonas Spindle atop a huge gray horse, a dainty white filly at his side. "It's Vortex! And Moonbeam!"

"Precisely. It appears that our good prince, whom you know to be an incurable romantic, did not feel he could take your beloved horse away from you. Neither could he see fit to part Vortex from his darling Moonbeam. So he has sent them both to you as a gesture of his best wishes—though he hopes you will make him a gift of one of their foals."

"Of course!" Angel sighed happily. She clung to Sebastian for a few seconds longer, loath to be parted for even the short time it took to walk to their bedchamber. At last she drew away and looked up into his face. "Oh, Sebastian," she murmured. "I love you, my wonderful husband and guardian."

"And I you, my dearest Angel."

Below, Jonas threw them a wave as he led the horses around the manor house in the direction of the stables.

Angel turned in Sebastian's arms and drew his lips down to hers for a long, tender embrace. Then, as the sun dipped sleepily below the western horizon, and Angel's glittering star peeped out from its place in the broad canopy of the sky, the earl and countess of Darcy parted for only the few moments it took them to enter the Abbey and embark upon another night of heavenly love.

ZEBRA REGENCIES
ARE THE
TALK OF THE TON!

A REFORMED RAKE   (4499, $3.99)

by Jeanne Savery

After governess Harriet Cole helped her young charge flee to France—
and the designs of a despicable suitor, more trouble soon arrived in the
person of a London rake. Sir Frederick Carrington insisted on providing
safe escort back to England. Harriet deemed Carrington more dangerous than any band of brigands, but secretly relished matching wits with
him. But after being taken in his arms for a tender kiss, she found
herself wondering—*could* a lady find love with an irresistible rogue?

A SCANDALOUS PROPOSAL   (4504, $4.99)

by Teresa DesJardien

After only two weeks into the London season, Lady Pamela Premington
has already received her first offer of marriage. If only it hadn't come
from the *ton's* most notorious rake, Lord Marchmont. Pamela had already set her sights on the distinguished Lieutenant Penford, who had
the heroism and honor that made him the ideal match. Now she had to
keep from falling under the spell of the seductive Lord so she could
pursue the man more worthy of her love. Or was he?

A LADY'S CHAMPION   (4535, $3.99)

by Janice Bennett

Miss Daphne, art mistress of the Selwood Academy for Young Ladies,
greeted the notion of ghosts haunting the academy with skepticism.
However, to avoid rumors frightening off students, she found herself
turning to Mr. Adrian Carstairs, sent by her uncle to be her "protector"
against the "ghosts." Although, Daphne would accept no interference
in her life, she *would* accept aid in exposing any spectral spirits. What
she never expected was for Adrian to expose the secret wishes of her
hidden heart . . .

CHARITY'S GAMBIT   (4537, $3.99)

by Marcy Stewart

Charity Abercrombie reluctantly embarks on a London season in hopes
of making a suitable match. However she cannot forget the mysterious
Dominic Castille—and the kiss they shared—when he fell from a tree
as she strolled through the woods. Charity does not know that the dark
and dashing captain harbors a dangerous secret that will ensnare them
both in its web—leaving Charity to risk certain ruin and losing the man
she so passionately loves . . .

*Available wherever paperbacks are sold, or order direct from the
Publisher. Send cover price plus 50¢ per copy for mailing and
handling to Penguin USA, P.O. Box 999, c/o Dept. 17109,
Bergenfield, NJ 07621. Residents of New York and Tennessee
must include sales tax. DO NOT SEND CASH.*

ELEGANT LOVE STILL FLOURISHES —
Wrap yourself in a Zebra Regency Romance.

A MATCHMAKER'S MATCH   (3783, $3.50/$4.50)
by Nina Porter

To save herself from a loveless marriage, Lady Psyche Veringham pretends to be a bluestocking. Resigned to spinsterhood at twenty-three, Psyche sets her keen mind to snaring a husband for her young charge, Amanda. She sets her cap for long-time bachelor, Justin St. James. This man of the world has had his fill of frothy-headed debutantes and turns the tables on Psyche. Can a bluestocking and a man about town find true love?

FIRES IN THE SNOW   (3809, $3.99/$4.99)
by Janis Laden

Because of an unhappy occurrence, Diana Ruskin knew that a secure marriage was not in her future. She was content to assist her physician father and follow in his footsteps . . . until now. After meeting Adam, Duke of Marchmaine, Diana's precise world is shattered. She would simply have to avoid the temptation of his gentle touch and stunning physique — and by doing so break her own heart!

FIRST SEASON   (3810, $3.50/$4.50)
by Anne Baldwin

When country heiress Laetitia Biddle arrives in London for the Season, she harbors dreams of triumph and applause. Instead, she becomes the laughingstock of drawing rooms and ballrooms, alike. This headstrong miss blames the rakish Lord Wakeford for her miserable debut, and she vows to rise above her many faux pas. Vowing to become an Original, Letty proves that she's more than a match for this eligible, seasoned Lord.

AN UNCOMMON INTRIGUE   (3701, $3.99/$4.99)
by Georgina Devon

Miss Mary Elizabeth Sinclair was rather startled when the British Home Office employed her as a spy. Posing as "Tasha," an exotic fortune-teller, she expected to encounter unforeseen dangers. However, nothing could have prepared her for Lord Eric Stewart, her dashing and infuriating partner. Giving her heart to this haughty rogue would be the most reckless hazard of all.

A MADDENING MINX   (3702, $3.50/$4.50)
by Mary Kingsley

After a curricle accident, Miss Sarah Chadwick is literally thrust into the arms of Philip Thornton. While other women shy away from Thornton's eyepatch and aloof exterior, Sarah finds herself drawn to discover why this man is physically and emotionally scarred.

Available wherever paperbacks are sold, or order direct from the Publisher. Send cover price plus 50¢ per copy for mailing and handling to Penguin USA, P.O. Box 999, c/o Dept. 17109, Bergenfield, NJ 07621. Residents of New York and Tennessee must include sales tax. DO NOT SEND CASH.

Taylor-made Romance from Zebra Books

WHISPERED KISSES (0-8217-3830-5, $4.99/$5.99)
Beautiful Texas heiress Laura Leigh Webster never imagined
that her biggest worry on her African safari would be the handsome Jace Elliot, her tour guide. Laura's guardian, Lord Chadwick Hamilton, warns her of Jace's dangerous past; she simply
cannot resist the lure of his strong arms and the passion of his
Whispered Kisses.

KISS OF THE NIGHT WIND (0-8217-5279-0, $5.99/$6.99)
Carrie Sue Strover thought she was leaving trouble behind her
when she deserted her brother's outlaw gang to live her life as
schoolmarm Carolyn Starns. On her journey, her stagecoach
was attacked and she was rescued by handsome T.J. Rogue. T.J.
plots to have Carrie lead him to her brother's cohorts who murdered his family. T.J., however, soon succumbs to the beautiful
runaway's charms and loving caresses.

FORTUNE'S FLAMES (0-8217-3825-9, $4.99/$5.99)
Impatient to begin her journey back home to New Orleans,
beautiful Maren James was furious when Captain Hawk delayed
the voyage by searching for stowaways. Impatience gave way
to uncontrollable desire once the handsome captain searched
her cabin. He was looking for illegal passengers; what he found
was wild passion with a woman he knew was unlike all those
he had known before!

PASSIONS WILD AND FREE (0-8217-5275-8, $5.99/$6.99)
After seeing her family and home destroyed by the cruel and
hateful Epson gang, Randee Hollis swore revenge. She knew
she found the perfect man to help her—gunslinger Marsh
Logan. Not only strong and brave, Marsh had the ebony hair
and light blue eyes to make Randee forget her hate and seek
the love and passion that only he could give her.

*Available wherever paperbacks are sold, or order direct from the
Publisher. Send cover price plus 50¢ per copy for mailing and
handling to Penguin USA, P.O. Box 999, c/o Dept. 17109,
Bergenfield, NJ 07621. Residents of New York and Tennessee
must include sales tax. DO NOT SEND CASH.*